D

KILL

Depth Force Thrillers
Book Seven

Irving A Greenfield

DEEP
KILL

Published by Sapere Books.

24 Trafalgar Road, Ilkley, LS29 8HH,
United Kingdom

saperebooks.com

ISBN: 978-1-80055-885-4

BATTLE STATIONS!

Admiral Jack Boxer switched on the Time To Launch clock. The missiles were armed and ready to go.

Suddenly the pinging of the Russian sonar invaded the Barracuda. *The pinging became louder.*

"Launch!" Boxer exclaimed. The Barracuda *moved slightly up, then immediately settled down.*

Seconds later the FCO reported, "ASROCS down."

"Roger that," Boxer answered.

The sound of two explosions rolled over the Barracuda. *The first shock wave caused the ship to heel to the port side. More explosions came from the surface.*

Boxer sucked in his breath. The fighting had finally begun…

CHAPTER 1

Aware that the bridge crew cast furtive glances in his direction, Admiral Jack Boxer came on the bridge of the *Novogorod*, a Russian attack submarine. Except for the constant hum of the ventilation system the boat was quiet. Three paces to his right, at the boat's Command Computer, sat his friend and sometimes enemy, Admiral Igor Borodine.

Boxer studied the COMCOMP and though he had no knowledge of the Russian language, he was able to read almost all of the instruments and even figure out the commands that Borodine now and then gave.

The *Novogorod* was down four-hundred feet, making fifty knots and traveling on a heading of thirty-one degrees. There were no targets on any of the sonar scopes.

Suddenly Borodine swiveled around, smiled and motioned him closer. "Dressed like that you could easily pass for one of us," Borodine said in English.

"Only as long as I kept my mouth shut," Boxer answered.

"Did you and your EXO have some good Russian food?" Borodine asked.

Boxer nodded. "Mister Cowly and your cook, with your EXO, Viktor, acting as interpreter, are exchanging recipes."

"Good that they have something to divert them for awhile," Borodine commented. "When we make contact with the *Shark* there will not be time to think about anything else."

"Any word about the *Shark*?" Boxer asked.

Borodine shook his head. "Sooner or later our SOSUS network will pick her up."

Boxer was going to comment, let's hope it's sooner than later, but instead he said, "I'm sorry that you lost so many boats."

"I still can't believe that one ship was able to do what the *Tecumseh* did... You know she downed a total of fifty aircraft, and your *Patterson* and the British guided missile cruiser, *The Indomitable* and four of my boats before one of our planes was able to put a salvo of missiles into her."

"But that was only after the first explosion," Boxer said.

"I don't understand."

"I'm not really sure that I do either," Boxer said. "But according to Cowly and the few men who were on the beach with me, the *Tecumseh*'s stern was blown open by a dolphin carrying an explosive pack. At the time I wasn't in any condition to know what was happening." He wasn't going to mention the fact that the same dolphin had saved his life, at least not now. That kind of story was best left for some time in the future, when they could sit across from each other in the dim light of a cafe or a cocktail lounge and reminisce...

Borodine rubbed his beard. "I know we have a similar program, but I never saw dolphins actually being used."

"Neither have I," Boxer admitted.

"How did your men know it was a dolphin that —"

"I think it surfaced and they saw the explosive pack on its back," Boxer explained. "But there was an explosion that ripped a huge hole in the *Tecumseh*'s stern because just after it happened, I managed to stand... About a half a minute later your plane came in to finish her."

"How many men do you think are aboard the *Shark*?" Borodine asked.

"I don't know. But everything can be controlled from the COMCOMP, including the firing of missiles and torpedoes.

The only thing that can't be done from the COMCOMP is the loading and arming of the torpedoes. That has to be done independently."

"Then we must figure that the *Shark* has all her torpedoes armed and ready to fire."

Boxer nodded.

"And the missiles?"

"They're in place and can be targeted from the COMCOMP," Boxer said.

"And the ASW?"

"All controlled from the COMCOMP," Boxer answered. "I would guess they were all armed before the *Shark* left the *Tecumseh*."

"We don't stand much of a chance against the *Shark*," Borodine admitted.

Boxer agreed. "Maybe we can damage her enough to force Bush to bring her to the surface. If we can do that before he reaches his launch position, then your surface fleet and aircraft could destroy her."

Suddenly the COMMO keyed Borodine. "Comrade Admiral, there is a message for Comrade Admiral Boxer."

"Roger that. Patch it through," Borodine answered; then to Boxer he said, "It is for you." And he handed Boxer a set of earphones and a mike.

"Kinkade here," the voice said.

Boxer identified himself.

"Why didn't you radio us that you were safe?" Kinkade asked.

"I intended to," Boxer answered. "But I have had other things to keep me busy."

"You know you're in the lion's mouth," Kinkade said.

"Listen, Kinkade, I'm just lucky I'm alive. A couple of hours ago I was almost food for the fish. And a couple of hours from now I still might be, so don't tell me I'm in the lion's mouth. Anything else?"

"Stark wants to speak to you."

"Roger that," Boxer answered. He was very much aware that Kinkade made no mention of his granddaughter's death, though the two of them had loved her. Perhaps any mention of Trish could be too painful? Perhaps —

"Stark here," the Chief of Naval Operations said in his gravelly voice.

"You're coming in loud and clear," Boxer said.

"What are your chances for getting the *Shark*?" Stark asked bluntly.

"One to ten. Maybe," Boxer answered just as bluntly. "That ten could change to a hundred."

"We can't send in any of our aircraft, or anything else for that matter."

"Even if you could, it might not help."

"What would help?"

"Anything about Bush and McElroy," Boxer answered.

"His brother and sister haven't seen him for years," Stark said. "Originally the family came from Kansas. Bush loves horses. But when he was a kid, a boy of five or six, he was scared out of his wits by them. Nothing else that is very different from most boys and teenagers. According to the shrinks at Bethesda, he is a very dangerous man. He reasons differently from the way we do and some of his insights might even be sharper than ours."

"I understand that," Boxer replied. "But if you get anything at all about him, let me have it. We're not only fighting the *Shark*, we're fighting a paranoid schizophrenic."

"Do you know the targeted cities?" Stark asked.

"Negative."

"If anything more on Bush comes up," Stark said, "I'll let you know. Good luck!"

"Roger that," Boxer answered, switching off the mike.

Borodine shook his head. "What I don't understand, Comrade, is how your security could have allowed a few men to steal the *Shark*."

"My guess is that more than just a few men were involved," Boxer said defensively. "And some of them had to be very high up in the government."

"Could not happen in Russia," Borodine responded. "The security is too tight."

Boxer uttered a weary sigh. "Ours was just too loose," he said. "But you can't have it both ways; you can't have freedom and a KGB. It is one or the other, Igor. There's nothing in between. The nature of the KGB makes that a certainty. Whatever the risk, I'd choose freedom anytime over tight national security."

Borodine didn't answer.

"I didn't mean to say anything political," Boxer said. "I was not criticizing your system, or even the KGB. I was only giving you my opinion."

"I understand," Borodine said in a low voice and then he turned to the COMCOMP and ran a systems check. "All systems are green," he reported, looking up at Boxer.

Before Boxer could answer, Cowly and Viktor came onto the bridge. The two men were as physically different as two men could possibly be. Cowly was tall, lean, almost ascetic looking. Viktor was chunky and Slavic.

"Captain Cowly now has all of our cook's secrets," Viktor told them with a broad smile.

"Skipper," Cowly said, "the man would make a fortune in the States."

"Don't tell him that," Borodine said with mock seriousness. "What I don't need is a discontented man aboard. Tell a man he's an artist and a good cook is exactly that; then that same man, who was happy before, begins to think he's someone special and becomes unhappy. He talks more about cooking than he actually cooks. Eventually he stops cooking altogether."

"Comrade Admiral," Cowly said, "I'm afraid the damage has been done. The man knows he's an artist."

"Oh?"

"Comrade Admiral," Viktor said, joining the conversation, "you told him that he was an artist. In fact you tell him that every time we eat."

"Only to keep him happy," Borodine said. "A happy man is a happy sailor, as the old saying goes. Besides, I like to give a man a feeling of —"

The COMMO keyed Borodine. "Comrade Admiral, SOSUS has verified the *Shark*'s position at north latitude eight-five degrees two-three minutes, east longitude three-five degrees one-eight minutes."

"Roger that," Borodine answered, as he fed the coordinates into the NAVCOMP. Within moments one of the COMCOMP's monitors filled with information. "We are less than four hours from the *Shark* at her present position," Borodine said. He pressed two buttons and a map came up on the monitor. "Our position is marked by the green dot in the lower left corner. The red dot marks the *Shark*'s position."

"Can you get a missile flight path from where she is to the major Russian cities west of the Ural Mountains?"

"I need to know the range of the missiles," Borodine said.

"Maximum six-thousand nautical miles," Boxer answered, "with a minimum of three-thousand yards from the launch point."

Borodine raised his eyebrows questioningly.

"With a ninety-eight percent accuracy throughout the entire range," Boxer said. "The *Shark* carries ten missiles with that kind of capability. Five of the ten are the cluster type."

"How many —"

"Each cluster has five independently targeted missiles."

Borodine shook his head. "Bush can launch from anywhere and destroy most of the cities west and east of the Urals. We must sink the *Shark* before he launches."

"Can we get a few more knots? Every bit of speed will help," Boxer said.

Borodine keyed his EO. "I need more speed," he said.

"We're pushing our luck now," the EO answered. "Everything is just below the red mark."

"Can we operate just into the red?"

"Yes. But with great danger."

"Go into the red," Borodine ordered.

"Aye, aye, Comrade Admiral," the EO answered. "But I cannot be held responsible for —"

"I will take full responsibility," Borodine said.

"Increasing pressure and steam flow."

"Roger that," Borodine answered; then looking at Boxer, he said, "We are now operating in the red zone."

Boxer nodded. He understood the risk. The reactor and the propulsion system were designed to operate within specific parameters. Borodine's order extended those parameters and if the safety factor of both systems was too close to the upper limit of their operational levels then anything from a runaway reactor to a boiler explosion could result…

"We will make a SYSCHECK every five minutes," Borodine said.

"Can you SYSCHECK on a continuing basis?" Boxer asked.

"No. Five minute intervals is the best we can do," Borodine answered.

Boxer watched the COMCOMP.

"We're up four knots," Borodine said.

Three red lights began to blink.

"Boiler pressure is one-hundred pounds more than its maximum operating pressure," Borodine explained. "The other two lights are temperature warnings."

Boxer said nothing. It was Borodine's show and he was playing it like the pro he was. *Novogorod* was now doing fifty-four and four-tenth knots.

The EO keyed Borodine. "Comrade Admiral we're running hot shaft bearings."

"Roger that," Borodine answered; then reported to Boxer what the EO had said.

"The *Shark* will pick up the sound of our bearings long before you'll pick her up on your sonar."

"At what range?"

"Depending upon the condition of the sea, between forty and fifty miles," Boxer answered. "And she'll be able to ID us."

"Without sonar?"

"Yes, without sonar," Boxer said.

Borodine keyed the EO. "Reduce power to cool shaft bearings."

"Reducing power," the EO answered.

Boxer watched the rpms diminish by two-hundred and fifty revolutions.

"We've lost two knots," Borodine said.

Boxer shrugged. He was a tall, lanky man with pepper and salt hair and beard and steel gray eyes that were bloodshot with weariness. The *Shark* was his boat. He knew every inch of her and now he had to destroy it before the men aboard her could start a war that would destroy the world.

"We're down another knot," Borodine reported.

"We're still operating in the red zone," Boxer answered, looking at the SYSSAT indicator.

Borodine ran a SYSCHEK. All systems were green. He looked at the clock. "Two hours at the most before we are in range," he said.

Boxer agreed.

Borodine switched on the MC. "All hands, now hear this... All hands now hear this... Two men at a time from each section will be permitted to go to the galley for coffee." He put the mike down and told Viktor to take the CONN; then to Boxer he said, "Come, Comrade and we will have coffee too."

"Good... I could use it," Boxer answered.

Kinkade, Chief of the CIA, Admiral Stark, Chief of Naval Operations, the members of the Joint Chiefs of Staff, the Cabinet and the President were seated in front of a huge electronic situation map in the War Room deep under the White House.

"Well, gentleman," the President said, speaking in a tired voice. "I don't see that we have much choice but to activate our emergency plans for the civilian population." He looked at Stark. "Have all of our ships put to sea?"

Stark shifted slightly forward. He was a tall, lean man with gray eyes and a full head of white hair. "All except those in drydock," he answered in his gravelly voice. "And we have moved all our land-based aircraft to areas away from known target areas. And all our missile-carrying submarines have been put on a yellow alert."

The President nodded and turned his attention to the Chief of the Air Force. "You ready to launch?"

"Ready," the general answered. "SAC is in the air and ready to go into Russia. We estimate that ten percent of our aircraft should reach their target area."

"What about the missiles?" the President asked. "How many of them will reach their targets?"

"If we wait until they launch first, we'll lose fifty to seventy-five percent of what we have before we ever launch. Of what is left, all of them should reach and destroy their targets. We could do a hell of a lot better than that if we launched first."

"I told you I don't want a pre-emptive strike," the President snapped.

"Mister President," Kinkade said, speaking slowly, "all of us here know your feelings about a pre-emptive strike. But given the circumstances it would certainly be to our advantage to make one."

Several of the men at the table agreed with him.

"You know that once the *Shark* fires its missiles, the Russians will retaliate by firing theirs at us," Kinkade said. "At least with a first strike we'll minimize the destruction that they can cause."

"Stark, what's your opinion?" the President asked.

"Either way, we won't come out a winner," Stark answered, studying Kinkade, who was very pale and almost fragile looking.

"Your missile-carrying subs can take out most of their strike capability," Kinkade said.

"Most but not all. Some of their birds will be launched and get through."

"I think the question we have to ask, Mister President," the Secretary of State said, "is what we will lose and whether the loss is acceptable."

"All right, what will we lose?" the President asked.

"This city for openers," Stark said. "New York, Chicago —"

"You're talking thirty million dead."

"More when you consider the after-effects," Stark said.

"But the losses could be four times that if the Russians launch first," Kinkade said.

"Is that true?" the President asked.

Stark nodded.

The President pushed his chair back, stood up and started to pace. He was a man of middling height with a slight paunch. Like everyone else in the room he needed a shave and his eyes were bloodshot from the lack of sleep. He stopped and faced the electronic situation map. "That's a damn big world to destroy," he muttered. "A damn big one and I don't want to be the one who gives the order to do it."

"Mister President," Kinkade said, "your counterpart in Russia has no such qualms. He knows that that advantage will be with the one who strikes first."

"I want a show of hands," the President said. "Those in favor of a pre-emptive strike. And now those against. There are equal numbers for and against it."

"That leaves it up to you," Kinkade said.

The President looked up at the clock. "Two more hours," he said. "We'll wait two more hours; then launch."

DB was one of the five men who survived the sinking of the American attack submarine *Neptune* by the *Tecumseh*. He slouched in a chair in the *Novogorod*'s small, crowded CIC room. He, Cowly and the admiral were the only three survivors taken aboard the *Novogorod.* The other two men, Captain Riggs and the cook, were left with the British marines.

DB looked at the three Russian sailors nearby. Like himself, they were very young. He was only twenty. But if he survived the mission he'd be twenty-one in two months. And like himself they were computer experts. They had rigged up a sonar broadcasting system. Over and over again the *Novogorod*'s active sonar was broadcasting code words that hopefully would access the central processing units of the *Shark*'s computer system.

But for the next ten minutes, the sonar was back under the control of the SO and DB had an opportunity to rest. He picked up a mug of coffee and drank. He started to drink coffee almost from the moment he had come aboard. Except for the few hours he had spent on the beach with the other survivors of the *Neptune*, he had spent all his time trying to break into the *Shark*'s computer system. His eyes burned from lack of sleep and every part of his body was stiff. Except for a few catnaps over the past four days, he hadn't slept.

DB's plan was to enter the system and find a computer whose password Bush hadn't changed. If he could find that, then he could wreak an enormous amount of havoc on the *Shark*. But if all the passwords had been changed, it might take days to crack the system and he knew they didn't have days. They didn't even have hours…

"You get the coffee," Borodine said. "And I'll see if the cook has some babka or pie."

"Good," Boxer answered and went to the urn, where there was always fresh coffee available. He took his black, with no sugar and called out to Borodine, "With cream and sugar?"

"Certainly with cream and sugar," Borodine answered. "Lots of sugar, if you please."

Boxer brought two steaming mugs of coffee to the table, where Borodine was already seated.

"Apple pie with ice cream," Borodine said, gesturing to the two plates in front of him.

Boxer sat down. "In my wildest dreams," he said, "I don't think I could have dreamed up this situation."

"We are strange bedfellows in more ways than this one," Borodine commented.

Boxer had started to lift his mug. "If you mean —"

"I mean," Borodine said, "we loved the same woman."

Without drinking from it, Boxer put the mug down.

"Trish," Borodine said.

He couldn't answer or think. He felt as if he had been thrust back into the sea with the surface far above him and depths deeper than he ever could have imagined.

"I loved her," Borodine said quietly.

"Did she love you?"

"She loved the two of us," Borodine answered.

Boxer picked up his mug and this time he drank. "Were you the reason she didn't want to go to New York?" he asked, holding the mug in his two hands.

"Yes."

Boxer remembered the morning he had returned to the apartment. Trish had not slept there the previous night.

"She would not have married you," Borodine said.

"Did she tell you that?"

"Not in so many words," Borodine answered.

"Would you have married her?"

"Even if I wanted to, I couldn't," Borodine answered.

"But you wouldn't. She was good enough to screw, but not to marry. Right?"

Borodine shook his head. "No," he answered in the same soft tone he had been using. "She was everything a man could want in a woman, except she couldn't find sexual satisfaction with just one man."

Boxer sipped at his coffee again.

"Didn't you suspect anything?" Borodine asked.

Boxer was about to answer, no. But he stopped himself. He was marginally aware that Trish was distracted.

"I told you now," Borodine said, "because I wanted you to know that two of us have lost her. That in the end she would have belonged to neither of us."

"I was going to ask her again to marry me," Boxer said.

"She wouldn't have. But I'm sure she would have told you about us. Yes, I am certain she would have told you."

"You know," Boxer said, "she was the only woman I was ever faithful to."

Borodine shrugged. "Sometimes, it happens that way. But for what it is worth, I wanted you to know that I loved her too."

"Is that why you told me?"

"No," Borodine said. "I told you because I would like you to be happy."

"Be happy that you were screwing her?" Boxer questioned, his voice suddenly becoming louder.

Borodine put his finger across his lips. "No… No… If we survive, I wanted you to put your relationship with Trish in its proper perspective. I wanted you to let go of the grief you feel and go on with your life. I wanted to free you of her and any guilt you have about her death."

"And what do I do for you in turn?" Boxer asked.

Without hesitation, Borodine answered, "Keep me as a friend and don't resent Trish. She gave us all she had to give." And he offered Boxer his hand.

Boxer took hold of Borodine's hand and shook it. "I guess I always knew she wouldn't marry me."

"Friends?" Borodine asked.

"Friends," Boxer answered. "Friends."

DB's tow head nodded. He felt someone shake him and snapped back to alertness. He realized the control of the sonar had been passed back to him. For a long moment he stared at the computer screen before he realized that the *Shark*'s computers were answering.

"I'm into the system!" he exclaimed, leaping to his feet. "Christ, I'm into the fucking system!"

The Russian sailors began to jabber to each other.

"Easy does it," DB said, "Easy... We only have a foot in the door; we still have to open the damn door." He watched the list of the *Shark*'s computers fill the screen.

COMCOMP — UNAUTHORIZED ENTRY

MINICOMCOMP — UNAUTHORIZED ENTRY

NAVCOMP — UNAUTHORIZED ENTRY

ENCOMP — UNAUTHORIZED ENTRY

ASWCOMP — UNAUTHORIZED ENTRY

In a matter of moments the list was complete. Every computer was closed.

"Now the fun begins," DB said, still standing. He turned to one of the Russian sailors. "Call your captain. I've made contact with the *Shark*."

The man just stared at him.

DB pointed to the screen. "The *Shark*," he said with growing impatience. "Call your Captain... Admiral Borodine."

The man nodded briskly and immediately went to one of the nearby officers...

Boxer and Borodine hurried into the CIC and before Boxer could ask any questions, DB said, "I'm into the *Shark*." And he pointed to the screen.

"Can you get control of any one of the computers?" Boxer asked.

"I'm sure as hell going to try, Skipper," DB answered.

Boxer nodded. "Maybe this will help," he said. "Put yourself in Bush's shoes. He's off the wall. But there's a certain logic to his madness. He sees and hears things that don't exist. His reality might easily be our nightmares."

"I think I understand," DB said.

Boxer turned to Borodine. "I want to notify my people that we've accessed the *Shark*'s computers."

"Wouldn't it be wiser to wait until we have control of one?"

Boxer motioned Borodine aside. "I don't want my people to make any rash moves."

"Rash moves?"

"A pre-emptive strike," Boxer said.

Borodine's eyes went wide. "My people might do the same."

"They might. All the hawks in the world don't live in Washington; Moscow has a few of them."

Borodine keyed COMMO. "Call headquarters for me and open a communication channel with Langley for Admiral Boxer. He will give you a call frequency. I am going to the bridge."

"Aye, aye, Comrade Admiral," the COMMO answered.

Borodine and Boxer left the CIC and went directly to the bridge.

"I have the CONN," Borodine told Viktor.

"Aye, aye, Comrade Admiral," Viktor said, relinquishing the chair in front of the COMCOMP to Borodine.

The COMMO keyed Borodine. "Comrade Admiral, you have an open channel to Moscow and a channel is open to Langley."

"Roger that," Borodine answered and handing a mike and a set of earphones to Boxer, he said, "Plug them where those two jacks are."

Boxer identified himself.

"Please wait for voice confirmation," a computerized voice said.

Boxer pursed his lips and drummed the fingers of his right hand against the edge of the COMCOMP.

"Voice confirmed," the computer said.

Within moments Boxer was speaking to one of Kinkade's aides. "I don't care if he's with the President," Boxer said. "I want this call patched through to him immediately... I mean immediately. If you hesitate a fraction of a second, I will have your ass, your fucking job and anything else you have... Understand?"

"Yes, Admiral," the aide answered.

"This is the President," a man said.

"This is Admiral Boxer. We have just accessed the *Shark*'s computers and we should intercept her within the next hour."

"We were not notified —"

"Mister President, I am notifying you," Boxer said sharply.

A moment later Kinkade was on the line. "Have you gained control of the *Shark*'s computers?"

"We will," Boxer answered, trying to sound more certain than he actually felt.

"That's not good enough," Kinkade said. "Not at all good enough."

"Put Stark on," Boxer told him.

"Stark here," the admiral said in his gravelly voice.

"Admiral, you must stop them from launching a pre-emptive strike. Either we'll get the *Shark* or other Russian ships will. Hopefully before Bush can launch. But if the United States launches first, we won't have a snowball's chance in hell of stopping the Russians from launching."

"What's going to stop them from making the first strike?" Stark asked.

"Borodine, I hope," Boxer answered. "He's speaking to his people now just the way I'm speaking to you."

"There's a clock here and it's running," Stark said.

"How much time?"

"An hour."

"Not enough. I need at least another hour. Can you get it for me?"

"I'm not sure."

"For Christ sakes," Boxer exploded, "those bastards are playing Russian roulette for the whole fucking world! They don't have the right to do that."

"Stay on the air," Stark said.

"Roger that," Boxer answered and drew the sleeve of his right hand across his brow to wipe the sweat away. He looked over at Borodine and realized he was having his problems too.

"You have thirty minutes more," Stark said.

Boxer shook his head.

"Did you hear me?" Stark asked.

"I heard you," Boxer answered. "But I can't believe those horse's asses don't understand —"

"Thirty minutes," Stark repeated.

"Roger that," Boxer answered. "Out." And he unplugged the mike and earphones. He was furious. For the first time in his life, he understood how stupid politicians were.

Borodine was finished with his conversation and turned to Boxer. "How much time did you buy us?" he asked.

"I'd guess about as much as you did," Boxer said.

"Thirty minutes."

Boxer nodded. "Thirty minutes."

"From when?"

"An hour from now."

"There must be something about politicians," Boxer said, "that makes them so much alike. I think they're like interchangeable parts. You can shift them from country to country and except for a few minor differences they will act the same and do the same stupid things."

"Are you telling me that your people have set the same launch time?" Borodine asked.

"To the minute," Boxer answered. "To the fucking minute!"

Sweating profusely, McElroy hunkered down close to the prostrate Bush. "Get up, you son of a bitch," he shouted. "Get up." He looked at the clock on the COMCOMP. The big hand pointed to twelve and raced. Bush was unconscious for more than an hour. The bastard had tried to kill him.

McElroy's eyes went from the clock to the depth gauge over the COMCOMP. They were three-hundred and fifty feet down. That was all he knew. He didn't even know where they were, except that Bush had changed their course before he became completely uncontrollable.

McElroy stood up. His knees hurt and his throat was very dry. To save himself and to save the cause, he needed the lunatic on the floor. He reached into his jacket pocket and took out the gun he had struck Bush with and shook his head. If he hadn't wrested it from Bush, the son of a bitch would have used it on him. Trying to keep that bastard under control was more than he had bargained for.

He sat down and wiped his brow with a handkerchief. He was feeling sorry for himself and he wasn't a damn bit ashamed of it. If it hadn't been for Boxer and that smart kike lawyer of his, he would have been able to prove that Boxer was at the very least a communist sympathizer and not fit to command the *Shark*, or any other American naval vessel. "Yeah," McElroy said aloud, "I would have been the hero of the American people and the country's next President. And Trish would have been First Lady. Trish, you couldn't keep your thighs closed. You had to crawl into bed with Boxer and then with Borodine!"

McElroy wiped his brow again. "I had it all in the palm of my hand," he said, "and it was stolen from me." He looked at Bush. "And now that son of a bitch just lies there and won't get up."

Angry, he left the chair and began to walk in a circle around the bridge. Then suddenly he rushed at Bush and kicking him in the side, he screamed, "Get up you bastard… Get up!"

Bush groaned.

McElroy kicked him again.

Bush's eyes fluttered open.

McElroy pointed the .38 at him. "If you're not on your fucking feet at the count of three, so help me God, I'll kill you."

Bush smiled. "If you kill me, you might as well kill yourself. Even for a mealy-mouthed coward like you, a quick death would be better than the slow one you'd have aboard the *Shark*."

McElroy's anger collapsed. He could feel himself go limp. "This is not the time for us to be arguing," he said weakly.

"I'm not moving unless you give me the gun," Bush said.

"What?"

"The gun, or I'll stay here."

"Bastard!" McElroy swore.

Bush smiled at him.

McElroy pointed the gun at him.

"Go ahead, shoot!" Bush challenged.

McElroy's trigger finger tightened. "You don't think I'll do it, do you?"

Bush shrugged.

Suddenly an explosion cascaded through the *Shark*. A single round pinged off the steel deck, struck a bulkhead and, spent, fell to the deck again.

Bush remained motionless.

The acrid stink of burnt powder made McElroy's eyes water. He felt the intense need to sneeze.

"The gun," Bush said, reaching up for it with his hand.

McElroy handed the weapon to him.

"Better," Bush said, scrambling to his feet. "Much better." He smiled. "First things first!" And he smashed the .38 across the bridge of McElroy's nose.

The burst of pain filled McElroy's skull. He dropped to his knees and blood gushed from his nose. The next blow sent him sprawling on the deck.

"Now," Bush said, "get to your feet and man your battle station, or I will kill you, Mister."

McElroy struggled to gain his feet.

"Good," Bush said. "Very good… In a little while from now, Mister, we will have made history!"

McElroy held a handkerchief to his bleeding nose. "I should have killed you," he muttered.

Bush smiled. "You didn't have the guts," he answered.

CHAPTER 2

"Target," the SO reported. "Bearing one-eight degrees... Range ten thousand yards... Speed three-five knots... Depth four hundred feet... Course two-seven-zero degrees... Sound ID the *Shark*."

"Roger that," Borodine answered; then turning to Boxer, he said, "Target just came on the sonar."

Boxer checked the scope. "Bush must have been tracking us for at least a half hour," Boxer commented.

Borodine switched on the MC. "All hands now hear this," he said, "All hands... Target picked up and identified... Rig for silent running... Rig for silent running."

With the exception of Cowly and Viktor, everyone not assigned to a duty station hurried to his bunk and stayed in it.

Borodine turned to Viktor. "Activate ECM."

"ECM activated," Viktor answered, changing the positions of several switches on the ECM panel.

The SO keyed Borodine. "Two targets... Bearing one-eight degrees... Range nine thousand yards... Speed five-zero knots... Torpedoes closing fast"

"Roger that," Borodine answered. "Helmsman, come to course three-two degrees."

"Coming to course three-two degrees," the helmsman answered.

Boxer watched the scope. The two blips moved rapidly toward them.

"Targets changing course to nine-eight degrees... Closing fast," the SO reported.

Borodine keyed the Fire Control Officer. "Activate Killer Dart control computer."

"Killer Dart control computer activated… Information being accepted and processed from CIC… Killer Dart battery one ready to fire."

"Fire," Borodine answered.

"Battery fired," the FCO answered.

"Roger that," Borodine answered. He pointed to a digital clock on the COMCOMP and in a whisper said to Boxer, "Ten seconds."

Boxer nodded and watched the scope. Two Killer Darts rushed toward their targets; then merged with them. The explosion thundered through the water and crashed against the *Novogorod*, making her yaw and pitch wildly.

"Helmsman come to one-eight degrees," Borodine said.

"Coming to one-eight degrees," the helmsman answered.

"How many torpedoes does the *Shark* have?" Borodine asked.

"Ten… Five sonar controlled… And five self-homing. They'll track by sound. Two of the ten are nuclear. But they need a special arming key."

"Does Bush have that key?"

Boxer looked at Cowly. "Do you think he has it?"

"It's in the combination safe in the CIC," Cowly answered.

"I never gave Bush the safe's combination," Boxer said.

"Neither did I," Cowly answered.

Boxer faced Borodine. "Scratch two nuclear fish," he said.

"At least we have something he doesn't have," Borodine answered.

"You also have the Killer Darts," Boxer said.

"Only four left," Borodine answered. "I need them to —"

"Skipper?" DB called.

Boxer swung around. DB was on the bridge.

"I did it," DB said. "I entered the *Shark*'s computer system."

"Where?"

"At the COMCOMP," DB answered, smiling broadly.

Borodine shook his head. "Too fast," he said. "I can't understand."

"DB is into the *Shark*'s COMCOMP," Boxer said.

"Can he —"

The SO keyed Borodine. "Target bearing two-five degrees... Range eight thousand yards... Speed forty-five knots... Closing fast."

"Roger that," Borodine answered, checking the scope. "The *Shark* is coming directly toward us."

"Four new targets," the SO reported. "Bearing two-five degrees... Range six thousand yards... Speed fifty knots... Closing fast."

"Save your Killer Darts," Boxer said. "Get those torpedoes with one of ours."

Borodine keyed the forward TO. "Load and arm N torpedo in tube one... Rig for CIC control."

"N torpedo armed and loaded in tube one... Range on CIC control," the TO answered.

Borodine keyed the CIC. "N torpedo armed and loaded... CIC direct."

"N torpedo under CIC control," the FCO officer answered.

Borodine keyed the forward TO. "Fire N torpedo."

"N torpedo fired," the TO answered.

The seconds flashed by on the digital clock.

Boxer sucked in his breath.

Borodine switched on the MC. "All hands brace yourselves... All hands brace yourselves..."

DB ran back to the CIC.

The explosion came when the DIGCLOCK stopped at 45. And the *Novogorod* was suddenly lifted up and thrown sideways.

Boxer lost his footing and crashed against the side of the hull. Viktor and Cowly piled on top of him.

The lights went out. An instant later the *Novogorod* dropped until she crashed onto the bottom.

The screams of the injured filled the boat.

The emergency generator kicked in and dim yellow lights flickered on.

Rolling from side to side, the boat began to rise.

Suddenly the screaming increased.

Viktor shouted something in Russian.

Boxer looked toward the COMCOMP. Borodine was slumped over it.

"Broken steam lines in the engine room," Viktor said, struggling to his feet.

Cowly stood up and reaching down, pulled Boxer up.

Red lights were flashing all over the COMCOMP.

Boxer went to Borodine. He was unconscious and bleeding profusely from two deep cuts on his forehead. Boxer set him down on the deck. "Get a medic here!" Boxer ordered.

Viktor shouted for a medic; then he said, "There are many injured and much damage."

Boxer looked up at the COMCOMP. At least half of the red lights had become green. They were at 400 hundred feet again. But they were off course and no longer operating in the red zone.

Borodine made a noise.

Boxer and Viktor hunkered alongside of him.

His eyes rolled toward Boxer and he tried to speak.

"Where the hell is that medic?" Boxer asked.

"There are only two on board," Viktor explained.

Borodine struggled to speak and coughed up blood.

Boxer looked at the COMCOMP. "Better take command," he said to Viktor. "Get a damage and casualty report and put us back on course."

"Yes, Comrade Admiral," Viktor answered. He looked toward the helmsman.

Boxer looked too. The man had been thrown to the deck and hadn't moved.

Suddenly all the lights came on.

"I'll take the helm," Cowly said.

"Good," Viktor commented and went to the COMCOMP. Within moments he said, "We have hull damage... Damage in engineering... One radar is out and we're taking on water."

"Can our pumps handle the water?"

"Yes," Viktor answered. "But we can't make more than two-five knots. Several ruptured steam lines."

Borodine began to cough again.

Boxer turned toward him.

"You and Viktor," he managed to croak. "You take command... Must stop the *Shark*... You must take command."

Boxer looked up at Viktor. "Your people in Moscow won't like it," he said.

"My people in Moscow aren't aboard this boat," Viktor answered.

Suddenly the medic came onto the bridge.

Viktor spoke to him in Russian and the man answered. Then Viktor said to Boxer, "We have five burn cases, several with broken arms and legs and many more with bad bruises."

Boxer nodded.

The DCO keyed Viktor. "Steam pipes repaired."

"Roger that," Viktor answered and told Boxer what had been reported.

The medic spoke to Viktor.

"The Comrade Admiral has internal injuries," Viktor said, "and should be brought to a hospital as soon as possible. The cuts on his forehead are deep but look worse than they are."

"Get him to his bunk," Boxer said; then pointing to the helmsman, he added, "Have the medic look at him."

The medic walked over to the helmsman, bent down, felt for a pulse and shaking his head, he said, "This man is dead."

Viktor translated what he said; he told him to remove the body.

Boxer turned his attention to the COMCOMP. He looked at the sonar display. The *Shark* was still on it. But it was to the west of where they were. "Come to course two-six-four degrees."

"Coming to course two-six-four degrees," Cowly responded.

Viktor stood alongside Boxer.

"Do a systems check," Boxer said.

Viktor ran his fingers over several keys and then he said, "Look at the panel on the upper right of the COMCOMP: the first two lights show operational status of the reactor; second two of the propulsion system; third, the hydraulic system; fourth, the air scrubbing system and fifth, the boat's electrical system."

A red light was flashing for the propulsion and the hydraulic system.

Viktor pointed to the propulsion system. "That's because we have lost steam pressure."

"Any way of shutting it off?" Boxer asked.

Viktor shook his head. "It will go off if we can go to our operating pressure."

The SO keyed Viktor. "Target bearing two-six-four degrees… Range eleven thousand yards… Speed forty knots… Closing fast."

"Roger that," Viktor answered and translated for Boxer.

The two men looked at the sonar display.

"Arm SUBROCS," Boxer said.

Viktor passed the command.

"Negative, Comrade Captain," the FCO answered.

"Explain… Malfunction indication on launch tube," the FCO said.

"It's not shown on the SYSCHEK," Viktor answered.

"I have it on the Launch Panel," the FCO said.

"Roger that. Stand by."

"Aye, aye, Comrade Captain," the FCO responded.

Viktor gave Boxer a shortened version of the conversation.

"Besides limiting our fire power, it also makes the operational status of other systems suspect too," Boxer said.

Viktor nodded, keyed the DCO and explained the situation.

"I'd trust the indication on the Launch Panel, Comrade Captain. And the American admiral is probably right about the operational status of the other systems," the DCO said.

"Roger that," Viktor responded and related the DCO answer.

"We're sitting in a goddamn bomb!" Boxer exclaimed.

The SO keyed Viktor. "Comrade Captain, Target bearing, two-six-four degrees… Range ten thousand yards… Speed four-five knots… Target closing fast," he reported.

"Roger," Viktor acknowledged and pointing to the sonar display, he said to Boxer, "If she comes closer, we can use our Killer Darts."

"If she comes closer and fires her torpedoes or SUB-ROCS we'll be blown out of the water," Boxer answered.

"Skipper," DB said, coming onto the bridge again, "you can talk to the *Shark*."

Boxer turned. "What do you mean, I can talk to the *Shark*?"

"I'm into the communication system," DB answered. "I can control it from where I am."

"Can you control the COMCOMP?"

"Still working on it, Skipper," DB said.

Boxer turned to Viktor. "It's worth a try. It might buy enough time for the surface ships to get here."

Viktor nodded.

"Patch me through," Boxer said.

"Aye, aye, Skipper," DB answered and hurried back to his place in the CIC.

"Bush, this is Admiral Boxer," Boxer said.

Startled, Bush leaped to his feet and knocked over the captain's chair in front of the COMCOMP.

"You're in a no win situation, Bush," Boxer said.

"Come out. I know you're here. I know you're on the *Shark*."

McElroy looked at Bush. His eyes were wide and staring.

"You were always out to get me," Bush said, looking around. "Come out where I can see you."

"I'm not on the *Shark*."

"If you're not here, where are you?"

"On the Russian submarine *Novogorod*. On the submarine that destroyed your —"

"Did you hear that, McElroy," Bush shouted with glee. "You were right all the time. Boxer is a fucking communist."

"Bush," Boxer said, "before there's more bloodshed, I'm asking you to surface and surrender."

Bush grinned. "No, Comrade Admiral Boxer. I know your boat is damaged. I know you've lost some of your fire power, or you would have used it against me. No, I will not surrender to you. But in the name of the World Federation, I demand that you surface and turn over your crew and boat to me." Then to McElroy, he whispered, "Turn on the UWIS... That switch there. Now set the second switch to three-six-zero degrees. Good."

"Bush, your offer is unacceptable," Boxer said.

"Then I will proceed to destroy you," Bush answered. He checked the UWIS. There were no other submarines within its 25,000 yard operational range.

"Bush," Boxer said, "even if you launch —"

"There isn't any 'even'," Bush shouted. "I *will* launch!"

"You will be found and destroyed," Boxer said, ignoring Bush's outburst.

"Launch now!" McElroy exclaimed.

"I'm prepared to die," Bush answered. "Are you prepared to die, Comrade Admiral Boxer?"

"Launch now!" McElroy demanded.

Bush ignored him.

"If my dying will stop you, I am prepared to —"

McElroy leaped at Bush and grabbed the gun. "Launch," he hissed. "Launch or I'll blow your fucking head off."

"Did you hear that, Comrade Admiral Boxer?" Bush chortled. "Did you hear what that puny man said to me? He's going to blow my 'fucking head off.' And he thinks that's going to scare me. He's pointing a gun at me and he doesn't know how to operate anything more complicated than a fucking car let alone something as complicated as the *Shark*."

"McElroy," Boxer said, "you still have a chance."

"No chance," McElroy shouted. "No chance... Launch those missiles... Launch them!"

"You heard the man," Bush said. "We're going to launch condition." He ran his fingers over several keys. The *Shark* began to lose headway.

"What's happening?" McElroy demanded to know.

"We can't launch at flank speed."

"Put the list of targets on the screen," McElroy said.

The target list came up on the screen.

"Good. Now eliminate those not in Russia," McElroy said, wiping the sweat off his forehead with his free hand.

"Now what?" Bush asked with a broad smile

"Launch!"

"Asshole," Bush exclaimed contemptuously. "You're a fucking asshole. Comrade Admiral Boxer, the pity is that I have to work with an asshole."

"Bush, you don't have to work with an asshole," Boxer said.

"It's the only way. Sometimes it's the only way to get the job done."

"Bush —"

"Listen asshole," Bush said to McElroy, "you just don't launch missiles by snapping your fingers. You have to arm them." And he switched on the red arming lever. Then he took two keys out of his pocket and threw one at McElroy. "That key goes in the lock on the other side of the bridge. Now listen to what I tell you and do exactly what I tell you." And he began to explain the missile launch sequence. "The missile lights are green, Comrade Admiral Boxer," Bush announced gleefully. "The firing sequence has begun!"

"Got it," shouted DB from the CIC. "I got it... I clicked into the missile firing sequence."

"Jam it!" Boxer shouted back. "Jam the fucking sequence!"

"Aye, aye, Skipper," DB answered.

Viktor grinned and switched on another monitor. "That's what your DB is looking at," he said. "Those spiked waves are the missile computers."

Suddenly the spikes went flat.

"Got it," DB yelled. "All missiles disarmed."

Suddenly Bush realized that the launch countdown clock had stopped. His brow furrowed. He heard the beeping sound. "Do you hear that? Do you hear that?" he yelled.

"It just started," McElroy said. "It started when that red light began to flash. What the hell does it mean?"

Bush looked up toward the red light. It was the signal that an unauthorized entry into the COMCOMP had taken place. "It's impossible... It couldn't happen... It couldn't happen!"

"What couldn't happen?" McElroy asked, coming to the COMCOMP.

"It couldn't happen," Bush screamed. "I changed the master code words..." Suddenly the horses began to run. He saw them coming toward him. "I changed the fucking master code words. Someone gave them the master code words. You gave it to them. You gave them the master code words..." A huge herd... "I'm going to kill you... I'm going to kill you before the horses get here!" And he flung himself on McElroy.

"Launch your Killer Darts," Boxer said.

Viktor nodded and keyed the FCO. "Stand by to launch Killer Darts," he said.

"Aye, aye, Comrade Captain," the FCO answered.

Viktor checked the COMCOMP. The *Shark* was still on a collision course with them. "Launch," he said.

"Killer Darts away," the FCO answered.

"Roger that," Viktor said.

Within moments the Killer Darts appeared on the scope.

"One-five-five seconds to impact," Viktor said.

Boxer nodded. Knowing that the *Shark* was going to die suddenly filled him with a great sadness. She had been his real home; she had also been his fortress…

McElroy squeezed the trigger; the explosion rang through the length of the *Shark*.

"Missed!" Bush shouted. "You fucking missed."

McElroy squeezed the trigger twice in rapid succession.

The two explosions merged into one deafening rumble.

Bush faltered. "Bastard!" he screamed, holding his right side.

"Look," McElroy shouted, "look at the screen… The UWIS screen!"

Bush shook his head. The horses were very close.

"Look!" McElroy yelled, pointing to the screen.

Bush slowly turned. "Horses … the horses are here," he cried. "They're here…"

"Five seconds to impact," Viktor intoned; he switched on the MC and said, "All hands rig for shock waves… All hands rig for shock waves."

Boxer braced himself against the COMCOMP and glanced over at Cowly.

"Doing fine, Skipper," Cowly said.

Boxer nodded and moved his eyes to the sonar display. "Now," he said under his breath.

An explosion thundered over the *Novogorod*; then another one.

Boxer was sweating and he could hear his heart thump.

A third and fourth explosion boomed through the icy arctic waters. And within seconds the *Novogorod* shuddered and began to drop.

Viktor keyed the DO. "Switching Dive Control to Auto... Venting all ballast... Diving planes going to one-zero degrees." Even as he spoke his fingers worked several switches.

"Not responding," Boxer said.

A second shock wave slammed down on the *Novogorod*, driving it deeper.

Viktor keyed the EO. "Give me full power... Go into the red zone."

"Going to red zone," the EO said.

A dozen more red lights began to flash on the COMCOMP.

A third shock wave grabbed hold of the boat, making it roll wildly from side to side.

The DCO keyed Viktor. "Comrade Captain, we're taking on more water."

"Roger that," Viktor said and gave Boxer the report.

Suddenly a fourth explosion smashed down on the *Novogorod*.

Boxer looked at the sonar display. All targets were gone.

The shock wave slammed the *Novogorod* onto the bottom. The lights went out again but immediately came back on.

"Christ!" Boxer exclaimed, as he was thrown to the deck.

The EO keyed Viktor. "Comrade Captain, we're running close to a meltdown."

"Reduce power," Viktor responded.

"Aye, aye, Comrade Captain," the EO said.

Boxer pulled himself to his feet. He looked at the depth gauge. They were down five hundred and fifty feet. But even as he was looking at it, the needle began to move counter clockwise. They were going up.

"Stand by to surface," Viktor announced over the MC. "Deck detail stand by… Bridge detail stand by." Then, turning to Boxer, he grinned broadly and said, "It's done."

Boxer nodded and grinned back; then he looked at his watch. There was only fifteen minutes left to the deadline. "Better radio our people," he said. "We don't want them to do anything stupid.'

Boxer entered Borodine's cabin.

Though his eyes were closed, Borodine was conscious. Slowly, he opened his eyes. "The *Shark* is down, isn't it?" he asked.

"Yes," Boxer answered, nodding.

Borodine reached for Boxer's hand. "Any missiles launched?"

"None," Boxer said.

Borodine uttered a deep sigh and said, "Good… Good… How did you do it?"

"DB guessed what the password was," Boxer said.

"It was Bush, wasn't it?"

"Yes… But how did you know that?"

Borodine shrugged and winced from the pain. "It came to me while I was sleeping, or at least I think I was sleeping."

"Better try and get some sleep now," Boxer said.

"Not now," Borodine said. "Now I want to talk to you for a few minutes."

Boxer pulled a gray metal chair close to Borodine's bunk and sat down.

"You know that some day in the future we will again face one another —"

"Igor, this is not the time to discuss that, or even think about it," Boxer said.

Borodine waved the objection aside. "Should that time come, I will follow my orders, just as I know you will. But in my heart, I will always keep you as my friend."

"We can never be anything else but friends, no matter what we must do for our respective countries."

Borodine nodded; then he said, "There's more that I want to say about Trish."

"Go ahead," Boxer answered.

"She did love the two of us," Borodine said.

Boxer uttered a deep sigh. "Yes, I suppose she did."

"I don't want you to be angry with her because —"

"I'm not," Boxer told him. "I'm really not. I can't say that I understand why she did what she did. But I do understand that—"

"It's enough for me that you're not angry with her," Borodine said, closing his eyes. "And that you're not angry with me."

"I'm not angry with you," Boxer responded.

"Good," Borodine said with a smile. "Good, now I can sleep..."

Boxer stood up and quietly left the cabin...

"Well gentlemen, as they say in Hollywood," the President said, "that's a wrap. We can go home and sleep peacefully in our beds."

Stark stood up first. "Admiral Boxer expects to be back in Washington by late tonight. His last message was from destroyer *Hanly*. He will be transferred from the *Hanly* to a carrier and flown here."

"I will want to see him the day after tomorrow," the President said.

"Yes, Mister President," Stark answered.

"You tell me what would be an appropriate decoration to give him, Captain Cowly, and the young sailor who managed to get control of those computers."

"You will have my recommendations first thing in the morning," Stark said; then turning to Kinkade, he said, "I'll give you a lift, if you want one."

Kinkade nodded. "I'll go with you," he answered.

The other men who were seated around the table began to stand.

Stark and Kinkade bid the President and the other men goodnight and left the situation room. Neither of them spoke until they were outside in the parking lot.

The night was cool, clear and crisp.

"How about walking a few blocks?" Stark asked. "I'll have my limo follow us."

"Good idea," Kinkade answered; then looking up at the sky, he added, "I have to say I'm glad we didn't have to launch. I'm very glad."

"So am I and so is the rest of the world," Stark said, "only they don't know it."

Kinkade nodded and after a few minutes of silence, he said, "I've written my resignation letter. It will be on the President's desk by the end of the week. I'm very tired and I want to enjoy myself before my time runs out."

"I understand," Stark said. "I will leave as soon as the *Barracuda* is finished. That should be in another six months."

There was another long period of silence before Kinkade spoke again. "Trish was really all I had in the world."

Stark didn't answer.

"I was hoping to see great-grandchildren," Kinkade said in a tight voice. "But I guess that was never in the cards."

"Probably not," Stark replied.

"I keep thinking about the three of them... Boxer, Borodine and Trish. Boxer and Borodine are like two sides of the same coin and she had to have both of them. For the life of me, I can't understand what made her the way she was."

"I don't understand either," Stark said. "But if I were you, I'd let go of it. It's all over. It doesn't matter any more"

"You're right," Kinkade replied, "it doesn't matter any more, except that now, with her gone, I have nothing. Absolutely nothing."

Stark knew Kinkade was right and he said, "I guess neither of us have anything. You lost your granddaughter and I never had the son who was really mine."

Kinkade stopped. "Boxer?"

Stark nodded and the two men continued to walk in silence...

CHAPTER 3

Boxer, Cowly, and DB, whose real name, Boxer finally learned on the flight to Washington, was Donald Butts, were met at the airport by a Navy limo and driven to Washington.

Cowly was dropped off at Cynthia's apartment and Boxer and DB went to the hotel where Boxer had previously stayed whenever he was in Washington. He could have gone to the apartment he had shared with Trish, but it held too many memories.

After they checked in, Boxer offered to buy DB a drink.

"If you don't mind, Skipper, I'll take a rain check," DB said, "I'm just beat to shit."

Boxer nodded. "I'll give you a call for breakfast. We're due at the CNO's office at eleven hundred."

"Good night, Skipper," DB said.

"Good night," Boxer answered and turning around, he crossed the lobby, went into the cocktail lounge and chose a stool at the bar. The maxi-screen TV was on and a new commentator was talking about how close the country came to war.

Boxer looked around. There were a few couples in the booths and at the tables and at one end of the bar there were two other men. None of them seemed to be the slightest bit interested in what the commentator was saying.

"What will you have?" the barkeep asked, coming up to him.

"A Stoli on the rocks," Boxer answered.

"One Stoli on the rocks," the barkeep echoed and added, "we close in ten minutes."

Boxer looked at his watch: it was ten minutes to two. "Had no idea it was that late," he commented, as the barkeep set his drink down. Then he looked up at the TV and asked, "Would you please turn that off."

The man gave him a peculiar look.

"The same story has been on all night," he said, trying to give the impression he had seen and heard it before.

"Leave it on, barkeep," one of the other two men at the bar said, speaking with a decided western twang. "Hell man, aren't you interested that we saved the world."

Boxer looked at him. He was a gray-haired man of middling height, expensively dressed and he wore snakeskin boots. The man next him was taller, as well dressed and his boots were made of tooled leather. Boxer looked at them and smiled. "We didn't," he finally said and picking up the glass, he drank.

"For shit sake," the man said, "what the hell do you mean by saying, 'we didn't,' when every asshole knows we did."

Boxer shook his head. He should have kept his mouth shut. He didn't need some drunk arguing with him.

"Mister," the man said, "I asked you what you meant?"

Boxer pointed to his empty glass and looking at the barkeep, he said, "Do it again."

"The trouble is we got too many Reds in this country," the man said, his voice becoming loud enough to attract the attention of the couples in the booths.

The barkeep put another Stoli in front of Boxer.

"If we didn't save this fucking world, tell me who did?" the man asked.

Boxer was about to answer when his picture came on the screen. And the commentator said, "This man, Admiral Jack Boxer, commanded our naval units in the action against the renegade submarine. He was solely responsible for its destruction and according to several highly placed officials, who prefer to remain anonymous, the Russian role was minimal."

Suddenly angry, Boxer exclaimed, "That's a lie, mister... That's a lie!"

"What the hell are you talking about?" the man on the stool asked.

Boxer pointed to picture on the screen. "That's me. I was there and that commentator doesn't know what he's talking about."

The barkeep looked at Boxer and then at the picture. "Son of a bitch, it's him," he said, "or his fucking double!"

"That really you?" the man asked.

Boxer nodded. "It's me."

"Hey," the man said, "how was I supposed to know —"

Boxer held up his hand. "It's all right. No harm was done. It's all right."

"Barkeep, the admiral's drinks are on me. Put them on my tab. Admiral," the man said, getting off the bar stool and coming toward Boxer, "my name is Jay Corless Archer. But my friends call me Jay." And he held out his hand. "It's a pleasure to meet you."

Boxer shook his hand.

"My friend is William White. But most people call him Billy. Com'on over here, Billy," Jay called.

Billy eased himself off the stool and came to where Boxer was seated. "Howdy," he said, pumping Boxer's hand.

"Billy and me are here to see some government people," Jay said. "But in a couple of days we're flying back home to Texas. Why don't you join us."

Boxer was about to say no, when Billy said, "Think on it, Admiral. It might be just what the doctor ordered."

"I'll think about it," Boxer said.

"Good!" Jay exclaimed with a smile.

"Closing time," the barkeep announced.

"Too bad," Billy said, "I was just getting to where I was ready to do some serious drinking."

"I know a few places just across the river —"

"Admiral, would you join us?" Billy asked.

Boxer shook his head. "Thanks, but not tonight. I'm very tired."

"Know what you mean an' how you feel," Billy said.

"Yeah, I guess it's best to call it a night," Jay commented; then to the barkeep, he said, "Now you remember, while I'm a guest here, the Admiral's drinks and food are on me. You make sure everyone knows that."

"I will, Mister Archer," the man said.

Embarrassed, Boxer mumbled, "Thanks."

Jay smiled. "It's my pleasure," he said.

Boxer stood up.

"I guess I'm ready for bed too," Billy said. "Besides, Holly is probably wonderin' where I am."

Boxer guessed Holly was Billy's wife.

Jay nodded and winked.

Boxer didn't understand the wink, but decided not to question it. And flanked by his new-found companions, he left the cocktail lounge.

"Billy and me," Jay said, "have the two penthouse suites."

"I'm on the twenty-first floor," Boxer responded.

They crossed the deserted lobby and entered the elevator together.

"Remember now," Jay said, as they rode up, "I want you to come back home with us."

"I'll certainly think about it," Boxer told him.

The elevator glided to a halt and the door opened.

"Been a real pleasure," Billy said.

"Thanks for the drinks and invitation," Boxer replied, stepping out of the car. "And goodnight."

As the doors closed, Jay called after him, "We'll be callin' ya."

Boxer waved, but didn't look back at them.

Boxer couldn't sleep. He stared up at the ceiling and worked to close down his mind. But the images wouldn't stop running through it. He had the feeling that he was empty inside. Or more precisely, that he was gray inside…

What had happened to Trish and what he had learned from Borodine about her, was just beginning to have an effect. But oddly enough, he wasn't angry either with her or with Borodine. He didn't even feel cheated. He knew that if he had been in Borodine's place, he would have done the same thing. Trish was an exciting, desirable woman…

Boxer left the bed and went to the window. What saddened him most was his blindness. He should have been able to see the signs. Maybe they would have had a chance together. As he filled and lit his pipe, he found himself wondering whether Trish would have eventually told him that Borodine was also her lover? Boxer was sure she would have. "Yes," he said aloud. "Yes, she would have…"

He sighed and went back to the window. "The truth was that I really did want to marry her," he said. "I really loved her…" He puffed on the pipe for several moments and slowly shaking his head, he knew that he had to get on with his life. "If I don't," he told himself, "I won't be any good to myself or anyone else, or I could wind up like Bush."

Boxer took the pipe out of his mouth and pursed his lips. That man never had a chance. He was a bomb that would have gone off anywhere any time. Boxer began smoking again.

Suddenly he found himself thinking about Jay and Billy and smiled. They were a set of characters. Boxer blew a column of smoke toward the ceiling. If their invitation was genuine, he just might visit them. "Hell," he said, "it just might be fun!"

He left the window, found an ashtray on the dresser, put his pipe in it and went back to bed. Now he hoped he'd be able to fall asleep.

Cowly looked down at Cynthia. Her eyes were lidded and her bare arms were around his neck. "Don't stop," she whispered.

"I love you," he said, moving again.

"I like the way you say that," she told him.

He kissed her lips. "Tell me again?" Cynthia asked.

"Marry me," Cowly said, close to her ear.

"What?"

"Marry me and I'll tell you that I love you," he said, looking down at her again.

Her eyes were no longer lidded. "You're not just saying that because —"

Cowly shook his head. "No. I was thinking about it while I was away. I think we'd do all right together."

"Just all right?" she asked and before he could answer, she said, "We're doing better than 'all right' now."

"Much better," he answered. "Will you marry me?" he asked again.

"Only if you finish what you started," Cynthia answered, looking up at him.

Cowly quickened his movements.

"Yes... Yes, my love, I will marry you," Cynthia whispered, her eyes becoming lidded again. "I love you... I love you." And she arched her body against his.

Cowly gasped. An enormous wave of pleasure rushed out of her body and into his. "I love you," he shouted. "I love you!"

Nine o'clock the following morning Boxer phoned DB and said, "I'll meet you down in the lobby in a half hour."

"Aye, aye, Skipper," DB answered.

Boxer smiled and put the phone down. Over the last few days he had come to like and admire the young sailor. Without him, the battle with the *Shark* might have turned out very differently. Just as the thought of what could have happened sent a shiver through him, the phone rang.

"Boxer here," he said, picking up the phone.

Cowly was on the other end. "Skipper, Cynthia and I are going to get married."

"Congratulations," Boxer said.

"Skipper, we wanted you to be the first to know."

"Thanks... I'm happy for the two of you."

"Cynthia wants to speak to you," Cowly said.

"Well put her on," Boxer responded. "Put her on!"

"Jack —"

"Me first," Boxer said. "I wish you the very best. You know that."

"Yes, I know that," she said.

"You couldn't find a better man, a better human being."

"I know that too."

"And he couldn't find a better woman," Boxer said. "I mean that, Cynthia. He's a lucky man."

"You're not a bad guy yourself," she said. "I mean —"

"Listen," Boxer said, sensing that she wanted to say something about past matters. "The two of you will always be my very good friends and Cowly is the best EXO any skipper could have."

"Will you be best man?" Cynthia asked.

"I'd be honored," Boxer said. "Really honored."

"Do you think Admiral Stark would come to the wedding?" she asked.

"Yes. I'm sure he would," Boxer answered. "And I'll tell you something else. There's not a man who served aboard the *Shark* who wouldn't come."

"Thanks, Jack," she sniffled. "Thanks… I'm suddenly teary… I'll give the phone back to Robert."

"Skipper, is it okay if I meet you at the CNO's office instead of the hotel?"

"Sure," Boxer said and added, "You tell Cynthia that not only will I be best man, but I'll make the wedding for the two of you. That will be my wedding gift to you."

"Skipper —"

"Don't say a word," Boxer said. "And that's an order. See you at eleven hundred."

"Aye, aye, Skipper," Cowly answered.

Boxer put the phone down and began to whistle. He was truly happy for Cowly and Cynthia. Then suddenly, as he started out of the room, his mood changed. He was suddenly flooded with sadness. It came from deep within him. It was dark gray and so heavy, he felt bowed by its weight. He uttered a ragged sigh, closed the door, and made sure the electronic lock was switched on. Then squaring his shoulders, he walked slowly toward the elevator.

As soon as Boxer stepped out of the elevator and into the lobby a man called out, "That's him… That's the admiral."

Boxer looked behind him. But the elevator door was already closed.

Two flashes went off and several video cameras were pointed at him.

A young woman thrust a mike in front of him. "This is Linda Johnson for Live At Five talking to Admiral Jack Boxer. Admiral, did you really save the world?"

Boxer looked past the crowd of newspaper and TV people and saw Jay and Billy. They were smiling broadly.

"Admiral, is it true that the Russians weren't much help?" Ms. Johnson asked.

"Admiral," a reporter began, "we understand that you were helped by —"

Boxer held up his hands. "I have no comment," he said in a loud, booming voice.

Ms. Johnson looked at him and burst into laughter. "Admiral, that might go down very well with your sailors. But this is a hotel and we're not your sailors."

Boxer flushed.

"The American people have a right to know what happened," she said. "The world has a right to know."

Boxer glared at her.

"If you're going to roar again," she challenged, "I'm just going to have to show you roaring."

"Come on," another young woman said, "be a sport."

"I have nothing to say now," Boxer responded. "I was told there would be an official press conference later today at the White House."

"Are you going to see the President?" Ms. Johnson asked.

Boxer nodded; then he said, "Now if you'll excuse me, I'd like to have my breakfast."

The reporters opened a way for him and he headed straight to Jay and Billy. "If that's some of your doing —"

"Careful, Admiral, they're right behind you," Jay said.

Boxer glanced over his shoulder. The reporters and the TV were only a few steps behind him.

"Well, Jay," Ms. Johnson said, "are you and the admiral friends?"

Billy smiled. "Go back a long way."

Boxer's jaw started to drop. But he stopped it. Now he was interested in learning who the hell Billy and Jay really were.

Ms. Johnson turned her eyes to Boxer. "Don't you think it strange that you have a long friendship with the two men who do more business with the Soviets than anyone else in the United States?"

"Not strange at all," Jay answered. "I knew his pappy. He was in on some of the early arrangements I had with the Russians."

"The admiral, here," Billy said, "is just like one of the family. Now if you'll excuse us, here comes the ladies we've been waiting for."

Ms. Johnson turned to her crew. "That's a take." Then smiling at Boxer, she said, "See you at the White House, Admiral."

"See you," Boxer managed to mumble.

The group of reporters began to disperse.

"Com'on, Admiral," Jay said, "and we'll introduce you to our ladies. Oh, Billy here isn't really married to his yet. But he's thinkin' about doin' it any day now."

"Someone is waiting for me in the restaurant," Boxer said. He felt as if he'd suddenly become a Loony Tune cartoon character.

"Fine boy, that sailor," Billy said. "We told him you'd be a little late joining him. We even told him to sit at our table."

Boxer stopped. "You two guys are —"

"Admiral, my wife, Louise," Jay said.

Boxer found himself looking at an exquisite brunette.

"A pleasure to meet you," she said, offering her hand. She spoke with a slight foreign accent.

"And this is Miss Holly Walker," Billy told him.

Boxer let go of Louise's hand and took hold of Holly's. She was also a dark-haired beauty.

"Billy was thrilled to meet you, Admiral," she said in a soft voice.

Boxer felt himself flush.

"He's blushing," Louise said.

"How sweet!" Holly added.

"I'm starved," Jay announced. "Let's have breakfast."

The five of them walked into the restaurant.

Boxer immediately spotted DB. He was seated at a table for six.

"We've been invited to the President's news conference," Billy said as the five of them came up to the table.

DB stood up.

Jay and Billy introduced their wives to him.

"Pleased to meet you," DB said, obviously somewhat flustered by meeting the two women.

Boxer helped Louise with her chair and DB did the same for Holly.

"Skipper," DB asked, "isn't Mister Cowly supposed to meet us here?"

"He called. He'll meet us at the CNO's office," Boxer answered.

DB nodded.

The hostess came to the table and starting with the women, she gave each of them a large, elaborately written menu.

"I tell you what," Jay said, putting his menu down, "I'm just a simple country boy and this here menu scares me. Can your fancy chef back there fix me some ham and eggs flipped over well done, and does he have some simple biscuits."

"I'm sure —" the hostess began.

"And will you bring a bottle of your best champagne to the table and have it chilled."

"But your waitress —"

This time Billy interrupted her and handing her a hundred dollar bill, he said, "Little gal, you take care of this table."

She flushed. "Certainly... Yes... Certainly... Have the rest of you decided what you'd like to order?"

Each of the women ordered something from the menu. Billy asked for bacon and eggs, with home fries. DB wanted pancakes with a side order of sausage and Boxer, now amused by Jay and Billy, decided on a cheese and herb omelette.

"Well now," Billy said, when the waitress left, "those newspaper and TV people can certainly be bothersome."

"You seemed to be enjoying it," Boxer said.

"That's because we set it up," Jay laughed.

"I guessed that," Boxer said. "But I was not amused."

"Could tell that for sure," Billy commented. "But Jay and me find it helpful to help the members of the fourth estate."

"So that they'll help us when we need it," Jay said.

"The Russians like to be mentioned in the press whenever Jay and Billy make deals with them," Louise said.

"That's true," Jay seconded.

Suddenly Boxer realized that Jay and Billy were not just millionaire ranchers, but they were two of the most unique businessmen in the free world. They did more business with the Soviets than anyone else in the west. If the Soviets wanted to buy tractors or soft drinks, they'd do it through them.

The hostess followed by two waitresses — one carried the cooler and the other champagne — returned to the table and showed the bottle to Billy.

"Is that the best you have?" he asked, looking up at her.

"Honey," Jay said, "let me have a look at that bottle."

DB leaned close to Boxer, "Skipper, what's going down?"

"Games," Boxer answered.

"Games?" DB echoed.

Boxer nodded.

"Twenty-nine wasn't a bad year," Jay said, giving the bottle back to the hostess.

"I guess it'll have to do, especially since you don't have anything better. But you tell your boss that nineteen-twenty-five was much better than twenty-nine."

"I'll certainly tell him that," she answered, motioning to her assistants to set up the cooler and put the bottle in it.

"Now to the media people —" Jay began.

"Before you make a mistake," Boxer said, "I want to set you two cowboys straight."

"Holly, did you hear what he called Jay and me?" Billy laughed.

Laughing, she answered, "I certainly did."

"You know, Admiral, that's mighty nice of you to call us that," Jay said. "Makes us feel proud to be from the state of Texas."

"But we ain't really cowboys," Billy said. "Never really were."

"I don't really give a damn whether you picked up cow shit or broke broncs," Boxer said, moving his eyes from Billy to Jay and back to Billy. "I don't want you to bullshit me."

Jay threw up his hands. "Just cashin' in on your good press," he said.

"The Russians would be pleased to know that we're friends," Billy commented. "I guess by now you know who we are?"

Boxer nodded. "I know and I still don't want you to bullshit me and I don't want you on my coat tails. You need good press, get it yourselves."

"Like this man!" Jay exclaimed.

Billy nodded. "Says what he means and means what he says."

"Okay," Jay said, "you win, Admiral. No more games."

Boxer looked at Billy. "No more games," he said.

"If that's the rule —"

"No 'if'," Boxer said, "that's the rule."

"You got it," Billy agreed.

"But this doesn't change the invitation," Jay said. "We want you to come down and visit us. You, this young man, and that Mister Cowly who was with you."

"Surely, Admiral, you could get away for a while," Louise said.

"I think I can manage it," Boxer answered. He liked the sound of her voice. It was soft, yet not so soft that he had to strain to hear her.

"Whenever you're ready," Billy said, "we'll fly you and your friends out."

"Skipper, are we going to Texas?" DB asked.

"Yes ... in a few days."

"Will I have time to visit my folks?"

"Where do you live, son?" Jay asked.

"Indian Town, Nebraska," DB answered. "My folks have a small farm just about three miles outside of town."

"When do you want to go there?" Billy asked.

DB looked at Boxer. "Skipper, when do you think I'll be able to go?" he asked.

"Probably by tomorrow morning," Boxer answered.

"We'll see that you get there," Jay said. "I'll have one of our planes fly you out. Your folks have a field where a small jet can land?"

DB's eyes opened wide. "You mean you're going to fly me to the farm?"

"Yes, and then when you're ready to return, fly you back."

"Skipper —"

"You just call your folks and tell them that a small jet is going to land on their property," Billy said.

"They're not going to believe it!" DB exclaimed.

"They will when they see it," Boxer said.

"Ah, here comes breakfast!" Holly exclaimed. "Would you believe that I wasn't the least bit hungry when I sat down, but now I'm famished. I think all the talking did it."

"But you didn't say a word," Louise chided. Then she asked, "Don't you think listening is work, Admiral?"

"Yes, especially when you're not the least bit interested in what you happen to be listening to."

Holly laughed. "Now, Admiral, how did you know that?"

"Because if I were either of you ladies, I wouldn't be interested either," Boxer said, as the hostess placed his cheese and herb omelette in front of him.

"Now there's a man who understands women," Louise said.

"No," Boxer answered, "that's stretching a point too far. I only said that if I were either of you, I wouldn't be interested."

"That," Billy said, "is enough for Louise to take a giant step and give you credit for understanding what no man understands … the workings of a woman's mind."

Boxer picked up his coffee and drank… He would have preferred to have a quiet breakfast with DB before meeting Stark. He wasn't in the mood to be part of — then suddenly one of the women rubbed her foot against his.

From the expressions on their faces, he couldn't tell which one was doing it. Both appeared to be concentrating on eating their food.

He moved his foot away and putting down his cup, he continued to eat. Whoever was playing footsy with him started again. But this time he didn't remove his foot; instead, he played the game and scanned the faces of the women for a reaction.

There was none!

"Certainly good food," Billy announced.

"Certainly is," Boxer said and then with a broad smile, he added, "I especially like the extras that come with it."

"You get what you pay for," Jay said.

CHAPTER 4

"Come in Comrade Admiral," the doctor said, motioning to Borodine, who stood in the open doorway of the Chief of Surgery's office in the Kronstadt Naval Hospital.

Borodine nodded, pushed the door open a bit more and walked into the office. He wore the regulation white terrycloth bathrobe over the hospital gown.

"Please sit, Comrade Admiral," the thin bespectacled man said.

"I am sorry I am a bit early," Borodine said, lowering himself into the chair at the left of the desk. The requisite photographs of the country's leaders were on the wall. But the office itself was spartan. There was a window in the side wall that overlooked a courtyard that was now covered with snow. And he saw that more snow was falling when he entered the room and glanced at the window.

"If I were you," the doctor said, "I would have been here at the crack of dawn. But then you would have had a longer wait, isn't that so, Comrade Admiral?" he laughed.

Borodine nodded.

"No doubt you're wondering when you will be released and when you will be able to return to duty?"

"Yes."

"Bored here after your adventures?" the Chief of Surgery asked.

"I am restless," Borodine answered. "I am not used to doing nothing."

"You should do more of it. You should learn that doing nothing has an important place in the scheme of things."

Borodine agreed and said, "That is something I will remember."

"Only as long as you're in this office," the doctor said with a smile. "You know that and so do I."

"At least you don't fool yourself, Comrade Doctor," Borodine responded.

"Ah, but I do. I like to think that some of the things I tell my patients actually matter. Like you for instance. You are well enough to leave here this afternoon, or this morning if you like. The doctors aboard the carrier did a good job on you. Besides, you were suffering more from internal bruises than anything else."

"You mean —"

"I mean you are free to go to Moscow. You're a hero and —"

Borodine put up his hands. "Please, none of that, Comrade Doctor. The credit belongs to Comrade Admiral Boxer of the American Navy. I was in the sick bay when the main action was going on."

The doctor laughed. "You've seen the TV and read the papers. That's not what they say."

With a wave of his hand, Borodine dismissed what the doctor said. "No matter," the Chief of Surgery commented, "you are free to leave. I have been informed that a plane is standing by to take you to Moscow."

"Is there anything I should not do?" Borodine asked.

"Your body will tell you what you should not do," the doctor answered. "But I will advise you to take a long rest. Several months if that is possible. I have spoken to Comrade Admiral Gorshkov and have told him the same thing. He assured me that when you return from leave you will be reassigned to Washington for at least six months."

"That certainly is limited duty," Borodine said.

"By the way, what is it like over there?" the doctor asked.

Borodine was about to answer: like nothing you could ever dream of, but then he checked himself. Even the Chief of Surgery could be KGB. "It's not nearly as good as it is here," he finally answered.

The doctor smiled and said, "I thought so. It's not someplace I'd like to visit."

"Any foods I should not eat?" Borodine asked, more to change the subject than from any real interest on his part.

The doctor shook his head. "You may have everything."

"I can continue to smoke?"

"It would be better for you if you stopped," the doctor said.

"I'll try," Borodine answered.

"You won't," the Chief of Surgery said.

Borodine stood up and shaking hands with the doctor, he said, "Thanks for everything."

"Perhaps this will sound foolish, even pompous," the doctor said, "but thank you for saving the rest of us and if you see that American, thank him too."

Borodine smiled. "I'll tell him," he said.

"And please take that rest."

"Yes ... yes... I'll do that too," Borodine told him; then letting go of his hand, he turned around and walked softly out of the office. The future looked wonderfully bright, especially that night, when he'd be able to eat a decent meal in a Moscow restaurant. As he walked to his room, he whistled and thought about what he would eat. Possibly a good hearty Russian dinner or perhaps something foreign. Something American?

That possibility made him smile and as Borodine entered his room, he said aloud, "It will be definitely something American!"

Boxer and DB were picked up by a Navy limo. Guessing that Cowly would want to tell DB himself, he said nothing about his wedding plans. Instead, he sat back and smoking his pipe, tried to figure out which of the women played footsy with him.

"Skipper, am I really going to be flown to Nebraska?" DB asked.

Boxer took the pipe out of his mouth. "Yes, if you want to?"

"And we're going to Texas?"

"Most probably," Boxer answered. "I think all of us can do with some vacation."

"I don't have much leave time left," DB said.

"Maybe we can get you a few more days," Boxer replied.

"That'd be great," DB said, then lapsed into silence.

Boxer put the pipe back in his mouth and began to smoke again. He had missed the christening of Louise's baby girl and wanted to see both the mother and child. He also wanted to make a trip to New York to see his son, John and —

"Skipper," DB said, "I have something to ask you?"

"Ask?"

"Is it possible for me to become a permanent member of your crew? I mean when you have your own boat to command?"

Boxer smiled. He had been expecting that question. "Are you sure that's what you want?"

DB nodded. "The only other thing would be to go to Annapolis. I have my application in. But I don't stand much of a chance. Besides I'm twenty-two and —"

"That's not a drawback, unless you make it one," Boxer said. "You'd be going in with experience and you wouldn't do some of the dumb things that plebes do."

"Maybe. But I'd probably do other dumb things," DB responded.

Boxer smiled. DB was not only smart when it came to computers but he also possessed a great deal of common sense.

"Could I transfer to your command?"

"Yes," Boxer said. "I'd be happy to have you aboard."

"Will you be getting a new boat soon?"

"I'll have you transferred even before that happens," Boxer said.

"You could do that?" DB asked in wide-eyed amazement.

"An admiral has to have some authority, otherwise he wouldn't be an admiral, would he?"

DB smiled broadly. "Guess not, Skipper."

By the time Boxer and DB arrived, Cowly was already in the CNO's office.

Stark came out from behind his desk and shook Boxer's hand. "Glad you made it," he said.

"So am I," Boxer answered; then he said, "Admiral, I want you to meet the young man who deserves much of the credit for the success of the mission... Electronics Specialist First Class Donald Butts. But everyone calls him DB."

"A real pleasure, DB," Stark said, shaking the young man's hand. "A very real pleasure." Letting go of DB's hand, he gestured to the empty chairs in front of his desk.

Boxer and DB shook hands with Cowly.

"How's Cynthia?" Boxer asked.

"Happy," he answered. "Happy."

"That's the way she should be," Boxer answered, as he sat down.

"Well, gentlemen, while we're waiting for Mister Kinkade," Stark said, "I want to know what I can do to make your lives somewhat more comfortable. Think a few moments before you answer." He sat down behind the desk and reaching across to the front of it, he took a cigar out of a humidor. "If any of you men want one, help yourselves."

"Don't mind if I do," Cowly said.

Stark nodded and lit up. "Boxer, is there anything you might want?"

"Some time for a vacation," Boxer answered.

"Three months enough? I'll arrange for transportation wherever you want to go. Now, Mister Cowly, what about you?"

"Admiral, Commander Lowe and I are getting married and—"

"Congratulations! She's a wonderful woman. Now tell me what you might want?"

"Would you do us the honor to be at our wedding?"

Stark smiled broadly. "The honor would be mine," he said in a deep gravelly voice. "Anything else?"

"Leave time."

"I'll make it simple," Stark said, shifting the cigar to the corner of his mouth, "every one of you has three months leave." Then looking at DB, he asked, "And what do you want?"

"To be assigned to Admiral Boxer's command," DB said.

"I have already done that," Stark answered. "Now is there anything else?"

"No, sir," DB replied.

"Admiral," Boxer said, "there is something else I would like."

"Oh! What is it?"

"I would like to have DB entered into the freshman class at the Academy."

"Is that what you would like?" Stark asked, looking at DB.

"Yes, sir."

Stark nodded. "I think that might be arranged," he said.

"Thank you, sir," DB responded, his face flushed.

"But before any of you go anywhere," Stark said, "you will have to be debriefed."

The phone on Stark's desk rang and he answered it, listened a few moments and said, "Have him come right in."

"Kinkade?" Boxer asked.

Stark nodded and said, "He took Trish's death very hard."

Boxer didn't answer, but he had the feeling Stark knew more about Trish than he would ever say.

The door opened and Kinkade entered the room.

Boxer stood up and turned toward him.

Cowly and DB did the same.

Boxer could see the changes in the man. His eyes were sunk deep in his head. He was even frailer than he had been after his heart attack.

When Kinkade reached them, he stopped and, nodding, he said, "Damn fine job… Damn fine."

"Thank you," Boxer said and introduced him to Cowly and DB.

He shook their hands.

"Let's move to the conference area," Stark said. "Given the situation I think something of a small celebration is in order."

"Have you told them what I want," Kinkade said, as all of them crossed the room behind Stark and followed him into a beautifully paneled room with a very large, highly polished oak wood table and twelve matching chairs.

Stark positioned himself at the head of the table. Boxer, Cowly and DB were on his right and Kinkade sat on his left.

"Help yourselves," Stark said, gesturing toward the tray, cut glass decanters and glasses. "There's vodka, scotch, and rye."

"DB, you pour," Boxer said.

"Aye, aye, Skipper," DB answered.

Stark made the first toast. "May good health and good fortune be with us all of the time," he said.

Boxer gave the second. "To the men of the *Neptune* who never made it, and to the men of the *Novogorod*, who made it possible for the three of us to be here today."

Cowly toasted peace.

And when DB's turn came, he flushed, stood up and said, "To you, Skipper and to you, Mister Cowly. The two of you are the best we have."

Boxer nodded. "Thank you," he said and added, "You're not bad yourself, or to put it another way: if you weren't the best, you wouldn't be here with us today."

"Without you," Cowly responded, "those missiles would have been fired."

"I have one more toast to make," Boxer said.

Stark nodded.

"To Captain Bush," Boxer said, raising his glass and drinking.

"We're due at the Oval Office in thirty minutes," Stark said. "The President will be holding a news conference with the three of you at his side. Are you up to it?"

"For myself, I think so," Boxer answered and he looked at Cowly and DB.

They nodded.

"Good," Stark said.

"There's just one thing I want to caution you about," Kinkade said. "And that is to keep your answers short and sweet."

"The skipper does that even when he's not in a news conference," DB said.

Boxer burst out laughing.

"Sorry, Skipper," DB said, "but I'm not used to drinking this early in the day. Besides, I think the combination of the champagne and scotch —"

"What champagne?" Kinkade asked.

Boxer explained how he had met Jay Corless Archer and William White the previous evening and how he and DB had breakfasted with them.

"Know them well," Kinkade said.

Boxer glanced at him. Kinkade didn't have to spell it out. Jay and Billy had obviously done some work for the Company.

"I know them too," Stark said.

"You'll see them at the White House," Boxer commented.

"They're very good friends with the President," Stark said. "He often goes down to Texas to spend time with them. There's some rumor about that he and Holly are uncommonly friendly."

"She's certainly a beautiful woman," Boxer commented.

"She's got quite a background," Kinkade said. "Some day we'll talk about it."

"We'd better get moving," Stark told them.

All of them stood up.

Boxer moved close to Kinkade. "Are you all right?" he asked.

"I miss her," Kinkade answered in a whisper.

Boxer nodded, sighed and in a low voice, he said, "So do I… So do I…"

Stark led the way into the Oval Office, where the President rose to greet them. Stark introduced Boxer, Cowly and DB.

The President shook each of their hands and said, "Well sit here a while before we go out to the press room to speak to the press."

Several chairs had been arranged in a circle to the right of the President's desk.

"Please," the President said, "sit down."

But all of them waited until he was seated before they sat.

"Admiral Boxer," the President said,"the world owes you—"

"Please, Mister President, with all due respect to you, the world owes me nothing. I did what I was trained to do. I am sorry that Captain Bush had to be killed. He was a very brave man."

"And disturbed," Kinkade added.

Boxer nodded. "Yes. Myself and Captain Cowly know that better than anyone else here. But there were other times when his acts of courage saved the *Shark* and the men aboard her."

"It's generous of you to say that here," the President commented, "but I wouldn't want you to be quite so generous when you speak to the press. What I mean is that they like to have their bad guys and their good guys. McElroy and Bush are the bad guys."

Boxer said nothing.

"Would you agree, Kinkade?"

"Yes."

"Admiral Stark?"

"If it must be that way, then it must be that way," Stark answered. "You're the one who calls the shots, Mister President."

"Now I want to hear what happened up there in the arctic," the President said, looking at Boxer.

"I'm afraid I'm not very good at the retelling of an event," Boxer said. "But I will tell you that because of the way the *Tecumseh* and the *Shark* fought, naval warfare will never be the same."

"Stark and Kinkade have already told me that," the President said. "And we have already initiated changes that will use the information gained in that battle."

"Mister President," Boxer said, "I have a special request to make."

"Yes. What is it?"

"DB would like to go to Annapolis," Boxer said. "And he doesn't know anyone back in his home state."

The President looked at DB. "Is that so, young man?" he asked.

"Yes, Mister President," DB answered.

"What do you say, Stark?" the President asked.

"Admiral Boxer thinks he will make a fine officer," Stark said.

"I'll write the necessary Executive Order," the President replied.

Suddenly the phone on the President's desk rang and he got up to answer it. "Yes, thank you," he said and putting the phone down, he announced, "The members of the press are waiting."

This time the President led the way out of the Oval Office and through the corridor that led to the press room. He took his place at the lectern. Boxer was to his right and Cowly and DB stood on his left. "Ladies and gentlemen," he said, "it gives me great pleasure to introduce you to the three men responsible for preventing the destruction of the world."

The newspaper reporters and TV people clapped.

Boxer spotted Linda Johnson and her camera crew. And he saw Jay, Louise, Billy and Holly sitting in the rear of the room.

Boxer listened to the President's short speech about how the American Navy "won the day and made the world safe again." And he didn't think much of it. But he didn't think much of the President either.

"And in conclusion," the President said, "I am going to give this nation's highest honor to Admiral Boxer. Admiral, it gives me great pleasure to present you with the Congressional Medal of Honor." He turned toward Boxer.

There was a burst of applause in the room.

The President took a half a step to the left and Boxer moved into position behind the lectern. "First, Mister President," Boxer said, "I feel truly humble and those who know me know I am anything but a humble man."

A flurry of laughter went around the room.

"And," Boxer went on, when the room was quiet again, "Captain Cowly and Electronics Specialist First Class Donald Butts are certainly more deserving of this medal than I am. But if there is one man who deserves it, it is not any of us. That man is a Comrade Admiral Igor Borodine, of the Russian Navy and I will personally give it to him. Mister President and the members of the press, in the final action it was the crew of the Russian submarine *Novogorod* that finally destroyed the *Shark*. If any honor should be given by this nation, or by Russia, it should be given to Comrade Admiral Borodine and his crew. Thank you." And he stepped back to his former position.

For a few moments, everyone in the room was absolutely silent.

Boxer glanced at the President. He was very pale.

Almost as if a signal was given, the room erupted into a combination of cheers and boos.

Boxer looked toward Stark and Kinkade. Stark's face was expressionless. But Kinkade's lower lip was trembling.

The President held up his hands. "Please... Please, ladies and gentlemen... Admiral Boxer will explain his position. I am sure he did not mean what he said —"

"I meant every word of it, Mister President," Boxer said, without waiting to be asked to speak.

The cheers and boos increased.

The President gestured Boxer back to the lectern.

"Ladies and gentlemen," Boxer said, "please quiet down. I will answer your questions one by one."

The noise diminished; then completely ceased.

Boxer noticed that Linda Johnson had somehow made her way forward and her hand was raised. He pointed to her.

"Do you actually mean that you will give your medal to Admiral Borodine?"

"Comrade Admiral Borodine deserves it more than I do," Boxer answered. "I would be cheating the American people if I took it and if I allowed them to have the mistaken impression that it was an American submarine which finally sank the *Shark*."

"Admiral," another reporter shouted, "where were you during the battle?"

"I was on the bridge of the *Novogorod*," Boxer answered. "Comrade Admiral Borodine had been injured."

"Who was in command?" the same reporter pressed.

"Comrade Admiral Borodine had turned his command over to me," Boxer answered.

"What?" Kinkade exploded.

"I was in command of the *Novogorod*," Boxer answered calmly.

"Do you speak Russian?" a third reported asked.

Boxer shook his head. "The EXO of the *Novogorod* speaks English. What orders I gave, he translated to the crew."

"Admiral Boxer, isn't it true that you and Comrade Admiral Borodine in the past have been adversaries?"

"Yes. But it is also true that we have become good friends."

"Given this friendship, would you again be able to face him as an adversary?"

"Yes, if the situation warrants it."

"How could you —"

"Ms. Johnson," Boxer answered, "we are professionals. We do what we must do to accomplish what must be accomplished."

"Then you would kill —"

"I hope it never comes to that," Boxer said. "But if it should, the answer is yes… I would kill him and I am certain he would do the same to me. But knowing this does not detract from our friendship."

Several more reporters began to shout for Boxer's attention.

Boxer held up his hands and when the room was quiet again, he said, "I want to make one more statement and it is this. I am proud that my country is my country. But I am even prouder that I have the right to tell the truth to you and to the American people. The blood that was shed to stop the *Shark* was American blood, Russian blood, British blood. But more important than the nationality of the men who shed it was the fact that they were men who gave up their lives for the rest of mankind. Thank you."

An explosion of applause filled the room. This time there were no boos.

The President took up the lead and Boxer, Cowly and DB brought up the rear.

"You pulled the rug out from under him," Cowly whispered.

"I told it like it was," Boxer answered.

Cowly grinned. "That's the one thing politicians can't stand. They're like vampires: they can't stand the light of day. But it will be fun to see what happens in the next few days."

"Kinkade nearly had a fit," Boxer whispered.

As soon as they were back in the Oval Office, the President went behind his desk, picked up the phone and told his secretary to hold all his calls; then he looked at Boxer and said, "That was quite a bomb you exploded, Admiral."

"Everything I said was true," Boxer answered.

"American admirals do not command Russian submarines," the President said in a low, flat voice.

"This one did," Boxer responded.

The President nodded. "You made a fool of me, Admiral," he said. "I knew you were aboard a Russian sub. But I sure as hell didn't know that you were commanding it."

"It's in my report."

"I didn't read your report," the President said; then turning to Stark and Kinkade, "Until further notice I want Admiral Boxer relieved of his command and I want a full-scale investigation of this incident."

"No need for that, Mister President," Boxer said. "Truth, Mister President, is what I believe in and what I gave to the American people and to the Russian people. If you can't live with truth, that is your problem." And turning around, he headed toward the door.

"Where are you going?" the President asked.

"Out to get some fresh air," Boxer answered, opening the door and walking out of the Oval Office.

Cowly and DB were escorted out of the Oval Office by Stark. "I don't have to tell either of you that what you saw and heard must not go any farther."

"I understand," Cowly said.

"And you, young man, do you understand?" Stark asked.

"Yes, sir," DB answered.

Stark accompanied them as far as the main entrance to the White House. "Did either of you know what Boxer intended to say?" he asked, as the three of them stopped.

"No," Cowly said. "But the skipper did tell the truth."

"He did," DB added.

Stark uttered a ragged sigh. "I didn't even know he commanded the *Novogorod*... I didn't read his report."

"What will happen to him?" Cowly asked.

Stark shook his head. "I sure as hell don't know. But this time he's in the lion's cage. I'll be in touch."

Cowly and DB saluted him.

Stark returned the salute and headed back to the Oval Office. He arrived a few minutes later to find the President pacing the length of the room and Kinkade standing off to one side and looking very glum.

The phone rang.

The President stopped pacing and motioned to Kinkade to answer it. Then to Stark, he said, "It hasn't stopped ringing since you walked out of here. Every fucking member of the Congress and the Senate has been trying to reach me, to say nothing about private individuals. Your Admiral Boxer has made a damn fool of me."

"I don't think it was intentional," Stark replied.

"That was Jay Archer, Mister President. He said he would like to speak with you now."

"He and Billy were in the back of the room," the President said.

"What should I tell him?" Kinkade asked. "He's waiting for an answer."

"Tell him to come," the President said. "Then call Security to pass him and Bill through the side gate." He looked at Stark. "Did you know he took command of a Russian sub?"

"The command was turned over to him," Stark said.

"Did you know?"

"No Mister President," Stark answered, "I failed to read his report."

"Kinkade, did you know?" the President asked.

"No, Mister President, I did not."

The President began to pace again. "Boxer is not a team man," he said. "And what we need is team men. Is there any way he can be reduced in rank?"

"Not unless he's court-martialed and then you'd have to charge him with a crime," Stark answered.

"For openers how about making a fool of his Commander in Chief?" the President asked.

Stark didn't answer.

"You could reduce him in rank by Executive Order," Kinkade said. "On the grounds that he did not supply the proper information."

"The information is in his report which none of us has read," Stark said.

"The Russians must be laughing up a storm over this," the President said. "To say nothing of the members of the other party and those bastards in my party who usually give me flack."

The phone rang again.

"That's probably Jay and Billy," the President said. "Kinkade, have them come in."

"Mister President," Stark began, "Admiral Boxer is not the usual naval officer."

"You sure as hell can say that again," the President exploded. "He certainly seems to make the rules, not obey them."

The door opened and Jay Archer and Billy White entered the room.

"Looks like a wake is goin' on here," Billy commented.

"Sure does," Jay agreed.

"What the hell did you expect?" the President challenged. "I just had the fucking political rug pulled out from under me."

Jay went over to the President's desk, opened the humidor and helped himself to a cigar and gave one to Billy. "Thank God we still have friends in Cuba," he said running the cigar under his nose and smelling it."

"Agents," the President said. "Kinkade's men."

Jay ignored the correction and as he snipped off the end of the cigar, he said, "That Boxer is one hell of man. I mean he's got the biggest set of brass balls I've ever seen." Then he laughed. "Of course I don't mean that I've really seen them. But —"

"This is no joking matter, Jay. I'm not doing that well with Congress right now to have this happen."

"The way I see it," Billy said, "the admiral handed you a golden opportunity."

"What the hell are you talking about?"

"You could agree with him," Jay said.

"What?"

"Go to Congress and ask them to vote a special medal for Admiral Igor Borodine; then ask the Russian government to send him here so that it could be presented to him in front of both houses. After all, you'd be doing something that could only be done in a democracy and the Soviets would respond. It might even make our job easier when we go over there to sell them —"

"Are you telling me to make a hero out of Boxer and Borodine?"

"They're already heroes," Jay answered. "I'm telling you to take advantage of the situation."

The President looked at Stark. "What do you think?"

"It's a good idea," Stark said. "And it certainly makes you look as if you're willing to honor not only your own people, but anyone who helped save us from destruction."

"Kinkade, what do you say?"

"It's workable," Kinkade answered.

The President went to his desk and helped himself to a cigar. "Boxer comes out smelling sweeter than a rose," he said.

"And so do you," Jay said.

The President nodded. "All right, that's the way we'll play it!"

CHAPTER 5

Two days later, Boxer was yesterday's news and he was glad of it. The furor he had inadvertently created was over.

He had received two phone calls. The first call came from Charles Spadaro, the boy whose guardian he had become when Captain Rugger had been murdered. Chuck told him that he had been suspended from high school for five days for fighting. Boxer had wanted to speak to Mr. De Mattao, the school's principal for some time and this had given him a reason. "I'll be there tomorrow morning," he said. "I'll see you at the school."

"Sure," Chuck answered.

Boxer hung up and was just about to phone his ex-wife Gwen to tell her that he was coming to New York and would like to see their son, John, when the phone rang. He picked it up and said, "Boxer here."

Stark was on the other end. "The President has decided to personally invite Borodine to Washington to receive a special medal!"

"I don't give a tinker's damn what the President has decided to do. I'm going to go up to New York for a few days to take care of personal business. I'll see you in a few days."

"If it means anything," Stark said, "I'd have done the same thing. But honestly," he added, "I wouldn't have had the guts to do it."

"Sometimes," Boxer answered, "you just have to find guts you never thought you had. For that time up there in the arctic we were all on the same side ... the side of survival. If the

President doesn't understand that, he doesn't understand anything."

"Jack," Stark said, "don't judge him, or anyone of us too harshly. We weren't there. There's no way we could know what you and those with you know."

"That's true," Boxer responded. "That's damn true."

"If you need anything," Stark told him, "just give me a call."

"Thanks," Boxer said and he put the phone down.

The next morning, dressed in uniform, Boxer flew up to New York to meet with Mister Roland De Mattao, the principal of New Dorp High School, to discuss his dead friend's son Charles Spadaro and see his own son, John.

By eight o'clock he landed at La Guardia airport and within five minutes was seated in a cab.

"Where to, Admiral?" the driver asked.

"New Dorp High School, Staten Island," Boxer answered with a smile.

The driver pushed down the flag and they were off.

"How did you know my rank?" Boxer asked.

"All officers are admirals," the man said.

Boxer accepted the answer with silence.

The ride was all highway until they crossed the Verrazzano Bridge; then they followed the signs to Hylan Boulevard and twenty minutes later they made a left turn on New Dorp Lane.

"Looks more like a prison than a school," the driver commented, as he pulled up to the main gate. "And it's got one of those crazy pieces of twisted metal in front of it."

Boxer looked at the driver's ID. "Where do you go from here, Mister Santana?" he asked, as he handed the man the meter rate and a generous tip besides.

"Back to the city. There's no business here."

"Suppose you wait for me?" Boxer suggested.

"With the meter running?" Mr. Santana asked, turning to look at Boxer.

"What do you make on a good day, including tips?"

"Two hundred... Two-fifty."

"Okay, you got two-fifty for the day and lunch," Boxer said with a smile.

"What about breakfast? I haven't had it yet."

"There must be a place around here. Be back in an hour," Boxer said, handing him another five dollars.

Smiling, Mister Santana said, "See you in an hour, Admiral."

At the door, Boxer signed in, was handed a guest pass and told that the principal's office was in "the south wing, on the right side at the end of corridor."

Boxer nodded and pausing a moment to remove his coat, he walked briskly away. When he had called Mr. De Mattao, he had said nothing about himself, other than that he was Charles's guardian and that he wanted to discuss the boy with him.

"It's coincidence that you should be calling now," De Mattao had answered. "Charles has been suspended for five days for fighting. School rules."

Boxer had said he understood that had been the case and had arranged for a ten A.M. meeting the following day.

Even as he walked down the corridor, Boxer was aware of a steady traffic of students. He was sure they belonged in class and found himself wondering why they were allowed to be in the hallway. When he went to high school, once the second bell rang, the halls were cleared: you wouldn't know there were students in the building. But that was a long time ago and ideas about what students should or should not be allowed to do have changed drastically.

Boxer entered the principal's office and found himself in an anteroom, where two secretaries were busy at their desks. Beyond him, he could see into a large conference room, where there was an oak wood table and a display case with several trophies in it.

The secretary nearest him looked up. She was a pinched-faced woman and wore metal frame glasses. "May I help you?" she asked.

"I have an appointment with Mister De Mattao," Boxer said.

"Who should I say —"

"Admiral Boxer," he answered.

She did a double take; then picking up the phone, she punched out three numbers and spoke in a low voice.

Boxer knew she had made the connection between him and the man whom she had seen on TV. He heard her say, "Yes, I'm sure it's him." He nodded and smiled at her.

She put the phone down and said, "Please go right in, Admiral."

"Thank you," Boxer said and walked through the gate. The principal's office was off to the left. When he entered it, Mister De Mattao was already on his feet behind his desk.

"It is a pleasure to meet you Admiral," De Mattao said, extending his hand.

Boxer shook it. De Mattao was a man of middling height and years. He had a dark complexion, a large hook nose, an underslung jaw, small black moustache, and a belly that hung over his belt.

"I had no idea that you were Charles's guardian," De Mattao said. "Please sit down." And he gestured to a chair next to the desk.

Boxer settled into the chair and placed his long coat and cap across his lap.

"I was just having coffee and some delicious Danish that one of my secretaries brought in," De Mattao said. "Would you care for some?"

"Coffee would be fine," Boxer answered.

"A wise man to avoid the Danish," De Mattao said. "But if we can't enjoy the small pleasures of life now and then, we really can't enjoy life, can we?"

"I generally forego the small pleasures to enjoy the larger ones," Boxer replied with a smile.

"There's something to be said for that philosophy too," De Mattao said and picking up the phone, he called his secretary and asked her to bring another cup of coffee. "With or without cream and sugar?" he asked, looking at Boxer.

"Black," Boxer answered.

"Black," De Mattao said into the phone and added, "Thank you." Then he put the phone down and turned his attention to Boxer. "Well, Admiral, I am certainly pleased to meet you. Charles must be very important to you —"

"Chuck is important to me," Boxer said. "Now tell me why he was suspended."

"He was fighting with another student and the school rules are such that anyone involved in a fight is suspended."

Boxer nodded. "What was the fight about?" he asked.

De Mattao shrugged. "Neither young man would say."

The secretary entered the office and excused herself; then she placed a cork coaster on the desk in front of Boxer and a mug of black coffee on top of it.

"Thank you," Boxer said.

She smiled at him and quickly left the office.

"Would you send for Chuck?" Boxer asked.

"I hadn't planned to make this a family type conference," De Mattao said.

"I hadn't planned to be here and wouldn't be," Boxer said, "if I hadn't gotten a phone call from Chuck telling me that he had been suspended."

Before he answered, De Mattao devoured the last piece of Danish and said, "Under the circumstances, I don't see why I can't spend a bit more time with you. After all, we both want the best for Charles, don't we?"

Boxer didn't bother answering.

De Mattao opened a manila folder and scanned a sheet of paper. "This is his program," he said. "He'll be going into homeroom in two minutes. I'll have security bring him here."

"That'll be fine," Boxer responded.

Once more De Mattao busied himself at the phone, giving Boxer a chance to examine the office. It was large, with the requisite bookcase on the other side of the desk, which was placed catty corner, almost behind the door. There were also copies of several famous paintings on the walls. He recognized two: Van Gogh's "Starry Night" and, Turner's "London Bridge." And there was also a copy of the Declaration of Independence on the wall. To the right of where De Mattao was sitting was a certificate announcing that De Mattao was a Danforth Fellow.

"Charles will be here in a few minutes," De Mattao said. Just as he spoke the bell rang.

Boxer picked up his coffee and began to drink it. "How is Chuck doing in his school work?" he asked.

De Mattao opened a large manila folder and looked at several papers. "For the last several months very much better… His teachers say that he is bright and cooperative. Essentially, there appears to have been a change in him."

Boxer nodded. He was satisfied that he had had some influence over the boy.

"Here at New Dorp," De Mattao said, closing the folder, "we are really one family: student and teachers alike. Many of our present teachers are past students. I myself attended New Dorp and played on its football team. I even student taught here."

"That doesn't allow for much outside world experience, does it?" Boxer said, lowering his coffee for a moment.

"Not in the broadest sense," De Mattao answered. "But it does have other advantages. People like myself who went to school here and now teach here have a real feel for this place and its students."

"Perhaps they'd have a better feel for the students if they were exposed to several different types of environments," Boxer answered. "I would think that a teacher should know something about the world outside school, after all, Mister De Mattao, that world out there is very different from the one in here."

"Our teachers are mothers, fathers and —"

The phone rang.

De Mattao answered and said, "Send him in."

A moment later Chuck entered the office.

Boxer stood up and shook hands with him.

Chuck grinned. "Glad to see you made it back," he said. "I mean you really did something out there, Skipper."

"Charles, why don't you bring another chair close to the desk," De Mattao suggested.

"I'd like to know what the fight was about," Boxer said, as soon as he and Chuck sat down. Dressed in Levis and a light blue football jersey, he was a tall, broad-shouldered young man with black hair and very bright, black eyes.

Chuck pursed his lips.

"Let me put it to you this way," Boxer said, "if you had a good reason to fight."

"Admiral, here there is never 'a good reason' to fight."

Boxer ignored the man. "I know you wouldn't have fought unless —"

"Skipper, I know why you did what you did with the medal," Chuck said. "I'd have done the same thing."

Boxer glanced at De Mattao. "Did you know it was about that?" he asked.

"It wouldn't have made any difference," De Mattao answered.

Boxer gave his attention back to Chuck. "Tell me what happened," he said. "No shit… Just the way it went down."

"Darrel — that's the other guy's name — said —"

"What did he say?" Boxer pushed.

"That maybe you're a commie," Chuck said. "And I said he didn't know what the fuck he was talking about because I knew that you weren't."

Boxer suppressed a smile. He was sure that several million people in the United States must be thinking the same thing. "Then what happened?" he asked.

"He said that if you wasn't a commie, then you must be the dumbest guy on the face of the earth. And I said, 'that dumb guy just saved all our asses.' Then he said his mother said, 'from what she's read about you, you're not even a good father.' Then I said, 'That's a damn lie because I know his son.' Then he said, 'You must be one of his bastards.' That's when I said I'd meet him outside of school and I started to walk away. But he grabbed hold of me, twisted me around and threw the first punch. Skipper, he wouldn't have gotten away with it if he—"

"Gotten away with it?" Boxer asked.

"He is the son of the president of the PTA," Chuck said.

"You mean he's not on suspension?" Boxer asked, directing the question to De Mattao.

"There was no reason to put him on suspension," De Mattao explained. "I had a very serious talk with Darrel's mother and she fully understands the gravity of the situation."

Boxer suddenly saw the picture. Chuck was just another tough kid in another fight with no one to stand by him, so it was easy to make an example of him and get away with it. Only this time, the man behind the desk didn't expect to be facing an admiral. It was time to pull rank and Boxer knew he was going to love every minute of it. "Mister De Mattao, I hope you understand the gravity of the situation."

"What?"

"Two boys fight, but only one boy is put on suspension," Boxer said. "I know a great many people, especially in the media, who might find that more than interesting."

"Are you suggesting —"

"Chuck," Boxer said, "wait outside and close the door when you leave."

"Leave the door open," De Mattao said.

"Chuck, close it," Boxer snapped.

"Aye, aye, Skipper," Chuck answered.

"Admiral, aren't you a little out of your depth," De Mattao said. "You know, I could call security and —"

"You could, but you won't," Boxer said calmly, "because I've got you by the short hairs. You do the wrong thing and I'll have the Feds down here so fast you'll think they were waiting just outside. I want Chuck's suspension lifted and I want it taken off his record."

"I can't do that," De Mattao said.

"You will do it," Boxer told him. "You should have guessed that I don't take no for an answer. Get it done now, in front of me."

"But —"

"Mister De Mattao, I don't have time to fuck with you," Boxer said in an icy voice. "I'm going to formally adopt Chuck and I don't want that suspension on his record. And just so that you understand where I'm coming from, I'm going to let him finish here and when he does, he will go straight into Annapolis."

"But his grades —"

"I can guarantee he'll be an honor student," Boxer said.

De Mattao hesitated.

Boxer looked at his watch. "You have three minutes. If you don't do what I asked you to, I will go outside and make a few phone calls. I do have some pull in government and I will use it."

"How will I explain the change on his permanent record?"

"I don't care how you explain it," Boxer said. "That's your problem. Mine is to see that it's made."

After a few moments hesitation, De Mattao nodded, picked up the phone and asked, "Will you please give me Charles Spadaro's permanent record card and type up a directive lifting his suspension."

"That was good," Boxer said smiling. "Very good. Now I'll just watch you make the change on the boy's record card and I'll be on my way."

De Mattao raised his eyebrows.

"I never said I trusted you," Boxer said and looking directly at the man, he added, "That's a mistake an old seahand like myself would never make..."

The rest of the day was perfect. Boxer had convinced De Mattao to excuse Chuck for the remainder of the day; then the two of them went into Manhattan to pick up John.

The boys seemed pleased to see each other again and though the day turned cloudy, the three of them had a wonderful time walking and riding around the city.

About five o'clock in the afternoon, Boxer met Gwen at the TV studio. She wore her long blond hair in a ponytail and was dressed in a lovely green pants suit.

As soon as she was in the cab, Gwen greeted each of them with a kiss and said, "I'm really glad to get out of that nut house. I swear sometimes I think I'm in the wrong profession." Then turning to Boxer she said, "I'm proud of you, Jack… I'm really very proud of you." And she possessively wrapped her arm around his.

For dinner, they went downtown to the Village to have dinner in a Spanish restaurant, called the Spain on 13th Street, just off Sixth Avenue.

At dinner Gwen wanted to know "what was it like up there?"

Boxer shrugged. "It's not easy to explain."

"Try," Gwen said. "I mean you did —"

"The men did it," Boxer said.

"And what about that Russian —"

"Comrade Admiral Borodine," Boxer said.

"Why do you call him that?"

"It's his rank and his name," Boxer answered.

"Please tell us what happened?" John asked.

Boxer finished his second vodka before he said, "Nothing pleasant. Many good men died. But we managed to prevent many, many millions of people from dying."

"That really doesn't tell us much," Gwen commented.

"I'm sorry," Boxer said. "I'm not much good at telling stories."

Later on the way back uptown to where Gwen and John lived, Boxer suddenly realized Chuck hadn't asked him any questions about the sinking of the *Shark* and just as suddenly he realized that boy intuitively understood that he didn't want to talk about it.

The cab pulled up in front of the building where Gwen and John lived.

"Are you coming up for a nightcap?" Gwen asked.

"Not this time," Boxer answered. "I'm just a bit too tired and Chuck here has school tomorrow."

Gwen kissed Chuck on the forehead; then gave Boxer a lingering kiss. "Won't that change your mind?" she asked in a whisper.

Boxer shook his head. "I'm sorry, Gwen… I really am tired."

She nodded and said, "You can be a hard man."

"Not hard," Boxer answered. "Just tired. I'll give you a call before I go back to Washington."

Gwen closed the door and the cab pulled away from the curb.

On the way back to Staten Island, Chuck suddenly asked, "Why did you and Gwen get divorced?"

The question seemed to come out of the proverbial blue. But Boxer realized that Chuck had been quiet for a while and probably had been thinking about it. "We wanted different things," he answered.

Chuck fell silent again.

Boxer closed his eyes.

"She's very beautiful," Chuck said. "And she's very smart."

"Yes on both counts," Boxer replied.

"She still has feelings for you."

Boxer opened his eyes. "I have feelings for her. We're friends and we share John," he said.

"I mean feelings... I mean she still wants you with her in her bed."

"What?"

"Skipper, I ain't cherry... I can tell what a girl wants by the way she looks at a guy."

"Gwen isn't exactly a girl," Boxer said, amused by Chuck's observations.

"You know what I mean," Chuck said.

Boxer suppressed a smile. It was obvious Chuck had a crush on Gwen. He could understand that. If he hadn't already been married to her, he too would have a crush on her.

"Skipper — You don't mind if I call you that?" Chuck asked.

"I don't mind."

"Skipper, I like Gwen and I like John," Chuck said.

"Good. I'm going to start the necessary wheels turning to adopt you. You'll be my son legally. Do you understand what that means?"

"I think so. Whose last name do I use?"

"Any one you want," Boxer answered.

Chuck was quiet for a few moments; then he said, "If it's okay with you, I'd like to be called Charles Rugger Boxer."

"It's fine with me," Boxer said with a smile. "It's really fine with me."

The window was very small and it overlooked Dzerzhinsky Square in Moscow. Snow was already on the ground and the sky was leaden with the promise of more. A lean-faced man stood with his back to the window and his arms crossed over his thin chest. He frowned at the fat, dark complexioned man seated in front of the desk and speaking in Russian, he said,

"The problem is, my dear Mister Morell, we can't get near Comrade Admiral Boxer. At least not in the usual way. To begin with, though he seems to be unaware of it, he is almost always guarded. If we take him out in the usual way, it will cause a furor. After all, he is not only a hero with a majority of his own people, but he is a hero with ours. Ordinary assassination would be stupid. But if he should be killed by the very man he seeks to kill, well now, everyone would understand that."

Morell shifted his weight. The man at the window was Deputy Director Valentine Makusky. He knew him very well. Over the years they had worked together on a variety of assignments and even had a social relationship that included going to the opera, ballet, and concerts together. "So you want to use me as bait, eh," Morell commented.

"The lure," Makusky corrected.

"Here in Moscow?"

"No... In Italy, where he expects you to be. Information will be passed to Sanchez that you are with your Mafia friends in Rome. Boxer will fly to Rome. You will lead him on a chase. Just to make it more authentic looking; then at the right moment and the right time, our people will step in and kill him."

"Suppose you misjudged the right moment and he kills me instead?"

Makusky launched himself away from the window and eventually settled behind the desk, where he picked up a pack of cigarettes, offered one to Morell and then taking one for himself, he struck a lighter and held it until they were both lit up. "Understand," he said, blowing smoke, "that we are willing to pay fifty thousand American dollars for this."

"Not much when you consider the wealth of the Kremlin," Morell answered nonchalantly.

"Boxer must be taken out before he takes command of the *Barracuda*, the new version of the *Shark*."

"Yes, I can understand that," Morell answered. "But if it is so important to take him, then why aren't your people willing to pay a decent price to have it done?"

"Seventy-five thousand."

"Two-hundred and fifty thousand dollars deposited in the usual Swiss bank," Morell said, his face expressionless.

"You're much too high," Makusky answered.

"Then get someone else. There are enough freelancers around, or use one of your own people for the 'lure'."

"You're the one he wants to kill!"

"Ah, then 'there's the rub', isn't it?"

Makusky didn't answer. He took several deep drags on the cigarette and blew the same number of smoke streamers across the desk. "I have to think about it," he said.

Morell shook his head. "No time to diddle around," he said. "I hate Moscow in the winter. It's too cold for me. You brought me here and I'm going to leave —"

"All right, you have your price. I don't like haggling. Two-hundred and fifty thousand dollars deposited to the same Swiss bank account number you always use."

"Yes. Half within the next five days and the remainder when the job is completed."

"I can't authorize half now."

"Half now," Morell insisted, "or we don't have a working arrangement."

"One third —"

Morell stood up. "We're wasting each other's time. I want to catch the four o'clock flight to Rome."

"This is a very important assignment," Makusky said.

"If it's that important, then why not stop playing games. I'll be the best fucking lure you ever saw. But I want to be paid at the highest possible price. You'll get quality service."

"Half within five days," Makusky said.

Morell dropped back into the chair. "Good. Now we can get some other business out of the way."

"I didn't know we had any other business."

"That's because you don't know a lot of things you should know," Morell said.

"Go ahead, tell me what I should know."

"Comrade Admiral Borodine and Comrade Admiral Boxer were sleeping with the same woman before she was killed by McElroy."

"Kinkade's granddaughter?"

Morell nodded.

"At the same time?" Makusky asked, reaching under the desk to switch on a tape recorder.

"Boxer didn't know it was going on. Several of my friends in the Company happened to see Trish and Borodine together and followed them for a while. They telephoned me in Rome and I told them I wanted a full-scale surveillance mounted. Borodine and Trish were lovers, but I'm certain Boxer didn't know."

Makusky let out a long low whistle. "So Comrade Admiral Borodine has finally given us something to beat him over the head with the next time he gives us trouble. Admittedly, it isn't very much. But for a man like that, this kind of information — well, it's going to be more difficult than ever for him to play Saint Borodine."

"And I'll tell you something else, Kinkade knew and didn't say anything," Morell said.

Makusky uttered a snort. "Why the hell should he? She was his granddaughter. He didn't want a scandal to touch either of them. But it's useful information and could probably be planted in the newspapers in America or any other Western country."

Morell agreed. "Now for the *pièce de résistance*, as they say. I happen to have in my possession photographs and tape recordings of Borodine and Trish doing, as we say, 'their thing'."

"I don't believe —"

"Here they are," Morell said, reaching into his jacket pocket and removing two sealed packets. "One is a tape the other contains slides in living color. Now Comrade, you tell me what these are worth to your people?"

"Another quarter of a million?"

"Going once… Going twice… Sold to the highest bidder!" Morell exclaimed. "The money for these two little babies is to be paid into my Hong Kong account within the next five days."

"It will be done," Makusky said, reaching for the two packets.

"Good porn," Morell said.

"I thought they were making love?"

"They are… But when you look at the slides and listen to the tape it will become porn."

"Always the philosopher," Makusky commented.

"It helps me stay alive. I want me alive, alive… I mean alive… *Cogito ergo sum*… Remember, I think therefore I am'."

CHAPTER 6

From the way Kinkade sat in his chair, Boxer knew it was going to be one of these meetings. He even knew what it was about. What he didn't know was why Kinkade wanted to meet him away from the office, rather than in Langley, where the old man would have the whole physical structure of the Company behind him. This way he had none of it: he was just another man who'd be trying to make a deal and who'd fail.

"Get everything done in New York?" Kinkade asked, caressing the outside of a martini glass.

Boxer nodded.

"New York's a great place to visit, but I wouldn't want to live there," Kinkade commented. "Ah, but I forgot, you're a Brooklyn boy, aren't you?"

"Born and raised there," Boxer answered, scanning the menu the hostess had put down, after she had led them to a table near the fireplace. He was beginning to think that a bowl of crab soup would be just fine for such a raw, windy day.

"I like this place" Kinkade said. "Has kind of rustic charm with the fireplace and the old wooden beams, don't you think?"

"I hope the food is as rustic as the place looks." Boxer answered.

Kinkade cracked a smile; then he said, "I brought you out here because there are several things I want to discuss with you."

"I thought as much," Boxer said.

"One is personal and the rest are Company matters."

"The waitress is coming," Boxer said. "I think we should order before we have any discussions."

"Have you decided on anything?" Kinkade asked. "I always have difficulty making up my mind."

"The crab soup and broiled red snapper," Boxer answered.

"Do you think?" Kinkade asked, looking at him over his half glasses.

"Only if you like them."

"The trouble is I don't like much of anything," Kinkade said. "I think I like it; then when I begin to eat, I find myself wondering why I ordered it. Trish and I played sort of a game —" He looked down at his drink and mumbled, "I'm sorry."

"It's okay," Boxer said. "You don't have anything to be sorry about. I could have just as easily mentioned her name."

"I promised myself I wasn't going to talk about her," Kinkade said, looking up at Boxer again.

"Talk about her," Boxer said. "It wouldn't be normal if you didn't."

The waitress came to the table. Boxer gave her his order and Kinkade ordered the same thing and when she left the table, he said, "Let's get the personal business out of the way first."

Boxer agreed, lifted his glass and drank the remaining vodka in it. Lunches with Kinkade, for that matter dinners too, were always three to five vodkas. Maybe more, depending on how difficult Kinkade would be.

"I'm retiring in a couple of months," Kinkade said.

"Any plans?"

"You don't seem surprised," Kinkade said.

"I'm not," Boxer answered. "I think it's a wise move."

"Wise or not, I'm going to do it. Anyway, the new man for the job hasn't been chosen. Several are in the running. But the President hasn't said who he wants."

"It won't be an easy choice to make," Boxer said.

"Because I am retiring and because Trish is dead, there are several things I must do and one of them is to make arrangements for the estate in the event that I die. My health, as you well know, is not the best."

Boxer nodded. He didn't see where this part of the conversation was going.

"Trish had her own trust fund," Kinkade said. "I happen to know she would have wanted you to have it."

"What?" Boxer's voice went loud.

"Her trust is worth a half million dollars," Kinkade said. "I have had the necessary papers drawn up giving it to you."

"I already have several million of my own," Boxer told him.

"You have a son and you're taking care of Rugger's son —"

"I'm adopting him," Boxer said. "And neither my son or Rugger's will ever want for money."

"Then with Trish's estate they'll want even less," Kinkade answered. "And though I have disagreed with you, I have always respected you; therefore, I have made you the sole executor of my estate, which totals twenty-five million in cash, stock and bonds. You will have full discretionary power as to how the money should be used."

Boxer was too surprised to speak.

"I have one request that I hope you will honor and that is that some sort of small, non-profit foundation be set up in my name. I'd like to leave something behind, if you know what I mean."

Boxer nodded. "A medical foundation?" he asked. He couldn't help feeling sorry for the man.

"Anything you choose, except one that has to do with studying ways to better relations between the United States and the Soviet Union. That's where I draw the line."

"I understand," Boxer replied, suppressing a smile.

"Now to Company business," Kinkade said.

The sudden hardness coming into the man's voice warned Boxer that next portion of the discussion was going to be difficult.

"You'll be starting your debriefing tomorrow," Kinkade said.

Boxer nodded.

"I'm going to ask you, Cowly and DB to give my men a complete description of everything aboard the *Novogorod*."

Before he answered, Boxer summoned the hostess and asked her to have the waitress bring another round of drinks; then he said to Kinkade, "I had the feeling you were going to get to that sooner or later and my answer is no. I don't care what Cowly and DB do give your pencil jockeys, but I'm not giving them anything about that Russian sub."

"They'll follow your lead," Kinkade said.

Boxer shrugged.

"It would help us a great deal," Kinkade said.

Boxer shook his head. "I was a guest aboard that boat. The men aboard that boat don't deserve to be betrayed."

"Your friend Comrade Captain Borodine would not hesitate to —"

"You're wrong, Kinkade. You're dead wrong. Borodine would do exactly what I'm doing. He would protect me and my crew."

"How can you be sure of that?"

"I'm not sure of too many things, at least those things that are abstract ideas, like courage, loyalty, even the belief in God. But I am sure that Borodine would not do what you're asking me to do."

The fresh round of drinks was brought to the table and the waitress assured them that their order would be out in a few minutes.

"No hurry," Kinkade, muttered and when she left the table, he said, "On this Stark will be on my side."

"Probably," Boxer answered, "at least from an official point of view. But no matter who's involved, I will not tell you about one single detail. I was a guest in the man's house, so to speak. I will not give you the information necessary to destroy that house at some future date."

Kinkade took a sip of his drink; then looking hard at Boxer, he said, "This man you're protecting wasn't exactly protecting your interests when he was screwing Trish, now was he?"

A sudden knot gathered in Boxer's stomach. He felt himself flush.

"How do you reconcile that with your idea of his loyalty to you?"

"I don't try," Boxer answered tightly.

"Don't you think you should?"

Boxer picked up the glass in front of him and drank half the vodka in it before he put it down.

"Had the situation been reversed, would you have done what he did?"

After a long pause, during which Boxer forced himself to look at what had been the situation, he answered, "I would have. I couldn't resist Trish any more than he could. I understand why he became her lover. I think I even understand why she let him become her lover. Trish wouldn't have married me, or if she had, she soon would have been unfaithful. She couldn't help it. She really couldn't."

Kinkade was silent and very pale.

"You know I loved her," Boxer said, after a short pause.

"Yes, I know. That's why I did what I did with her trust fund and my estate."

Boxer finished off the remaining vodka.

"We need that information," Kinkade pressed. "It could make the difference in some future combat situation."

"I know that better than anyone else," Boxer said. "But I can't give it to you. I really can't."

"Think about it before you give a definitive no."

Boxer shook his head. "I won't change my mind. I owe those Russian sailors. Hell, we all owe them. You don't pay your debts by —"

"Suppose you tell just about those devices that are different from ours?"

"No."

"Why the hell do you have to be so pig-headed about it?"

"Because," Boxer answered softly, "when I look at myself in a mirror, I want to be able to do it without having to say to myself, if I had it to do all over again I would have done it differently: I would have done it right. I want to do it right the first time around."

"You're a damn hard man," Kinkade said.

"So I've been told," Boxer replied. "So I have been told."

"This is the last session," the debriefing officer announced at the end of the third debriefing session.

"I'm sure glad it is," Cowly said, "I couldn't have lasted another session."

Boxer, Cowly, and DB filed out of the room. They were exhausted and in some strange way, still back in the arctic, tracking the *Shark*.

"I'm going to go home and get under a hot shower," Cowly said, as they left the debriefing room and walked along the corridor of the west wing in Langley.

"I just want to sleep," DB said. "Go back to the hotel and sack out."

"What about you, Skipper?" Cowly asked.

"I just want to walk and get the cobwebs out of my head," Boxer answered, as they stepped into the elevator and rode down to the garage, where a limo was waiting to take them back to the city.

"Remember," Cowly said. "The wedding is on Saturday."

"Can't forget it," Boxer said.

"Me neither," DB assured him.

The three of them settled into the car and forty-five minutes later, Cowly was dropped off in front of the building where he and Cynthia were living and a few minutes later, Boxer and DB were deposited outside their hotel.

"I'm going upstairs," DB said, as they entered the lobby.

"See you around," Boxer responded and he walked over to the desk to see if there were any messages for him.

There were none.

"You're a hard man to find," a woman said from behind him.

He turned and though she looked familiar, he didn't recognize her.

"Linda Johnson," she said.

"The TV reporter," Boxer responded.

"Yes, that's me."

Boxer looked around for the rest of her crew.

"I'm here solo," she said, smiling up at him.

He realized that even in high heels, she was at least a half a head shorter than he. She was wearing a mink coat over a light tan skirt and jacket that accentuated her well-proportioned figure. A single strand of pearls graced her neck and she wore her dark brown hair shoulder length. Her eyes were green and intense looking.

"Well, Admiral, do I pass inspection?" she asked.

Boxer nodded. "You certainly do."

"Well, you sure as hell don't. You look terrible."

"Thanks," he said.

"I want to talk to you," Linda told him.

He was going to say that he didn't want to talk to her, or anyone else. He wanted to be left alone. But she reminded him of another woman from his past and instead, he said, "If you're willing to walk, I might be persuaded to talk."

"I'll walk," she said.

Boxer nodded. They crossed the lobby together and as soon as they were outside, she wrapped her arm around his.

"What do you want to talk about?" he asked.

"Several things. For openers, who is the real Jack Boxer?"

"That's the wrong question to ask now," Boxer said, stopping at the corner to wait for a walk signal to come on.

"How about telling me if it's true that you were saved by a dolphin?"

"That's what I was told," Boxer answered.

"Are you and this Russian admiral really good friends?" she asked.

"Yes."

She fell silent.

"No more questions?" Boxer asked.

"I'm thinking," Linda answered.

Boxer smiled, but didn't say anything. He was thinking too. But not about any of the questions she'd asked. He was wondering why she wanted to see him.

"You know," she said, after being silent for a few moments, "I knew about you — that is to say, I heard about you — before Jay and Billy set up the interview in the lobby."

"Oh! How?"

"You dated a newspaper reporter named Tracy Kimble and—"

Boxer stopped. Tracy and he were lovers and after their passion had cooled, friends until she was murdered. But all of that had happened several years ago.

"She was my half-sister," Linda said. "She used her father's name and I used my father's name."

Boxer nodded.

"Does it upset you that I'm Tracy's half-sister?" Linda asked.

"I'm not sure," Boxer answered, starting to walk again.

"I was a freshman in college when she first met you," Linda said. "I remember her telling me she met the most spectacular man and that man was you."

"I was very fond of her," Boxer said quietly.

"I know she knew that," Linda answered.

Boxer felt a momentary increase of pressure on his arm.

"I'd like to do a full length interview on you. I mean something with depth… Something that will give the reader an understanding of why you did what you did and said what you said."

"I don't think so," Boxer responded. "Besides, you'd have to get clearance from —"

"Whatever clearances are necessary, I can get," she said.

Boxer glanced at her. He knew she wasn't just making an idle boast. "The no stands," he said. "I really don't have any desire to be in the public eye. I am paid to do a certain job and I do it to the best of my ability."

"Com'on Skipper — I hope you don't mind me calling you Skipper. Do you?"

"I don't think any woman has ever called me that," Boxer said.

Linda smiled. "It fits you. Besides, I want to be the first woman to call you that."

Boxer shrugged. "I can't very well stop you," he said.

"As I started to say, Skipper, you do much more than just your job. You know that. The people you work for know it and certainly your men know it."

Boxer remained silent. He was beginning to feel uncomfortable. Like Tracy, Linda went after what she wanted. But she wasn't nearly, or at least didn't seem to be, as brash as Tracy had been.

"That story would mean a lot to me," she said.

"I'm certain it would, but I can't really help you," Boxer told her. "By tomorrow, or the next day, I'm going to be leaving for a few weeks vacation and —"

Linda stopped. "The network would be willing to pay a million —"

"No," he said, starting to walk.

She came after him. "Just tell me that you'll think about it," she urged. "Can't you do that?"

Boxer shook his head. "I won't think about it, because I'm not in the least bit interested in having it done. Linda, I really don't want to continue this conversation."

"What do you want to do?"

"You really want to know?"

"I asked, didn't I?" she responded sulkily.

"Get drunk, go to sleep, get laid, but not necessarily in that order. Now why don't you leave me alone so I can decide which of the three I intend to do first."

"Why are you so angry?"

"I'm tired and —"

"I can help you with one of the three, perhaps two of three," she said.

"A roll in the sack won't get you the story," Boxer said.

"Did I ask for a trade-off?"

"Sorry," Boxer said. "But you must admit —"

"I'm getting tired of walking," Linda said, "and I feel kind of horny myself, so that brings up the question whether or not you want to come back to my place and get laid, or do we part company here and now, which would be a pity since I am sure we would be able to give each other a great deal of pleasure."

"Put that way, I don't see how I could refuse," Boxer said.

A few minutes later they settled into the back seat of the cab. Linda gave her address to the driver; then turning to Boxer, she pressed her lips to his.

Boxer found her tongue. He was wrong. She was every bit as brash as Tracy had been...

Linda unlocked the door and pushed it open. "Go in," she said. Boxer nodded and stepped into a large room that was a dining area, bedroom and anything else the person occupying it wanted it to be.

"It's a studio apartment," Linda explained.

Boxer nodded and looked around. There was a small kitchen area on one side and the door to a very small bathroom was open on the other side.

"A drink?" Linda asked, slipping out of her fur coat and dropping it over a chair.

"Vodka on the rocks," Boxer answered, removing his cap and coat. He set them down on the back of another chair and looked around. There were shelves with more video tapes than books. A combination VCR, TV and hi-fi systems occupied several shelves. A convertible couch was against one wall and above it was a large copy of a poster advertising a rock group. A video camera lay on an end table and there were a half a dozen trade magazines in various places around the room. Boxer was disturbed by the sense of organized confusion.

"What shall we drink to?" Linda asked, handing him a glass.

"Anything you want to," Boxer answered, beginning to feel more and more uncomfortable.

"To the good time ahead," she said, touching her glass to his.

Boxer drank.

"I'll open the couch," Linda said, putting her drink down on a small round table.

Suddenly Boxer began to sweat. This was where he wanted to be. But he didn't really know where he wanted to be. "Look," he said, "this isn't going to work."

Linda stopped what she was doing, straightened up and looked at Boxer. "I don't understand?"

"I mean, it just won't work between us," he said. "I'm sorry. But I'm going to leave."

"You mean —"

"I mean that I'm not going to make love to you," Boxer said.

"I never said anything about you making love to me," she answered. "I said I was horny. You want to get laid and I wanted to screw. I don't remember either one of us mentioning the word love."

Boxer put his glass down next to hers and picked up his coat and hat. She was a lot harder than he would have thought. "I apologize," he said.

"You apologize?"

Boxer put his coat and hat on. He was still sweating profusely and his heart was beating very fast.

Linda crossed the room and stopped in front of him. "Is it because I'm Tracy's half-sister?" she asked.

"No. It's not you. It has nothing to do with you. It's me. I can't explain it. But —"

"Are you some kind of weirdo?"

Boxer didn't answer. He turned and walked toward the door.

"Man, did I make a mistake about you," she called after him. "I thought you'd be something else in the sack."

Before he left the apartment, Boxer glanced back at her. In the elevator, he became panicky. When he reached the lobby, he couldn't restrain himself any longer and ran into the street. He ran until he was too exhausted to continue; then he stopped and leaned against a lamp pole. After a while, he realized he was sobbing...

Boxer walked with his collar up and his head bent into the windblown sheets of rain. With no idea of where he was, or how long he had been walking, Boxer was aware that the gray afternoon slowly had dissolved into the sad short twilight of a November evening.

He tried to pull himself together. But he couldn't. He was dangling over a huge, bottomless pit and the rope holding him was snapping strand by strand.

Suddenly Boxer saw a man and woman walking down a flight of stone steps. He saw the woman look at him and putting his head down, he quickened his pace.

"Admiral... Boxer... Jack Boxer?" she called.

He stopped and faced her.

"My God!" she exclaimed and went to him.

"Do you know who I am?" she asked.

"My lawyer, Francine Wheeler."

"What's wrong with you?"

"I'm all right," Boxer told her.

She shook her head. "No you're not. Come with me!"

"Please… I'm all right," he repeated.

"Pete, I'm sorry," she said to her companion. "I can't go out with you. This is an old friend. He needs my help."

"I have tickets —" Pete started to say.

"I'm sorry," Francine said. "I'm really sorry." And she took hold of Boxer's right arm.

"I won't call you again," Pete threatened from the curb side where his white sports car was parked.

"Suit yourself," she answered.

"There's no need to bother yourself with me," Boxer said.

"There's every need," she told him. "Can you make the steps?"

He nodded. "I guess I have to. You can't very well carry me."

"No, I couldn't. But I sure as hell would try."

Boxer smiled and with Francine supporting him on one side, he grabbed hold of the iron railing and slowly mounted the steps.

A few minutes later Boxer was settled in a large easy chair in front of a roaring fire.

Francine was standing off to the left of the fireplace.

He looked at her. She wore a green gown with a neckline that left the tops of her breasts bare and accentuated all the other curves of her body. He drained the remainder of the vodka in his glass.

"When was the last time you had something to eat?" Francine asked, coming to him and kneeling in front of him.

"Toast and coffee for breakfast," Boxer answered; then he added, "I'm really sorry about your friend and —"

"How about a bowl of soup and some of yesterday's stew?" she asked.

"That will be fine," he said, trying not to look at the bare tops of her breasts.

"I'll microwave everything. It'll be done in a few minutes," Francine told him as she stood up. "While I'm getting dinner, why don't you go upstairs, have a hot shower and put on the blue terry cloth robe that's in the guest room closet."

Boxer was about to object.

"You're not going anywhere tonight," she told him authoritatively. "I didn't give up going to dinner and a concert just to have you eat and run."

He nodded and asked, "Is it okay if I have another drink?"

"Why don't you wait until dinner?" she asked.

Boxer looked at her; then at the glass. After a few moments, he said, "Good idea." And he handed her the empty glass.

She bent down, kissed him lightly on the forehead and turning started for the kitchen.

Boxer stood up. He enjoyed watching the movement of her hips as she walked...

"Feeling better?" Francine asked.

Boxer looked down at the empty plate; then at her. While he had showered, she had changed from the evening gown to a more practical black jumpsuit. He smiled and said, "I'm stuffed."

"That's not what I asked. I want to know if you feel better."

"Will not nearly as bad do?" Boxer asked, reaching for the vodka and filling half his glass. "I have a very good Russian friend who assures me that vodka will have absolutely no effect if you eat."

"Your Comrade Admiral Borodine?"

"My Comrade Admiral Borodine," Boxer said, lifting his glass. "To you and to him. My very good friends."

She touched her unfinished glass of red wine; then drank. 'What were you doing in this part of the city?" she asked.

Boxer shrugged. "I really didn't know where I was. I had been walking for hours."

"Do you want to tell me about it?"

Boxer drank again.

"You have more courage than that can ever give you," Francine said and reaching across the table, she gently stroked his hand.

"Courage is a very strange word," he answered. "Much of what you and other people might deem courage is really professionalism. Courage has very little to do with it."

"I'll clean up here and we'll go into the living room and talk," she said.

Boxer helped her gather the soiled dishes and place them in the dishwasher; then he washed down the table, while she cleaned the microwave oven. It took less than ten minutes of teamwork to get everything done.

As Boxer settled into the same easy chair he had sat in before, she put two large faggots on the andirons and stirred up the ashes until the flames began to chew on the wood above them. Then she came back to where he was and sat down on the floor in front of him. The zipper of her jumpsuit was open just enough to let him see that she wasn't wearing a bra.

"What happened to you?" she asked, looking up at him.

"I panicked."

"I believe that. But I also know more than that happened."

Boxer pursed his lips.

"It won't go any farther than this room," she assured him.

"I never thought it would."

"Talking about it might help whatever it is that's bothering you," Francine said.

"Are you sure you want to hear it?"

She nodded. "I'm sure."

Boxer started with the end of the debriefing session, his subsequent meeting with Linda Johnson and his discovery of her relationship to Tracy.

"That didn't bother you?" Francine asked.

"Why should it?"

"The fact that you were about to screw the sister of a former lover?"

Boxer shook his head. "We were consenting adults. We had no illusions —"

"Do you have any illusions about anything anymore?" she asked.

"Probably," he answered. "Though, I would have to admit they're few and far between."

She nodded and told him to continue.

"Suddenly I began to sweat… I mean really sweat and my heart started to race. I knew I couldn't stay. I had to leave. When I told Linda that she became very upset. I guess in her place I would have also."

"She did expect something," Francine said.

"I'm not faulting her," Boxer replied.

"You left the apartment?" Francine asked.

"Yes… I got into the elevator and —" Boxer stopped. His throat suddenly tightened and his hands began to shake.

Francine reached up and took hold of his hands in hers. "Easy, Jack," she whispered. "Take it easy… You're all right."

He nodded and forced the words out of him. "As soon as the doors closed, the fucking world collapsed. I felt… I felt as if I was going to be crushed. I had to stop myself from beating on the walls… I was terrified… I mean terrified… Believe me, Francine, I have been in situations where there was real danger of being crushed. But this was far more frightening to me than anything I've ever experienced."

"I believe it," she said gently.

"I thought I'd collapse before I reached the lobby. I don't believe I ever made it to the lobby. I think I stopped at one of the lower floors and ran down the stairs. Finally I was out in the street and I ran until I was too tired to run any more. I wound up hanging onto a lamp post; then I began to cry, I don't remember having started walking, but I obviously had. Then you happened."

"I'm glad that I happened and not someone else," she said.

Boxer leaned back and closed his eyes. "You can't be claustrophobic and be a submariner. The two are —"

"One episode doesn't qualify you as claustrophobic. Besides, now there are all sorts of ways of treating it that didn't exist a few years ago."

"I'd still be one hell of a risk," Boxer said, opening his eyes.

"I don't want to sound Pollyannaish about it," she told him, "but you've had two hard missions, a few personal troubles in between them and no rest. Just how long do you think you could drive yourself without something happening?"

"I never thought about it," he answered.

"You just had a signal from your body … from your brain. You need time out. You need some tender loving care."

"Is that what the doctor prescribes?" he asked.

She nodded and in a choked voice, she said, "Yes, I think so. But it's not a doctor who's doing the prescribing, it's your lawyer."

"And who'll administer the tender loving care?"

"Would you mind if I tried?"

"I wouldn't mind at all," he said, wrapping his hands around hers and squeezing them gently.

For several moments neither one of them spoke; then she said, "I don't think you just happened to come by here."

"Oh?"

"I think you were coming to me," Francine said. "I think you wanted to come to me."

Boxer shrugged. "Maybe."

She shook her head. "There isn't any 'maybe' about it. None at all."

"You don't mind that I did?"

"I don't mind," she answered.

Boxer let go of her hands. "I'm not the easiest man in the world to get along with," he said.

"I never thought you were."

Boxer rubbed his beard.

"You look perplexed," Francine said.

He nodded. "I am… I'm not quite sure how I should act… I mean —"

"You mean you want to go to bed with me, but you don't want to rush me for fear I might bolt and run."

Boxer flushed.

"True?" she asked.

"Sort of," he answered, aware that the wavering firelight touched her red hair and made it glow.

She smiled up at him. "I promise you I won't bolt and run… I'd stay around to enjoy it."

Boxer bent forward and taking hold of her, he pressed his lips to hers. Her perfume had a delicate floral note.

"Are you sure this is what you want?"

"Yes," she whispered. "Are you sure you're up to it?"

"I'll do my best," Boxer said, nuzzling her ear. "And if I can't, you'll be the first to know."

She drew away, stood up and took hold of his right hand, "This is no place for a labor of love. Come with me to a softer, better place."

Boxer let himself be pulled out of the chair; then he scooped her into his arms.

"Will you do this when we're old and gray?" she asked, as he carried her upstairs.

"Only if you don't put on any more weight and I don't happen to have a hernia," he answered, moving sideways through the door into the darkened room. "Bed or floor?" he asked.

"Floor first; then bed."

CHAPTER 7

The wedding reception was held inside Mrs. Lowe's house. The living room and dining room had been cleared of furniture to allow the caterer to set up the buffet tables.

Everyone in the *Shark*'s crew came and so had Admiral Stark and Kinkade. Boxer wanted to bring Francine with him, but she had convinced him that another time would be more appropriate for her to meet his crew. And as he stood off to one side and watched the bride and groom mingle with the guests, he realized she was right. But he was anxious to return to her.

"Ah, there you are!" Stark exclaimed, coming up to him.

"Been here for a while," Boxer grinned.

"How about a drink?" Stark asked.

"Could use another," Boxer said, looking at his empty glass.

"The bar is set up in the foyer."

"It might take a bit of pushing to get there," Boxer told him.

"It will, but I'm game."

"Lead the way, sir... You have the rank," Boxer said.

"But you have the youth."

"Rank," Boxer exclaimed and pointed to the foyer.

Stark pushed forward and Boxer brought up the rear.

"Doesn't the bride look beautiful," Stark commented.

"Very."

"And Cowly actually looks nervous."

"As a cat," Boxer answered.

The two men laughed.

"Are you going down to Texas to visit Jay and Billy?" Stark asked. They had reached the bar and Boxer asked the barkeep for a vodka on the rocks for himself and a scotch on the rocks for Stark, before he answered. "I almost forgot about that," he said, handing Stark his drink.

"To the bride and groom," Stark toasted.

"May they be happy," Boxer added.

"I might take a few days off and join you there," Stark said.

Boxer rubbed his beard. "I may not go."

"Oh? I thought it was definite."

Boxer shook his head. "I never gave those characters a definite date. They took charge and arranged my life."

Stark laughed. "They're good at doing that."

"I was actually thinking of asking you if I could use your place for a few days."

"Now?"

Boxer nodded.

"It's bleak as hell down there, and cold too."

"I —"

"Alone?"

Boxer hesitated for a moment; then said, "No … with Francine Wheeler."

Stark raised his eyebrows. "I didn't know that you had anything more than a client-lawyer relationship with her."

"It somehow progressed from that," Boxer said.

"Sure, you can use the place. After all, it will eventually be yours."

"Thanks," Boxer said.

"Just how serious is it between you and the lady lawyer?" Stark asked.

"Hard to tell," Boxer answered. "But I have the feeling that it could become serious."

"You think she feels the same way?"

"I hope so," Boxer answered, lifting the glass to his mouth again.

"As serious as those two?" Stark asked, gesturing toward the bride and groom, who were making their way out of the living room and into the foyer.

"The possibility has occurred to me," Boxer said.

"Well now, I'll drink to that!" Stark exclaimed.

"Why the hell not!" Boxer responded.

As the afternoon wore on, each of the men had come over to Boxer to shake his hand and introduce him to their wives and sweethearts; then finally Cowly quieted everyone down and said, "First, I want to thank everyone for taking time to be here this afternoon. I know many of you came from as far away as California and Washington State... Then I'd like to thank my newly gotten mother for letting me and Cynthia use her house to give this reception. And I'd like to thank my own mother, father, sister and brother for being here." He paused and then said, "But there is one man who's responsible for myself, Cynthia and the rest of us who served aboard the *Shark*, for being here today. Ladies and gentlemen, a hand for Skipper."

The men clapped and began to chant: "Skipper... Skipper... Skipper!"

Boxer stepped forward and held up his hands.

A sudden silence fell over the room.

"As much as I'd like to take the credit," Boxer said, "I can't. I'm here because of all of you. But more important, we're all here because of Mister Cowly and his beautiful bride, Cynthia. And we're here because as every man who ever served with Mister Cowly knows that there isn't a better man, a better officer on any boat in the Navy."

The men began to cheer...

Rejoining Stark, Boxer stepped back and said, "Now I could use another drink."

Stark nodded.

"Ladies and gentlemen," Cynthia called above the hubbub of conversation, "may I have your attention for a few moments."

The room became silent again.

"A few moments of silent prayer," she said, "for those shipmates who will never again be with us in body, but whose memory always will be locked in our hearts."

Stark bowed his head, while Boxer found himself looking straight at Cynthia. Dressed in a simple black cocktail dress with a princess collar and with her long blond hair touching her shoulders, she was a strikingly beautiful woman. That they had been lovers now seemed so distant that it was as if it never existed. Suddenly Boxer realized that she was looking at him. He smiled at her.

She smiled back.

Boxer knew she was telling him she was happy. And he was happy for her.

The few moments of silent prayer passed and once again the sound of people talking filled the downstairs rooms.

"I'm surprised Sanchez isn't here," Boxer said, after he had gotten another vodka on the rocks.

"Are you certain he was invited?" Stark asked.

"At least ninety-five percent," Boxer replied. "Here comes Cowly now. Why don't we ask him?"

"I led the way to the bar. You can do the asking," Stark said.

"Fair enough," Boxer answered.

"Everything all right?" Cowly questioned.

"Just fine," Stark told him.

"I don't mean to pry," Boxer said, "but did you invite Sanchez?"

"Sure," Cowly answered. "He couldn't make it. Said he had to take care of a few things. That man is something else. You know what he did?"

"No way for us to know," Stark said.

"He bought us a house for a wedding present," Cowly told them. "He sent us all the papers yesterday and said that if we didn't like it, we could sell it and buy what we liked. The house is worth about three hundred thousand dollars."

Boxer utter a long low whistle. "That's one hell of wedding present."

"We're not sure that we should take it," Cowly said.

"Take it," Boxer responded. "If you don't, you'll hurt the man's feelings. I'll tell you what: you take the house and I'll furnish it."

Cowly's eyes went wide.

Boxer nodded. "Cynthia will do the choosing," he said.

"Just a minute," Cowly told him, "I want to get Cynthia."

"Get her," Boxer answered and as soon as Cowly was gone, he commented to Stark, "I think I put him in a state of shock."

"You might have. He's coming back with Cynthia in tow."

"Skipper, tell her what you told me," Cowly said to Boxer.

Boxer repeated his offer.

"Oh my God, I don't know what to say!" Cynthia exclaimed.

"Don't say anything," Boxer said. "Send all the bills to me. Buy whatever you need."

"But —"

Boxer put his finger on her lips. "Happiness is not having to worry about certain things. You have a house and now you can fill it with the things you need."

"But how much should we spend?" Cowly asked.

"I leave that to your good judgment," Boxer answered with a smile. "Now stop bothering me and enjoy yourselves."

Cynthia threw her arms around Boxer's neck and kissed him on the lips; then she whispered, "You know you're a wonderful man."

"I know," he laughed.

Cowly gave Boxer his hand. "You know there'll always be a place for you."

Boxer nodded and said, "Now go back to your guests."

"Is he ever going to take a command of his own?" Stark asked, when he and Boxer were alone again.

"I hope so. He's the best officer you've got."

"Speaking about officers," Stark said, "Captain Riggs has applied to serve on the *Barracuda*."

"A good man," Boxer said.

"Does that mean you'll take him?"

"If he's willing to share the EXO duties with Cowly," Boxer said.

"I think he'd be willing to wash the deck, if it meant he could be under your command."

"Have you been scouting around for a man to lead the assault team?" Boxer asked.

Stark nodded.

"There are two men I'm considering. One is a Marine; the other is a Delta Force officer. I'd like you to meet them soon."

"Soon," Boxer said, suddenly remembering how De Vargas had died.

"Are you all right?" Stark asked.

Boxer nodded. "I'm hungry."

"You sure?"

"Let's move over to the buffet and you will see just how sure I am."

"This time you lead the way."

"Aye, aye, sir."

Stark grinned.

"Everything looks too good to eat," Boxer said, looking over the trays of food.

"That's not going to stop me," Stark responded, placing two slices of turkey on his plate.

Boxer took roast beef, ham, several cubes of cheese, potato salad and two slices of bread. "I have enough for the first round," he said.

"I'm set too," Stark answered.

The two of them moved away from the buffet and into the living room, where Boxer spotted Kinkade standing near the window. "Have you spoken to him yet?" he asked.

"No," Stark replied. "I didn't even know that he was here."

"Let's keep him company," Boxer said.

"He certainly looks as if he could use some company," Stark answered.

The two of them headed for Kinkade and when they reached him, Boxer asked him how he was feeling.

"Well enough to attend this," he answered grumpily. "How's the food?"

"Good," Stark said.

"I'll get you some," Boxer offered. "Tell me what you want."

"I'm well enough to get my own food," Kinkade answered testily.

Boxer didn't answer.

For several moments neither of them spoke; then Kinkade asked, "Is that turkey as good as it looks?"

Boxer nodded. "Here," he said, "hold my plate and I'll get you some."

Kinkade took the plate. "Get some potato salad too and a couple of pieces of cheese."

"Will do," Boxer said and headed back to the buffet table, where he began to pick up those things Kinkade had asked for. He was just about to pick up several toothpicks on which small cubes of cheese were impaled, when suddenly he was looking at his men whom the Libyans had impaled. The vision lasted a fraction of an instant, but it was enough to make him stagger. He began to sweat and his hands were trembling.

"Skipper, are you all right?" Mahony asked.

Boxer looked at him. "I'm okay," he managed to say.

"Let me take that plate from you."

"Would you bring it to Mister Kinkade, the man with Admiral Stark. Tell them I had to go to the head and I'll be with them in a few minutes."

Mahony nodded.

"Thanks," Boxer said and forcing himself to smile, he added, "Got to answer nature's call."

"Always," Mahony answered.

Boxer made his way to the bar, started to ask for vodka on the rocks and remembering Francine, asked instead for "club soda on the rocks." He drank it quickly and walked to the door, opened it and stepped out into the raw November afternoon.

The sky was the color of lead and the trees were bare. "Had I my way," he whispered, "I'd —" He stopped, knowing that he did not know what he'd do and pursing his lips, he stepped back inside the house and closed the door behind him.

Coming up to him, Cynthia asked, "Is there anything wrong?"

"Just needed a breath of fresh air," he said.

"You look kind of strange. Are you sure you're okay?"

"Positive."

"Jack, thanks for the gift."

"Just be happy."

"Are you happy?" she asked.

"I think I could be," he answered looking straight at her. "This time I think I could be."

She smiled. "You deserve it."

"I think so too," he said; then added, "I told Stark and Kinkade I'd be right back."

"Don't leave without saying goodbye to us," she told him.

Boxer took hold of her hand and squeezed it. "I promise I won't." And he walked back to where Stark and Kinkade were standing.

"Turkey is good," Kinkade said. "But there's too much pepper in the potato salad."

"We just have to make the best of the fact that we live in an imperfect world," Stark said. "What do you think, Jack?"

Boxer grinned. "Oh absolutely... There is no doubt about it."

Boxer lay with his hands behind his head. Francine was beside him. Her body was warm and had a fresh, clean scent.

"Don't worry about it," she said, running her finger over his bare chest. "Sometimes it happens."

"It never happened before," Boxer said, not looking at her.

"There's always a first time."

"I couldn't make love because —"

She touched his lips. "Tell me ... but don't be angry at yourself about something that's not your fault."

"I'm in bed with you, aren't I?"

"You know exactly what I mean," she said.

Boxer turned over and held her to him.

"Now tell me what stopped you," she said.

"I saw the men with their pricks stuffed into their mouths," he said. "That's the way they were when we came out of the water."

"I don't understand. You're not making any sense."

"Before I met you on the flight home from Rome," Boxer said. "We were in action."

"Yes, you told me."

"What I didn't tell you is that most of my assault team had been wiped out and those men who were captured were impaled on the beach and mutilated."

He felt her tremble.

"You mean their —"

"Yes. They were left to bleed to death," Boxer answered tightly. "This was the second time I saw them today. I saw them when I was at the wedding reception."

"You poor darling," Francine whispered. And she kissed his lips. "Don't you understand that it will take time for you to get over that."

"And time to get over the claustrophobia?"

"Yes ... and time for whatever else might manifest itself," she said.

"I feel as if I am coming apart."

"You're not coming apart; you're only reacting to some pretty ugly things."

Boxer caressed her hair. For several moments he remained silent. He wanted to believe that what was happening to him would pass. He loved Francine and he didn't want to burden her with an emotionally twisted individual.

"Did you speak to Stark about using the house for a while?" she asked.

"He said we can use it any time."

"It will take me a couple of days to clear my desk," she said, gently rubbing his chest.

"There's no real hurry," he said; then he mentioned his invitation to visit Jay and Billy in Texas.

"I didn't know you knew those two," she responded. "In this town, they're the power behind the throne."

"So I have been told, though not exactly that way."

"Do you want to go?" she asked.

"No real burning desire."

"I'll tell you this about those two 'good ol' boys' — they just didn't invite you to be friendly. They have another reason."

"You make them seem as if they're the world's greatest schemers."

"They are. They've been dealing with the Russians so long they even think like them."

Boxer laughed. "Borodine should hear you say that."

"You'll find out when you go."

"I was actually thinking of not going," Boxer said. "I'd rather stay here with you."

"Aren't you even a little bit curious?"

Boxer shook his head.

"Well, I certainly am," Francine said.

"You don't seem to like them very much," Boxer commented.

"On the contrary… I neither like or dislike them. But what I dislike is the power they have."

"I'm beginning to suspect that you've dealt with them," Boxer said.

"Indirectly… I dealt only with their lawyers."

"And you lost."

"I won the judgment," Francine said. "But only because the judge was honest and I wasn't about to be bought."

"Money —"

"Not something as mundane as that. No, I was offered a federal judgeship."

Boxer let out a long, low whistle.

"Not by them, or their lawyers, but by a third party. An oily looking man named Julio Sanchez."

"I know him," Boxer said. "He's a good friend of mine." He felt her stiffen.

"Is he really?" Francine asked, her voice becoming tense.

"He has been in some very tight spots with me," Boxer said.

"What do you know about his business?"

"Only that he works for the same people I do now and then."

"He works for anyone who'll pay," she said bitterly. "He's filth!"

Boxer didn't answer. He wasn't about to get into an argument with her over Sanchez.

"He's a toady for powerful men," she said. "He does their dirty work and some of his own."

"Well," Boxer finally commented, "I'd have to agree that he's not exactly a schoolboy." He was sorry now that Sanchez had come up in their conversation.

Francine gave a snort of disdain; then she said, in a low hard voice, "He almost ruined my life."

"Do you want to tell me how?" Boxer asked.

"No," she answered quietly. "I'll tell you some other time. Now I want you to hold me."

Boxer kissed her on the lips.

"Jay and Billy want something from you," she said. "I think you should go just to find out what it is."

"I'd rather stay here with you," Boxer responded, nuzzling her ear. "I'd rather be where you are."

"Think about going for a few days."

"Will you come with me?"

"No. My presence would spoil it. I want to know why they're so interested in you. There must be a reason."

"Sure, I'm charming."

"True, but that wouldn't be enough."

"Holly, or Louise... I don't know which one, was playing footsy with me at breakfast a few days ago. Maybe —"

"They do a lot more than play footsy," Francine said.

"I guess I'm just not as curious as you," Boxer responded. "Besides, I just don't feel up to becoming involved with characters like Jay and Billy."

"Believe me, if they want something from you, you won't have any choice. But you suit yourself," she said.

"If you're right and they want something from me, I'd prefer it if they came to me."

After a few moments passed, she said, "Maybe you're right. Maybe it would be better that way."

"I really want to be here with you," Boxer said, caressing the hollow of her stomach.

"Somehow I'm beginning to get that idea."

Borodine walked slowly alongside his father, a man now bent with age. They said nothing to one another. Even though it started to snow lightly, neither one suggested they return home.

Finally the elder Borodine said, "I didn't want your mother to hear our conversation. She is already too upset about the matter to —"

"What matter?" Igor asked.

His father stopped and looked back at the house. "When I'm gone," he said, "the house and half the land you can see all around it will be yours. It's good land and gives me a good income."

Igor nodded.

"Even without my pension I'd be a wealthy man," his father said.

Again Igor nodded.

"The house and the land will go to you," the old man repeated.

"If you want to leave it to someone else," Igor said, "I —"

"It's yours… You're my eldest… The land is yours." The man's voice became shrill.

"I only meant that like yourself, I'll have my pension when I retire."

"Not enough," his father grumbled. "Not enough. This far in one year it has an income five to eight times the value of my pension."

"I never realized it was that much," Igor said.

"Well, it is," his father grumbled.

Borodine realized that the wind had shifted from the west to the northeast and it had picked up. That meant another storm was coming in. He hoped it wouldn't be a blizzard. The following day he was planning to take his mother and sister to town to shop.

After a long pause, his father asked, "Why haven't you married again?"

Igor suppressed a smile. "I haven't found anyone I loved," he said and as he spoke, he suddenly thought about Trish. Had he really loved her, or had he loved the way she screwed? He bit his lower lip. She wasn't the kind of woman a man could forget easily…

"Are you listening to me?" his father asked.

"Sorry, I was just thinking about a woman I had met in the United States. She was —"

"I don't care what she was. You must marry a Russian woman and have a son so that this land stays in the family. If there are no heirs then the government will take it back."

"I just can't marry and have children —"

"You don't understand."

"What don't I understand?"

The old man took a deep breath and slowly blew smoke from his nostrils and mouth. "There is a young widow who lives in town. She is a school teacher. Her husband was an administrator at the Ragakusa Metal plant. He drowned two years ago while they were on a summer vacation. She's twenty-five and never had any children. Her name is Tanya Suntsov. I've already had someone speak to her about you and she's willing to meet you."

Borodine didn't know whether to laugh or be angry. He took a third way and said, "Let's go back to the house. I'm getting cold standing here."

"I've arranged to have her come here tomorrow night for dinner."

"I will not be here," Igor said, starting to walk back to the house.

His father came after him. "You must be here. Why would she come here if you're not going to be here?"

"I have no idea," Igor answered. "But I suddenly remembered that I haven't visited the local tavern since I've been home and I think I'd like to do that."

"Walk slower," the old man commanded.

Igor slowed his pace and his father said, "She's a good woman."

"I don't want a good woman," Borodine said. "I want a woman who really knows how to —"

"You want a woman who can give you a son," his father shouted. "You don't have to love her! You have to make her pregnant!"

"You make her pregnant," Borodine shouted back.

"This land must be protected," the old man answered.

Borodine stopped. "The land, the land... Since when did you want to own land, or for that matter anything else. You're a communist, a member of the Party. A hero of the Second World War. This land isn't yours... It belongs to —"

"Me," his father roared. "I earned it with my blood and I worked to make it the best farm in the district. I own it and I don't want to know that when I'm gone, the government will take it back. It's mine. Don't you understand that? And because it's mine, it's yours."

"How much money do you have?" Borodine asked.

Smiling, his father answered, "Almost a million rubles... I'm a wealthy man."

Borodine nodded. "You certainly are."

"Meet the woman," his father said and added, "it would make your mother very happy"

Knowing that as long as he was home he'd be badgered, Borodine sighed and said, "All right, I'll meet her... I'll meet her to please you and Mom. But I am telling you now, I will not marry her to please the two of you."

"One step at a time," his father answered gleefully. "Take one step at a time."

Borodine was too annoyed to answer.

As soon as they returned to the house, his father announced, "He's agreed to meet Tanya."

"I'm so happy," his mother exclaimed. "I'm so happy!" She rushed to him, threw her arms around his neck and kissed him. "You'll see," she assured him, "you'll like her."

Borodine kissed his mother's forehead. "I agree to meet her," he said. "I didn't agree to like her, or do anything else."

"One step at a time," his father repeated.

Borodine took off his cap and coat, hung them in the closet and went to the refrigerator, where his father kept the vodka.

"Good idea to celebrate," the old man said. "Pour me a drink too and we'll drink a toast to Tanya."

"I am not celebrating," Borodine said, "and I will not drink a toast to her."

The two men faced each other with drinks in their hands.

"All right," the elder Borodine said. "You make the toast."

"To Trish," Borodine said.

"Trish? What's a Trish?" his father asked.

"She was the American woman I made love to," Borodine answered.

His father hesitated; then he raised his glass and said, "To Trish." And he drank.

Borodine lifted his glass again. "To Comrade Captain Boxer."

"To Comrade Captain Boxer," the old man echoed.

Borodine lifted his glass a third time. "To Tanya," he said.

His father smiled broadly and entwining his arm with his son's, he said, "To Tanya!"

The dinner was late Sunday afternoon. A special table was set up in the living room and covered with a white linen tablecloth whose edges were embroidered with blue scallop shapes. Napkins, made of the same fine cloth and decorated the same way, were rolled and placed in highly polished wooden rings.

The best china and silverware in the house were on the table. And at each setting were two crystal glasses: one with a graceful long stem for wine, and a small, round one for vodka.

From early in the morning, the house was filled with the wonderful odors of food. Borodine's mother prepared a roast goose, a leg of lamb, a huge fish pie, several noodle dishes and a potato pie. She even baked her own bread, cake and cookies.

Borodine smoked cigarette after cigarette as he paced back and forth waiting for Tanya to arrive, while his father sat in his favorite chair and looked at the grandfather clock every few minutes. And his mother and sister, wearing their best dresses, took turns looking out of the window.

The appointed time for the dinner had been set for five o'clock and it was already ten minutes past five.

"Do you think she got cold feet and wouldn't come?" Borodine's mother asked.

"She couldn't do that," his sister said. "She'd send word to us."

Borodine looked at his parents and suddenly was concerned that they might be disappointed. He went over to his mother and putting his arm around her shoulder, he said, "She'd be a fool to miss your cooking." And he kissed her on the cheek. She was a whole head shorter than he and like his father, bent with age. Her hair was gray and long. She had put it up in a bun on the back of her head.

"I see headlights!" Nadia exclaimed from her post by the window.

"Must be her," her father said, starting to stand.

"Come away from the window," Borodine called. He could see the headlights now.

"Igor, go upstairs," his father said.

Borodine smiled. "I'm not exactly the coy schoolgirl type."

"You don't want her to think that we've been concerned about her coming, now do you?"

"Just one look at us and she'll know that."

The car turned into the driveway and stopped in front of the house.

"I'll answer the door," Borodine's mother said.

"Let Nadia do it," Igor said, motioning to his sister.

Suddenly there was a knock at the door.

Nadia stood very still.

Borodine pointed to the door.

She shook her head.

There was another knock.

"Igor, you go," his mother said.

Borodine took a deep breath and as he slowly exhaled, he walked to the door.

"Open it," his father told him.

Feeling foolish, Borodine put his hand on the knob, turned it and eased the door open.

"I'm sorry I'm late," Tanya said. "But I had some trouble starting the car."

Borodine nodded. "That can happen," he answered. She was very different from what he imagined she would be. She was neither tall and skinny or fat and dumpy. She was somewhat shorter than he and had blue eyes, a dimple on the left side and one on the right. She wore a black sable coat and a matching hat that covered her short blond hair.

"And the roads were none too good," she added.

"They seldom are this time of year," he said, stepping back and allowing her to enter.

She was warmly greeted by Nadia and Mrs. Borodine. Then Mr. Borodine took hold of her right hand, kissed the back of it and said, "We're happy you were able to join us for dinner, Mrs. Suntsov."

"And I am very pleased to be here. But please, everyone, call me Tanya."

"Igor, take her coat and hat," his mother said.

Borodine stepped up behind her and as she slipped out of her coat, he took hold of it. Her perfume had a lavender scent.

She gave him her hat and said, "Thank you."

He nodded and realized that the situation must be as awkward for her as it was for him … perhaps even more?

"Well, let's sit down," Mrs. Borodine said. "Everything is ready."

Borodine put Tanya's coat and hat in the closet and turning toward the living room, he studied her for several moments. She wore a simple black dress, with buttons down the front, a wide belt of red leather and black boots. She had small breasts, a narrow waist and wide hips.

"Come, Igor, and sit down," his father called from the head of the table.

Tanya looked at him, flushed and turned away.

Borodine came to the table and sat down next to Tanya.

"Well, I think we're ready to eat," his father announced. "I know I am." He picked up the bottle of wine. "Tanya, would you like some?" he asked. "I made it myself some ten years ago."

"Yes," she answered. "I'd love some."

When he finished pouring wine into everyone's glass, he said, looking at Tanya, "You make the first toast."

She hesitated for a few moments; then lifting her glass and looking at Borodine, she said, "To peace."

"To peace," Borodine echoed.

"To peace," the others at the table said.

Nadia excused herself and began helping her mother serve.

"How does it feel to be home for a while?" Tanya asked, breaking the silence that had fallen over the table.

"Good, but strange," Borodine answered. "I haven't been home for two years."

"Closer to three," his father said.

"Are you really going to America to receive their highest decoration?" she asked.

"Yes," he answered.

She smiled at him. "You must feel very good about it."

He nodded. "I do and I think our government should reciprocate and give Comrade Admiral Boxer our highest decoration. After all, he was the one who was really responsible for sinking the *Shark*."

"I remember reading that," she said.

"It's true," Borodine answered. "It really is true."

"First course," Nadia announced, carrying in the fish pie.

"That smells heavenly!" Tanya announced.

"And tastes even better," Borodine said.

Mrs. Borodine and Nadia returned to the table.

"Igor," his father said, "you do the slicing this evening."

Borodine glanced questioningly at his mother. It was the first time that his father had relinquished that function to anyone.

"Go ahead and slice," his father urged.

Borodine picked up the knife, marked the center point, pierced the crust and began to cut…

The hours slipped by and soon it was almost nine and Borodine was finishing his second cup of coffee. The conversation at the table had touched on many different topics. Borodine had discovered that Tanya loved classical music and was an amateur naturalist.

Finally, the table was cleared.

Tanya offered to help wash and dry the dishes, but Mrs. Borodine assured her that Nadia and she could do it alone.

"Would you like to take a walk?" Borodine asked.

"Yes," Tanya answered. "I'd like that very much. I haven't had so much to eat in a long time."

"Neither have I," Borodine said. "I'll get your coat and hat."

A few minutes later, the two of them left the house.

"Would you mind if I held onto you?" Tanya asked.

"Not at all. Here, wrap your arm around mine," he said.

"How cold do you think it is?" she asked, as they left the driveway and turned onto the road.

"I wouldn't even be able to guess," Borodine answered.

For a few minutes, they walked without speaking; then suddenly Tanya said, "If you don't want to, you don't have to walk with me. Just take me back to the house so I can thank your mother and father before I leave."

"Did I give you any reason to think that I didn't want to walk with you?"

She remained silent.

"Did I?"

"This whole thing was a bad idea," she said. "I should have never agreed to come to dinner."

Borodine stopped, forcing her to stop. "The dinner was probably my father's idea and not yours."

"It was your mother's," Tanya said.

Borodine laughed.

"What's so funny?"

"The whole situation," he answered.

"There's nothing funny about it," Tanya told him. "I'm a widow and I want to marry and raise a family. I want a house of my own, a life of my own. I love my work, but I want something more out of life. I don't see anything funny in that."

"It didn't strike me funny that way," Borodine said. "It's funny the way my parents —"

"They're not funny either," Tanya said, cutting him short. "They love you and want to see you happy. They want to hold your children, your son, in their arms. That's not funny. Maybe that's what life is all about."

Borodine started to walk again.

"Why aren't we going back?" Tanya asked.

"Because," he answered, "we're not finished."

"What haven't we finished?"

"Talking," he said. "We haven't finished talking."

"I've said all I'm going to say and probably more than I should have. But I will say one more thing. I didn't want this meeting any more than you did. But your mother convinced me that it would be a good idea. I want to marry again. I can understand if you do not. I liked being married and I understand that marriage is for some people and not for others. Obviously, you're in the second category. That's all I have to say."

"There's no cause to be angry," Borodine told her.

"I'm not angry," she shouted.

"If you're not, then your voice is," Borodine said.

"All right, I'm angry," Tanya answered. "I'm angry because I feel humiliated. Even if you are the great Comrade Admiral Borodine, our national hero and I'm just a widow teaching school, I have feelings too and right at this moment, I feel as if you're laughing at me." Without giving him a chance to answer, she turned and started to run back toward the car.

Borodine went after her, caught hold of her and spun her around. "I'll marry you," he said.

They were both breathing hard and their steamy breaths joined in the cold night air.

She swallowed twice before she asked, "Why?"

"Because… Because, I'll never get a better offer," Borodine answered.

"When?" Tanya asked.

"As soon as possible. I want you to come to Moscow with me and then to the United States."

"You mean it? You won't go back on your word?"

Borodine put his arms around her. She was trembling. "I meant everything I said and I won't go back on my word."

She closed her eyes and tilted her face up to his.

Borodine pressed his lips to hers.

Then in a low, breathy voice, she said, "I haven't been kissed like that since my husband died. I haven't had a man's arms around me."

Borodine sensed that she was going to cry and with his gloved hand, he gently touched her cheek. "I guessed that," he said.

"I don't expect you to love me," she said, lowering her eyes. "But if you're kind and gentle, I will try to please you."

"And I will try to please you," he responded and taking hold of her hand, he said, "Come, let's go back to the house and tell my parents what they want to hear."

After a short silence, Tanya said, "You can still change your mind. I won't —"

"Do you want to change your mind?" Borodine asked.

"No," she answered. "No."

Borodine squeezed her hand and they continued to walk without speaking.

When they were close to the house, she said, "I have something else to say to you before we go inside and tell your parents."

Borodine stopped.

She turned toward him. "If —" she began.

"If what?" he asked.

"If I do not satisfy you," Tanya said struggling with the words, "and you find you need someone else, I won't stand in your way. I mean, I understand that what we're doing has nothing to do with love. You want children and I want a family. It will be a good arrangement, but I want you to know that I —"

"There's no need to talk about that," Borodine said.

She shook her head. "This is the time to talk about it, not later when it happens."

"What if you fall in love with someone else?" Borodine asked.

A thin smile touched her lips. "It's not the same with a woman. After all, I will be the wife of a famous man."

Borodine smiled. "That wouldn't and shouldn't prevent you from falling in love."

"There's something else I want to say," she told him.

"Say it," he said. He was beginning to admire her frankness.

"If you want me to remain here, I will… I will continue to teach."

"I want you with me," Borodine said. "From time to time I will be away for long periods of time. But when I'm not at sea, I want us to be together."

"Thank you," she said. "I appreciate that."

"Now there's something you should know," he said.

"I know about your two previous marriages," she told him. "Your mother was very honest about things."

"There was a woman in America I loved," he said quietly.

"Do you still love her?"

"She's dead," Borodine said.

"Do you still love her?" Tanya asked again.

Borodine nodded.

"I still love my husband," she said softly.

"That's as it should be," Borodine told her. "I could not be jealous of a dead man."

"Nor I of a dead woman," Tanya said.

"There might be a time when I will not come back. I might be killed."

"Should that happen I will return here to raise your … our children," she said. "I cannot say or promise you anything more."

He took hold of her hand. "What you have said is enough. Come, let's go tell my parents." They started for the house and just before they reached the door, Borodine stopped. "When are we going to tell your parents?" he asked.

"They're dead," she answered. "I have a sister. But she lives in Vladivostok. Like you, she's in the Navy."

"Do you want her here for the wedding?" he asked.

"Can you do that?" she asked.

"I think so," Borodine said. "But we'll talk about that later. Now let's go inside."

Tanya smiled at him. "You're an honest man, Igor."

He kissed her forehead. "And you're an honest woman," he said, as he turned the knob to open the door.

His mother, father and sister were standing in a group on the far side of the room.

"We decided to get married," Borodine said.

"Good," his father exclaimed.

His mother and sister ran to Tanya and hugged her; then they hugged him. His father crossed the room more slowly and when he hugged Tanya, he said, "Now I have another daughter." Then he kissed her and turning to his son, he hugged and kissed him too…

CHAPTER 8

Boxer and Francine left Washington on Wednesday in rain that turned to snow before they arrived at the house. On the way down they stopped at a mall and did a week's shopping in a supermarket.

"I can't remember the last time when I was in one of these," Boxer said, as they waited their turn on the checkout line.

Francine laughed. "That loss of memory is a thing of the past. I'm not a very good solo shopper… I need someone to consult with."

Boxer touched her hand with his. "I just need you."

"That's what you say now, but what will you say when I'm old, fat, and ugly?"

"And I'll still be young and handsome?"

"Well, not exactly."

"How not exactly?" Boxer asked.

"You'll be old, fat and ugly too."

"Old, I'll accept; ugly too. But not fat. I refuse to accept fat."

"Fat," she giggled.

Boxer shook his head and was about to answer, when suddenly he felt that he had to get outside.

"Are you all right?" Francine asked.

"No… I have to get out of here… I'll be all right as soon as I'm outside." He walked quickly past the checkout counter to the front of the store and through the automatic sliding door. Even though it was snowing, he stood outside. After two deep breaths, he felt much better and waved to Francine, who had moved up to the checkout clerk.

Boxer joined her when she came out with the shopping cart.

"Feeling better?" she asked.

"Better," Boxer said, taking over the job of wheeling the cart. "It looks as if we bought enough food for a month," he commented.

"We probably did," she answered.

When they reached the car, Boxer opened the trunk and moved the bags of food into it; then he said, "You drive."

She took the keys from him and slid behind the wheel.

Boxer settled next to her.

"How much further is it?" she asked, turning out of the parking lot.

"About an hour's drive," Boxer said, closing his eyes and resting his head on the head rest. "I could sleep for a week."

"You'll be able to do just that," she told him.

"Some music?"

"Why not," he answered.

"A string quartet," Francine commented. "Must be coming from Washington or Norfolk. Too long-hair for you?"

Boxer smiled. "No. But if you want something more bouncy, change it."

"I rather like it. Sounds Russian to me," she said.

"Sounds sad to me," Boxer responded. "Very sad." Then he added, "There's more than an outside chance that you made a mistake."

"What kind of mistake?"

"I won't grow old, ugly and fat. I won't even grow old. I'll just develop phobia after phobia until … until —" He opened his eyes and straightened up. "You can still change your mind. We can turn around and —"

"And do what?" she asked.

"Go our separate ways."

"After you've taken my virginity? Not on your life!"

"I'm serious."

"So am I," she said, taking hold of his hand and putting it on her thigh. "No matter how many times a woman has been laid, she still can be a virgin until she finally makes it with that one special man. After having been with you, I'm no longer a virgin."

Boxer squeezed her thigh.

"I told you before and I'll tell you again, your reactions are reactions; they're nothing more."

"That's what I'm trying to believe."

"Believe it," she said. "Believe it, my darling, believe it!"

By the time they reached the house, the snow became heavy enough to coat the roadway.

Boxer transferred the bags of food from the trunk to the kitchen and then phoned the caretaker to let them know who was in the house. Still on the phone he asked Francine, "Do we need a cook?"

"No," she answered. "I'll do it." Then in a lower voice, she said, "I want us to be alone."

Boxer nodded, thanked the caretaker's wife for the offer and hung up.

"Aren't you going to show me around?" Francine asked.

"Sure. But I've only been here once myself and that was for an afternoon."

"As soon as I put the food away, we'll explore this place together. How does that grab you?"

"I can live with it," Boxer said, beginning to remove items from one of the bags and set them out on the table.

"This is a lovely kitchen," Francine commented.

It took the better part of a half an hour to put everything away and before they explored the house together, Boxer went out to the car and brought their luggage in.

"It's mean and cold out there," he said, glad to be back in the house.

"I hope it has central heating," Francine responded.

"It does. The thermostat is in the master bedroom," Boxer said.

"That's a good reason for going there first," she told him, taking her valise from him. "Lead the way."

Boxer switched on the lights and started up the steps. "The admiral has left this to me," he said. "The house, the marina and a boat."

"I know," she answered. "I drew up the papers."

He glanced back at her. "You never said a word about it."

"It's called confidentiality," she said. "I had no idea that you knew it was left to you. But since you do know, I —"

"No need to explain," Boxer told her, entering the master bedroom and switching on the light before he set his nylon bag down.

"Not bad, not bad at all," Francine commented.

Boxer nodded. The room was decorated in a colonial motif, complete with a canopied bed.

"I would have thought the admiral would have preferred a nautical decor," Francine said.

"Stark is full of surprises," Boxer said. "It wasn't until a few years ago that I discovered he and my parents had been good friends practically all of their lives."

"Probably has something to do with some old law of the sea."

Boxer shook his head. "I hardly think so."

"What would you think if I asked you to make love to me?" Francine said, looking at him.

He took her in his arms. "I'd think you were no longer a virgin."

"Is that bad?"

"It's good," he said, kissing her. "It's very good." And he moved his hand over her breasts. She was wearing a sweater, but not a bra.

Francine moved out of his embrace, pulled the sweater over her head and dropped it on one of the two chairs in the room.

Boxer placed his clothes over the chair.

Naked, they held each other.

"I love you," Francine said.

Boxer ran his hands over her nude body. "Enough to marry me?" he asked.

"Is that an academic question or a proposal?"

"A proposal," he said, caressing her behind.

"I'll have to think about it," Francine answered. "I love you, Jack and I think you love me, or are falling in love with me."

"I love you."

"Listen to me," she said, taking hold of his hand and leading him to the bed. "Help me to turn it down... Take the other side."

Boxer went to the other side of the bed, did what she did and when the bed was ready, he joined her under the blanket.

"You were telling me something," he said.

"I'll tell you afterwards," she said. "Now I want you to make love to me."

"Are you ready, already?" he teased.

"Yes... Oh yes."

Boxer rolled off Francine and drew her to him. "You started to tell me something."

"If we were married," she said, "I'm not sure I could live with the fact that any time you went to sea I might lose you; and you might not be able to live with the fact that I have my own career, which would be separate and apart from our marriage and frequently would interfere with it."

Boxer sighed. "I can't deny what you said about my going to sea," he answered.

"Or what I said about my career."

"Then you're completely satisfied with the kind of relationship we have now?"

Francine hesitated for a few moments before she said, "I love you Jack… I want to be your wife —"

"Then be my wife."

"I want you to be aware of the difficulties that we would face," she said.

"Every marriage has difficulties," he answered.

"What if you fail to come back?"

"That's —"

"That's what I will have to live with each time you go away. I'm not sure I can do it."

"You'll have to live with it whether we marry or not, won't you?"

"Yes. But being married would intensify it."

"It's a decision you'll have to make," Boxer said. "I have already made mine. I want to marry you. I want someone to come back to. I want a home of my own."

"What about children?"

Boxer kissed her forehead. "Yes, children too. I am going to move Chuck to school in this area. I'd like to give him a home and I'd like my own son, John, to know that my home is his. I certainly have enough money to take care of them and —"

"How will you deal with my career?" she asked.

"I won't," he said. "That's something you'll have to do. You'll have to come up with the answers."

"And what if you don't like them?"

Boxer ran his hand over his beard. "I guess that's something I'll have to deal with. But I would hope that we'd be able to—"

"Compromise?"

"That's as good a way of putting it as any," he said.

"Are you angry with me?"

"No."

"But you are disappointed, aren't you?" Francine asked.

"I'd be lying if I said I wasn't."

"I still want to think about it," she said.

"Think about it," he told her.

"You know I love you, don't you?" she asked.

"Yes, I know that," Boxer answered.

She kissed his chest and asked if he was hungry.

"Now that you mention it, I am," he said.

"I am too," she responded, moving away from him. "I'll go down and fix something to eat. How about a sandwich and cup of soup?"

"That will be fine," Boxer said, watching her slip back into the slacks and sweater she wore on the drive out.

Francine paused in the doorway. "How does ham and cheese strike you? Or would you prefer something else?"

"Make it on toast and you have a taker."

"On toast it'll be!" she answered and left the room.

Boxer put his hands behind his head and listened to the wind-driven rain beat against the window. He understood that he really wasn't a good marriage risk. But he really did want a wife, a home and a family…

By the next morning, the storm had blown out to sea and a bright sun glistened off the cove's water.

Boxer was up early, dressed and was out of the house before Francine awoke. Nothing of the snow that had fallen was left and though the wind had died down, it was still cold.

He walked around the marina and inspected Stark's boat, which was resting on blocks. Using the ladder that was resting on the boat's side, he climbed aboard and inspected everything above and below deck. Satisfied that it was in good shape, he climbed down the ladder, returned to the house and began making breakfast.

"How long have you been up?" Francine asked.

"For a while," Boxer answered, without looking at her. "I walked around the marina, checked out Stark's boat; then I decided to come back and make breakfast."

She came up behind Boxer and putting her arms around his waist, she pressed herself against him.

"How am I supposed to work?" he asked.

"I missed you," she said, ignoring his question. "I wanted you next to me when I woke up."

Boxer put down the egg he was holding and faced her. She was wearing a light blue bathrobe over a white, see-through nightgown. "Are you trying to tell me that I missed something?"

Francine nodded. "I like to make love in the morning," she said.

"How about after breakfast?"

"Is that a firm offer?"

"Firm until it becomes firmer," Boxer answered. "Now let me get back to my work."

"Not until I tell you that I've decided to marry you," she said, looking up at him.

"Is that a firm answer?"

"Very firm," Francine answered.

Boxer put his arms around her. "We can make it work," he said and kissed her lips; then he kissed the side of her neck.

"I hope so," she answered.

He was about to open her robe and caress her breasts, when he suddenly realized the bacon was beginning to burn. Separating himself from her, he turned back to the stove and with a pair of tongs, he began to lift each strip out of the frying pan. "I hope you like well done bacon," he said, "because this bacon on a scale of one to ten is easily ten and a half."

"You want me to finish up?" Francine offered.

"No, you sit down at the table and start thinking about what kind of wedding you want."

"Something simple," she answered. "A few of your friends and several of mine."

"That's fine with me," Boxer said. "What about the reception?"

"You'll want your crew, won't you?"

Boxer glanced at her. "You don't have to do —"

"I think they'd be hurt if they weren't included," she said. "And I have many friends who would feel the same way if we didn't invite them."

"All right, crew and friends," Boxer replied, turning back to the stove. Then suddenly he turned fully around. "You know I never asked whether or not you had family. Well, do you?"

"Mother, father, married sister and brother, with two children apiece," Francine answered. "All of them live in New York."

"Fine, we'll have them all come down."

"I'm not sure my parents will come … my mother might. But my father —" She stopped and walked to the window.

Boxer put the last strip of bacon down on the paper towel and went to her.

Wiping her eyes with the back of her hands, she apologized for crying. "Dad blames me for my husband's death."

"He died in a car crash, didn't he?"

Francine nodded. "He was leaving me," she explained. "We had a terrible row. I knew he was into drugs and — well, he said, I wasn't much of a wife, to say nothing about not being much of a woman. I told him to get out. He did and twenty minutes later a state trooper came to the door to tell me that my husband had been killed in a two-car smash-up."

Boxer turned her around. "Invite him," Boxer said gently. "Leave the decision as whether or not he will come up to him. Don't have it on your conscience that you didn't invite him."

She nodded.

"Now go wash your face," he told her, "and let's sit down and have breakfast."

She smiled at him. "I love you," she said in a soft passion-filled voice.

"And I love you," he answered, swatting her backside. "Go and wash your face!"

"Yes, sir," she laughed and crossed the room.

Boxer stood at the window and looked out at the sea. He was beginning to like this place more and more. He could understand why Stark liked it. It was almost as if the place existed for itself and didn't need the rest of the world.

"Ready," Francine called, reentering the kitchen.

Boxer was just about to turn when he saw a long, gray limo turn onto the road that went along the shore before it came to an end at the house. "We've got company," he said.

Francine joined him at the window.

"It's not a government limo," Boxer said.

The two of them watched the car roll up to the front of the house and stop. The driver got out, walked around to the other side and opened the door.

A man wearing a tan, belted coat and a brown, wide-brimmed hat, got out of the car, turned and looked up the house…

"Christ, it's Sanchez!" Boxer exclaimed.

"How the hell did he find us?" she asked tightly.

"Probably through Stark or Kinkade," Boxer said, looking at Francine. She was very pale.

"Why is he here?"

"I guess we'll find out as soon as we let him in," Boxer said.

"I hate the man!" Francine exclaimed.

Boxer left the window.

"Where are you going?" she asked.

"To let him in."

"Well, I'm going upstairs. Call me when he leaves."

"Francine —"

She turned out the palms of her hands. "I don't want to be in the same room with him."

"What about breakfast?"

"I just lost my appetite," she said, walking away.

Boxer went to the door and opened it.

"Why this Godforsaken place?" Sanchez asked, as he came up the steps.

"Don't ask questions," Boxer said.

Sanchez took off his pigskin gloves and shook Boxer's hand. "I had one hell of a time finding you," he said.

Boxer closed door. "Didn't you ask Kinkade or Stark?"

"Sure," Sanchez said, "but they're tight-lipped. No, I had to find out through my own sources."

"How about some breakfast?" Boxer asked, taking his coat and hat. "I have bacon, eggs, toast and coffee."

"Coffee and toast," Sanchez said. He sat down at the table and looked around. "You here with someone?"

"I'd have thought your sources would have told you that too," Boxer said, pouring coffee for both of them. "The toast will be ready in a minute or two."

Sanchez fitted a cigarette into a cigarette holder. "I'm sorry I missed Cowly's wedding. I wanted to be there but business before pleasure."

"That was a very generous gift you gave them," Boxer said, answering the ring of the toaster by leaving the table and getting the toast.

Sanchez shrugged. "They certainly deserve it."

Boxer put two slices of toast on a plate and set it down in front of Sanchez.

"I found him," Sanchez said.

Boxer's heart skipped a beat and began to race.

"I told you I'd find Morell," Sanchez said, "and I did."

Boxer broke two eggs and dropped them into the frying pan before he asked, "Was that why you weren't at the wedding?"

"That and two or three other things."

"Where is he?"

"Rome," Sanchez said. "The bastard is in Rome."

With a spatula, Boxer turned the eggs over. "Guarded?" he asked.

"What do you think?"

"How heavy?"

"Two men go wherever he goes," Sanchez answered.

Boxer flipped the eggs out of the pan and onto a plate, put four strips of bacon over them and brought the plate to the table. "Can he be gotten at?"

"With help."

Boxer cut a piece of the egg and speared it with a fork before he asked, "Will you help?"

"Yes."

"How long has he been in Rome?"

"A month at the most," Sanchez answered, holding his cup of coffee with two hands.

"Is there anything else I should know?" Boxer asked.

"You'll be contacted by my people when you're in Rome. They'll take you to him."

"Good," Boxer said, biting into a slice of toast.

"Are you sure you want to do it yourself?" Sanchez asked.

Boxer nodded and said, "If I wanted someone else to do it, I would have asked. I want to do it."

"If you change your mind, just tell one of my people and it will be done for you."

"I won't change my mind," Boxer growled. "I want that fucker dead and I'm going to make sure he is dead."

"When do you expect to be leaving here?" Sanchez asked.

"Probably —"

"Not for a while, Julio," Francine said from the doorway. She had changed into a long sleeved gray jumpsuit.

Sanchez's jaw went slack.

"Close your mouth, Julio," Francine told him. "It's me."

Sanchez looked at Boxer. "I didn't know —"

"Well, that's something new," Francine commented, "you didn't know something."

"I'll be going now," Sanchez said.

"In case either of you didn't know, killing is illegal."

Sanchez stood up and said to Boxer, "You know where to contact me. If you're going to do it, I suggest you do it quickly."

"I'll get your coat and hat," Boxer said, getting up.

At the door the two men shook hands. "Thanks," Boxer said.

"I owe you a lot more than this," Sanchez answered. "A lot more." And turning around, he walked down the steps to the limo.

Boxer waited until the limo was out of sight; then he closed the door and walked back into the kitchen.

Francine was seated at the table drinking coffee. Boxer poured himself another coffee and sat down opposite her.

She remained silent.

"I guess we have some serious talking to do," Boxer said.

"There's nothing to talk about," she responded. "You have made up your mind to kill a man and that weasel Julio is going to be the finger man."

Boxer looked down at his coffee. "That's something you should not have heard."

"But I did," she snapped back.

"Let's deal with you and Julio first," he said.

"There's nothing to deal with," she answered.

"I can't buy that," Boxer told her.

"Already told you about his offer."

"Yes, but you also said there was more and that someday you'd tell me. That someday is now."

Francine started to stand.

"You can't run from it," Boxer said.

She sat down again. "You're not going to like it. You're not going to like me and you're not going to like Julio."

Boxer said nothing.

"After my husband died, Julio contacted me again. He had read about the accident in the newspaper and asked me if he could do anything to help me. I said 'no' and thanked him.

About two months later we happened to meet in a restaurant. He asked me if he could phone and I made the mistake of saying 'yes'."

"Mistake?" Boxer asked.

"We became lovers," Francine said.

Boxer's stomach balled into a knot.

"I can see by the expression on your face that you're not too pleased. Well, there's more that you're not going to be pleased about, a lot more. How much do you really know about Julio's various businesses?"

"I only know he works for the Company the way I do," Boxer answered.

Francine nodded. "He deals in anything that can be sold or bought. Drugs —"

"I don't want to know!"

"It's time you did know," Francine told him. "He sells arms, women —"

"What the hell are you talking about?"

"I'm talking about Julio," she answered. "He may work for the Company but he also works for himself. He has his own thing going."

"How do you know all of this?"

"Because after we broke up I had him investigated. Yes, that's what I did."

"But that's crazy!"

Francine smiled at him. "For any normal person to do, yes. But you see I wasn't normal. I looked normed, I acted normal but I wasn't. Do you want to know why?"

Boxer nodded, though he was beginning to feel very uneasy. This was a side of Francine he had not seen, or suspected existed.

"Julio took me to a party. He said there was some very important people he wanted me to meet and there was one man in particular he wanted me to be nice to. 'How nice?' I foolishly asked. 'Go to bed with him,' he said nonchalantly. I was sure he was joking. But he wasn't; he was deadly serious. I told him to take me home. He wouldn't.

"At the party I was introduced to the man. He was from one of those small Arab countries that has nothing but oil. He was very attentive, so attentive that I realized that Julio must have told him about me."

She paused and bit her lower lip; she said, "I told Julio I was going home, he shook his head and signaled to two of his goons. 'They'll cut that pretty face if you don't behave yourself…'

"Well, to make this very long, ugly story shorter, I was drugged and wound up in bed with the Arab."

"Christ!" Boxer swore.

"That's right — I wound up in bed with him and he took me, while five of his friends waited their turn."

Boxer gripped the edge of the table so hard his knuckles turned white.

"It was the following morning when Julio finally came to the bedroom to get me. On the way home he said, 'Count yourself lucky… I could have sold you for a hundred thousand dollars.'"

"I'll deal with Julio in his own way," Boxer growled.

"It was after that I spent three years in analysis. That is your friend Julio." She bowed her head and softly began to sob. "He made a zombie out of me. A zombie!"

Boxer went to her. He put his hands on her shoulders. He didn't know what to say. "I know a different Julio," he told her.

"I'm sure you do," Francine said. "I'm sure you do."

Boxer bent down and kissed the top of her head. There wasn't any way he could know the hurt and degradation she had experienced, but neither was there any way for her to understand his feelings about what Morell had done.

She took hold of his hands. "I'm yours. No matter what I did in the past or what happened to me I'm yours."

"I know that," Boxer said gently.

"I'm asking you not to go," she said, looking back at him.

Boxer moved away from her. "This has nothing to do with Sanchez," he said, "at least not in the way you think. The man I want was responsible for the deaths of almost a hundred men. Yes, a hundred men. They were my men and they died on a beach in Libya."

She nodded. "Will killing him bring one of those men back?"

"It will prevent him from doing it again."

"And who made you his executioner?" she asked.

"The men who died," Boxer answered.

Francine stood up. "I think we should go back to Washington," she said. "Staying here is a waste of time."

"Is that the way you see it?" Boxer asked.

She nodded. "That's the way I see it."

Boxer pursed his lips, but didn't say anything…

An hour later, they were packed and on their way back to Washington.

Francine sat in the far corner of the seat with her arms crossed and looked out of the window.

Boxer wanted to speak, but whatever he thought of saying seemed to be off the mark.

Finally Francine asked, "When will you be going?"

"As soon as possible … tomorrow, or the next day at the latest."

"Has it occurred to you that you might get killed?" she asked, turning to look at him.

He nodded.

"Just a nod, nothing more?"

"It's a chance I'll have to take," he said softly. "I know it's there. But —"

"You're not afraid, are you?"

"I'm afraid," Boxer said. "I'm afraid because of — you know the things that are wrong with me. But if I don't do it now, I might not ever get another chance."

"It means that much to you, that you'll risk going even though you're not well?"

"It has to be done."

"Then for godsakes, let Julio do it!"

"I sent two men to kill him and he got away," Boxer said. "This time, he won't."

Francine turned toward the window and lapsed into silence again.

"I promise you," Boxer said, "I'll even the score for you with Sanchez."

She faced him. "Will you kill Julio too?"

"What?"

"I asked you if you will kill him," she said. "That really would be the only way to even the score... No, there's one other way: you can cut off his balls. You look shocked. Why? If you had the chance to do that to Morell, wouldn't you?"

Boxer didn't answer.

"One deserves killing as much as the other," she told him.

"I said I'd settle with Sanchez in my own way," he answered.

"I don't want you to 'settle' with him," Francine said. "I survived and whether he lives or dies means nothing to me."

"You don't want revenge?" Boxer asked.

"Not any more," she said. "I didn't see it then, but in analysis I came to understand that I let myself be used. I knew exactly what he was when I went to bed with him the first time. But because I was trying to deal with my husband's death and the memory of a marriage that was on the rocks, I needed someone to belong to. I knew what Julio was, but I closed my eyes and let things happen that never should have."

"I didn't let Morell happen," Boxer said tightly. "He was given to me. I didn't get to pick him."

Francine didn't answer.

When they turned onto the Beltway, Boxer asked, "Where do we go from here?"

She shook her head. "I think you'd better stay at a hotel for the next few nights," she said.

Boxer swallowed. "Does that mean —"

"It means that you're free to do what you want," she said haltingly. "And I'm free to do what I want."

"Is that the way you want it?"

"No," she said. "That's the way you want it."

Boxer continued to drive in silence. He wasn't going to beg her to change her mind. She knew he loved her and he knew she loved him. A half hour later, he parked in front of her house, and brought her luggage up to the front door. "I'll come by for the rest of my clothes when I get back," he said.

"And if you don't come back, what do I do with them?" she asked in a choked voice.

"Whatever you want," Boxer answered, suddenly angry. "Whatever the hell you want!" He turned and without looking back, he hurried down the steps.

CHAPTER 9

The 787 crossed the southern coast of France and started its descent into Rome's Di Vinci Airport while still over the Tyrrhenian Sea. From his window seat in the first class section, just forward of the portside wing, Boxer looked down at the Italian coast and wondered how long he'd be in Italy? Not too long, he hoped. As soon as he took Morell out, he intended to return to Washington to patch things up with Francine. By then, he hoped, they would be able to reach some sort of understanding. He didn't want to lose her.

The stewardess came on the PA and starting with Italian, she announced in a total of four different languages that they would be landing in Rome in fifteen minutes and asked that everyone fasten their seat belts and obey the non-smoking sign when it came on.

"I was having such a wonderful dream," Sanchez said, stretching. "I dreamt the dark-haired stew that served us dinner was..."

"Wishful dreaming," Boxer interrupted, buckling his seatbelt.

"I don't know," Sanchez said. "I'm going to ask her to have dinner with me. Should I also ask her if she has a friend for you?"

Boxer shook his head. "All I want to do while I'm here is to do what I came over to do."

"You don't mind if I —"

"As long as it doesn't interfere," Boxer said.

"It won't... I have a unique talent for keeping business and pleasure separate."

Boxer accepted Sanchez's statement without comment. He hadn't said a word about the story Francine had told him and didn't intend to until after he finished with Morell. And Sanchez didn't say anything about having found him with Francine, or try to explain her hostility toward him. Maybe he too was waiting for the right time.

"I booked us in to the Elisio; it's a small first class hotel across from the Villa Borghese," Sanchez said.

"Do your people know exactly where Morell is?"

Sanchez nodded. "He was living in the Trastevere section in a small apartment on Viale del Quattro. Five days ago when I was here, he was still living there."

"You saw him?" Boxer asked.

"I made discreet inquiries."

The plane banked sharply to the left.

Boxer suddenly realized Sanchez was looking at him. He wanted to ask him why. But he knew if he opened his mouth, he'd scream. He gripped the edge of the armrests and shut his eyes. He could feel the sweat stream down his face.

"What's wrong?" Sanchez asked. "What the hell is wrong with you?"

Boxer shook his head.

"I'll call the stewardess," Sanchez said.

"Don't," Boxer forced himself to say. "For the love of God, don't!"

The plane banked right.

Boxer clamped his jaws together until both sides of his face were slashed with pain.

The plane straightened out and began to lose altitude very fast.

Boxer forced himself to speak, "I'm all right. It'll pass."

Sanchez didn't answer.

The plane touched down, roared down the runway and began to slow down.

"I'm all right," Boxer said, letting go of the armrests. With a handkerchief, he wiped the sweat from his face. "I'll be fine as soon as I get out of here."

"Do you want some water?" Sanchez asked.

Boxer held up his hand. "I'll stop and have a drink as soon as we clear customs."

"One of my friends is going to meet us at the airport," Sanchez said. "And we'll go through customs quickly."

The plane rolled up to the gate and Boxer and Sanchez were in the main terminal within a matter of minutes. When they got to customs, Sanchez summoned one of the guards and spoke to him in rapid-fire Italian.

The guard nodded several times; shook his hand, smiled and picking up their bags, he motioned them to follow him.

"What was that all about?" Boxer asked.

"A fifty dollar handshake," Sanchez answered.

The guard led them through customs, touched his fingers to his cap and gave them a big smile.

"Smile," Sanchez said under his breath.

Boxer smiled.

"My friend will be at the information desk," Sanchez said. "But she'll wait, if you want to go in the lounge for a drink."

"I'm fine now," Boxer assured him and pointing to a fountain, he said, "I'll settle for water."

"Be my guest."

Boxer bent over the fountain and turned the water on. He took a long drink and when he was finished, he said, "Don't worry about me… I really am fine."

"You sure as hell weren't fine a few minutes ago," Sanchez replied. "In fact you looked as if you were having a stroke."

"That's my new act," Boxer said, as they walked into the main plaza of the terminal building.

"Could have fooled the shit out of me," Sanchez told him.

Sanchez's name suddenly came over the PA; then the woman said, "Your party is at the Al Italia information desk." The announcement was repeated twice.

Boxer nodded and said, "Your friend is on time."

"She wants to impress me," Sanchez replied.

"The last time I was in this airport," Boxer commented, "I was on my way home after the *Turtle* went down."

"I wouldn't want to go through that again," Sanchez said.

"Neither would I. But I feel that way about all the missions. They're all one of a kind."

"I know what you mean. I feel the same way about the couple that I've been on."

The two of them approached the information desk, when Boxer suddenly saw De Vargas's sister, Diana. He slowed his pace.

"She works for me," Sanchez explained.

Boxer gave him a questioning look.

"She wanted a chance to get out of the south Bronx, out of the place where she's living. You were there. What future did she have there?"

"How long?" Boxer asked.

"A few weeks ... maybe two months," Sanchez answered.

"What about her parents?"

Sanchez shrugged. "She told them she's working for me. They seemed to like the idea."

Boxer frowned. De Vargas was the Marine officer who led the *Shark*'s assault team. He had been severely wounded in the attack on Libya and couldn't make it to the surface after the

Turtle had to be abandoned. Boxer provided financial support for the family.

"Listen," Sanchez said, "it's not as if she was cherry. She knows what it's all about."

"I'm sure she does," Boxer answered.

Diana spotted them. She flashed a big smile and started to wave.

"Nothing like the exuberance of youth," Sanchez commented.

"Good to see you again, Admiral!" Diana exclaimed, throwing her arms around Boxer's neck and kissing him on the lips.

"Good to see you too," Boxer said, aware that she was expensively dressed and was wearing a very provocative perfume.

She embraced and kissed Sanchez.

"You'll like the Elisio," Diana said, when she separated from Sanchez. "It's very Italian."

"Right now I'd like any place where I can sleep," Boxer answered. "Until a few moments ago, I didn't realize how tired I was."

"The car is in the parking area," she said. "There just wasn't any way I could bring it closer."

The three of them left the terminal and a few minutes later, Boxer was sitting in the rear of a white Ferrari; Diana was at the wheel and Sanchez was seated next to her.

"I'm really glad to see you," Diana commented, glancing back at Boxer.

"You can tell him that later," Sanchez said. "Now you'd better pay attention to the road, or one of these wild Italian drivers will be up your ass."

She shook her head and laughed. " Not on your life."

Sanchez put his hand on her thigh and squeezed.

"Julio told me that Mister Cowly and Cynthia were getting married," she said.

"They were married. I was best man," Boxer said.

Diana nodded her head approvingly. "Nice people," she commented.

During the time it took to go from the airport to the hotel, Boxer had very little to say. He was concerned that Sanchez had seen him go into a claustrophobic episode and because of the story that Francine had told him, he was more than bothered by the fact that Diana was working for Sanchez, which was another way of saying she was his mistress. Sooner or later, he knew he'd have to explain his condition to Sanchez and that meant exposing part of himself that he wanted to keep hidden. And sooner or later, he was going to have to discuss Francine. And now there was also Diana to think about. But all of these had to be put aside until he had finished with Morell.

"Have you ever been here before?" Diana asked, half turning her head toward Boxer.

"Only for a few days," Boxer answered.

"Well, maybe you'll spend a few more days here. Rome is a wonderful city."

"I can't promise I will," Boxer said.

"Let's not make any long-range plans," Sanchez said. "Let's just take one day at a time."

Diana turned into the Via Veneto and crawled along with the late morning traffic.

"That businessman I told you about," Sanchez said. "I'll try and see him toward evening."

"Business ... business," Diana chirped. "That's all you ever think about."

"Not all," Sanchez laughed, easing the hem of her dress up and putting his hand inside her thighs.

She snapped her thighs shut. "Remember, I'm driving," she said. "Don't start playing games until you're able to really play."

Boxer suddenly felt embarrassed.

"Hotel is close by," Sanchez said. "We go to the top of the Via Veneto and make a left turn. It's only a few hundred yards in on the Porta Pinciana."

"I checked the two of you in," Diana said. "Just drop off your passports at the desk and pick up your keys." She laughed. "Would you believe they have each key attached to a big round wooden ball so that you can't put it in your pocket and take it out of the hotel?"

"It's the same way all over Europe," Sanchez told her.

"Maybe," she said. "But that doesn't make it less funny."

Boxer smiled and tried not to watch Sanchez's hand work its way up toward her crotch.

Diana squirmed. "Hey, I can't drive with you playing with me," she complained.

"You're doing a good job of it," Sanchez said. "But if you really don't like it, all you have to do is open your thighs and let go of my hand."

She stuck her tongue out.

"Admiral, you heard me give her a choice, didn't you?" Sanchez asked, turning to look at Boxer.

Boxer waved the question aside and looked out of the window.

A few minutes later, they pulled up across the street from the hotel and got out of the car.

"I like it," Sanchez said, "because it has a quiet dignity."

Boxer nodded and looked up at the red brick building. It was old. Built perhaps at the turn of the century, or at the very latest during the twenties.

The three of them crossed the street, entered the small lobby and went straight to the desk.

The clerk and Sanchez greeted one another warmly in Italian and continued speaking, giving Boxer a few moments to be alone with Diana. "How long have you been working for Julio?" he asked.

"About a month," she answered; then lowering her eyes, she added, "He's very good to me."

"I'm sure he is now," Boxer said.

"He doesn't know it yet, but I think he's falling in love with me." She raised her eyes and looked straight at him. "You know I'm in love with him."

"I know," Boxer said.

Sanchez waved to Boxer. "Your passport and your signature," he said.

Boxer detached himself from Diana, went to the desk and handed the clerk his passport.

In English, the man said, "Ah, Admirale, please sign at the bottom of the form." And he placed a registration card in front of Boxer.

"I thought we were already signed in," Boxer said, looking at Sanchez.

"Diana had the rooms held in our names," Sanchez answered. "But she couldn't sign for them unless she was going to rent them."

Boxer scribbled his name and handed the card back to the clerk.

"Room six ten," he said, as he put the key in front of him. "And for you," he added, smiling at Sanchez, "room six twelve." Then he called a bellhop to take their bags.

"This way," the bellhop said, leading them to the elevator.

After a moment's hesitation, Boxer entered the small car and stood in front of Diana. Sanchez was to his right and the bellhop to his left.

The elevator moved slowly.

"Suppose we meet at six at Harry's bar," Sanchez said. "It's just down the street from here at the Via Veneto."

Boxer coughed. His heart was racing.

"Is that okay with you, Skipper?" Sanchez asked.

"Fine," Boxer managed to say. "Just fine."

The elevator came to a stop and the bellhop was the first out of the car. Boxer followed and immediately realized that he should have stepped aside to allow Diana out. He apologized.

She smiled at him and said, "You're a sweetheart!"

"If he's a sweetheart, then what am I?" Sanchez asked.

"I've been trying to figure that one out," Diana answered.

The four of them trouped down the corridor and in a matter of minutes, Boxer was alone in his room. He went to the window and looked down on the pine trees in the Villa Borghese across the street. Then he lowered the shade, took off his coat and hat and jacket and started to unpack. He brought enough clothes for a week's stay, but he hoped he'd be on his way back to the States in three days at the very most.

The phone's high-pitched ring made him jump. He squinted at it, wondering who would be calling him; then picking it up, he said, "Boxer here."

Stark was on the other end.

"How the hell did you know where to find me?" Boxer asked.

"Sanchez is a creature of habit, at least as far as his choice of hotels is concerned and his treatment of women," Stark answered in his gravelly voice.

"What's the bottom line?" Boxer asked. "Why did you call me?"

"Kinkade is in the hospital. He doesn't have much chance of making it out."

Boxer was very quiet.

"Are you still on the damn line?" Stark growled.

"I'll be there as soon as I've finished my business here," Boxer answered.

"Give it up!"

"I can't do that, Admiral," Boxer said. "It has to be done and I have to do it. I'll call you the moment I know when I'm coming back."

"Why the hell do you have to be so difficult?"

Boxer didn't answer.

"I can order you back to the States," Stark told him.

"You can, but you won't because you know I won't come back."

"You know I had to inform my Italian counterpart," Stark said.

"I didn't know," Boxer said. "Did Sanchez?"

"Even if he did know," Stark answered, "it wouldn't matter. It would only make it more exciting. He doesn't give a shit about anyone's dont's, he just goes ahead and does what he wants."

Boxer had to laugh.

"Why the hell did you leave in such a damn hurry?" Stark asked.

"I'll tell you some other time," Boxer said. "Send Kinkade my best and tell him I'll be up to see him as soon as I get back."

"I'm sure that's going to thrill him."

"I'll be in touch," Boxer said and hung up. That Kinkade might not make it out of the hospital gave him pause. He and Kinkade had battled one another too many times for him to remotely suggest to himself that he liked the man, even though Kinkade had made him his sole heir. Kinkade was Trish's grandfather and Boxer knew that the old man loved her more than he loved anything else, including himself…

Boxer pulled his thoughts away from Kinkade and Trish and finished unpacking. Then he undressed, showered, and crawled into bed for a few hours sleep…

Rather than risk an episode in the elevator, Boxer used the stairs to get to the second floor, where he took the elevator down to the lobby. And even during that short ride, he began to sweat.

The lobby was empty, except for a man sitting in a high-backed chair and reading a newspaper.

The clerk coughed twice and politely smiled at Boxer.

"Has Mister Sanchez gone out?" Boxer asked, putting his key on the counter.

"No, Admirale … but I have only been here for an hour. You may call him on the house phone," he said, pointing to a white telephone on the counter.

"That's all right," Boxer said. "If you see him would you tell him I went out for a while and will meet him at six."

"Yes," the clerk said and asked if he wanted a cab.

"No," Boxer said, "I think I'll walk."

"The Spanish Steps are not far from here," the man offered. "And the late afternoon and early evening are a good time to see them, though of course it's better in the late spring and summer. Then it's very colorful."

Boxer was about to say that he had already seen them, but suddenly he decided it would be a good idea to pretend he was just another tourist, or a businessman with some time on his hands to do a little sightseeing. "How would I get there?" he asked.

The clerk gave him directions.

Boxer listened attentively, thanked him when he was done and started toward the door.

The man in the chair folded his newspaper and standing up, said in perfect English, "I'm sorry, but I couldn't help overhearing your conversation with the clerk. I'd be pleased to show you exactly where the Spanish Steps are."

Boxer stopped and looked at him. He was tall and lithe, with a well-trimmed gray moustache and black hair with gray sideburns. He had high cheekbones, black eyes and good teeth, which were visible because he was smiling.

"It would be no trouble at all," the man said.

"Thank you," Boxer responded.

The man offered his hand. "Captain Luigi Visconti, Naval Intelligence."

"Then you must know who I am," Boxer said, not touching the man's hand.

Visconti nodded and lowering his hand said, "Why don't we start to walk toward the Spanish Steps?"

Boxer shrugged. "Stark worked fast," he commented.

"What?" Visconti asked.

"It's not important," Boxer said.

The doorman opened the door for them.

Boxer stepped out of the hotel first. Off to one side he spotted the Visconti's chauffeured limo. He pointed to it and said, "You could give me a lift to where Morell lives."

"I think we had better walk," Visconti replied, falling in alongside Boxer.

For a few moments neither of them spoke, then Boxer said, "You wouldn't be walking alongside of me if you didn't know why I was here."

"That's right," Visconti said.

"And you're going to try and talk me out of killing Morell and if that doesn't work, then perhaps you'll try to have me deported?"

"The first part of what you said is right," Visconti answered. "As for the second, well — I hope it doesn't get to that."

Boxer reached into his coat pocket, took out his pipe and tobacco pouch and carefully filled it.

"I thought you'd be a pipe smoker," Visconti commented.

Boxer said, "I'm going to save you a lot of time, Captain, and a lot of unnecessary aggravation." He took a few moments to light his pipe. "I came here to kill Morell and that's what I'm going to do."

"Not in Rome," Visconti answered. "Not any place in Italy."

Boxer puffed on his pipe.

"Whatever this Morell did, or didn't do —"

Boxer stopped. He pointed his pipe at Visconti and said, "Captain, the only way you're going to stop me is to kill me before I kill Morell."

"I could have you arrested and —"

Boxer shook his head. "You won't. You won't arrest me because if you do, there are people in my government, in my country, that would demand your balls. And the balls of everyone involved and I'd simply tell the press that the Italian government took it upon themselves to act on an unfounded rumor. It might cause you to be reassigned and it might cause a crisis in the government. Besides, if you stop me, there are other people who will kill him for me."

They came to a red traffic signal and stopped.

"Your own people have asked us to stop you," Visconti said.

"If they couldn't stop me, what makes you think you could?"

"I am not sure that I could," Visconti answered. "But I will certainly try. As you people say, just for openers let me tell you that you'll be under a twenty-four hour surveillance and my men have orders to kill you if you attempt to kill Morell."

Boxer accepted what he had just heard with a nod.

"Then there's the matter of your friend, Mister Sanchez," Visconti said.

The light went to green and they crossed the street.

"Sanchez is a most interesting man," Visconti continued, "a most interesting man. We know, of course, he works for your government from time to time. But the times when he doesn't work for your government, he is gainfully occupied in the buying, selling and distribution of arms, drugs and women."

Boxer didn't answer. Francine had given him the same information. But hearing it again from Visconti was, he had to admit, a bit of a jolt.

"You have nothing to say about your friend's other activities?" Visconti asked, taking a cigarette out of a silver case and placing it between his lips.

"Nothing," Boxer said.

Visconti flicked on a lighter, lit his cigarette, blew smoke out of his nostrils and mouth and said, "Besides fingering Morell for you, he's here for other business."

"Am I supposed to ask, what other business? Okay, what other business?"

"He is going to sell Diana De Vargas," Visconti said calmly.

Boxer pulled up short. "What the hell are you talking about?"

"I shouldn't say sell," Visconti explained. "The deal was made weeks ago. He's going to hand over the merchandise after you kill Morell, or Morell kills you."

Boxer started to walk again; this time his pace was anything but slow. "Who's the buyer?"

"Another trader in flesh," Visconti said. "She's bound for a brothel in Saudi Arabia."

"How much —"

"She went for ten ounces of pure cocaine."

"Christ!" Boxer swore.

"A blond, a real blond, would have brought half as much again."

"Why don't you stop him from —"

"Because there have been times when he has been very helpful to us and there might be times in the future when he can be helpful again. It isn't a moral world we live in, but it is certainly a real one."

"Does that mean you're going to let him turn Diana over to the buyer?"

"That depends on you," Visconti said. "I deliver her into your hands."

Boxer stopped again. "That's blackmail!" he exclaimed.

"Certainly it is," Visconti said. "And you don't have to go along with it."

"But —" Boxer stopped himself and started to walk. This time his pace was slower.

"Think about it," counseled Visconti. "There is still time before Sanchez will turn Diana over to the buyer."

Boxer puffed violently on his pipe.

They came to another street crossing and Visconti stopped. "I'll leave you here. The Spanish Steps are to your right. I'm sorry we had to meet under these circumstances."

"Morell was responsible for the deaths of almost a hundred of my men," Boxer told him.

"Whether you believe it or not," Visconti said, "I understand why you want to kill him. I might even agree with you. But — and it's a very important but — my government, like your own, does not sanction individual justice."

"But it does sanction blackmail."

"Rather than thinking of it as blackmail, think of it as an exchange. Think of what will happen to Diana if Sanchez hands her over to the man who bought her. That should be enough to convince you that killing Morell isn't half as important as preventing Sanchez from completing this end of the business deal."

"Is there a number where you can be reached?" Boxer asked.

Visconti handed him a card. "The number in the top right-hand corner is my office number, the one in the bottom left-hand corner is my residence."

Boxer took the card and pocketed it.

"Before we go our separate ways," Visconti said, "I think you should know that Morell is waiting for you."

"What?"

Visconti nodded. "Think about it," he said; then he added, "I don't have to caution you not to say anything to Sanchez about our conversation. He would think nothing of having Diana killed to protect himself." Then he turned and without looking back, he turned and walked away.

Angry, Boxer headed for the Spanish Steps. The situation was more complicated than it should be. He paused to knock his pipe empty against a lamp post. Sanchez's wheeling and dealing was fucking things up. Boxer came out of a side street and in a matter of moments found himself at the top of the Spanish Steps. He had no desire to be there and hurried down the several flights to find a cab. At the bottom of the steps, he changed his mind and crossing the plaza, he chose a side street to walk down.

The Via Veneto was brightly lit and crowded with Romans and tourists seeking a place for cocktails.

Boxer moved quickly through the crowds and headed straight to Harry's Bar at the top of the famous avenue. When he arrived, Sanchez, Diana and a strange man were seated at a table behind the window.

Sanchez motioned through the window for him to join them.

Boxer entered the restaurant and checked his hat and coat. Then he went up to the maître d' and pointing to Sanchez, he told him he had friends at a table who were waiting for him.

"We got here a few minutes ago," Sanchez explained, when Boxer sat down. Then gesturing toward the strange man, he said, "Admiral, I'd like you to meet Mister Blanchard."

Boxer's eyes went to Blanchard. He was a short, barrel-chested man with piercing gray eyes and thick hair on the back of his hands.

"A pleasure, Admiral," Blanchard said, extending his hand.

"A pleasure," Boxer repeated, shaking his hand before he sat down.

"Well, what have you been doing?" Diana asked.

"I walked to the Spanish Steps," Boxer answered.

"It's not as lively there now as it is when the weather turns warmer," Blanchard said.

Boxer looked around for a waiter.

"I've already ordered a vodka on the rocks for you," Sanchez said. "And a few tidbits to eat while we're here."

"And he's made reservations for dinner at —"

"What's your line of work, Mister Blanchard?" Boxer asked.

"I'm in the import-export business."

"We do a lot of work together," Sanchez said.

Boxer said nothing. He looked toward the window. The street was crowded and traffic moved very slowly.

"Ah, here comes our drinks and something to munch on," Blanchard said.

"The Campari to me," Sanchez told the waiter in Italian, "and to the lady. Vodka to that man," he said, pointing to Boxer, "and the scotch to the only person without a drink."

"To you, Admiral," Blanchard toasted. "Its truly an honor to be with you."

"I'll drink to that," Sanchez said, raising his glass.

Boxer looked at Diana; then at Sanchez and finally at Blanchard. There was no way of knowing if he was the buyer, or as he claimed to be in the import-export business.

"Admiral, how long do intend to say in Rome?" Blanchard asked.

"Not long," Boxer answered.

"I'd be pleased to show you around," Blanchard said. "My wife and I know a great deal about the history of this area." Then with a smile, he added, "We're amateur archeologists."

Boxer nodded and reaching for a cracker with a small piece of cheese on it, he answered, "If I have the time, I'll let you be the guide."

"Oh, I drove over to see if our friend was still living at the same address," Sanchez said. "I didn't get to see him. But I was assured by his neighbors that he still lives there."

Boxer made no comment. He picked up his glass and drank the remaining vodka; then he said, "I want another drink."

"I think we can all use a refill," Blanchard commented and this time he summoned the waiter and in perfect Italian ordered drinks for all of them.

"You speak the language like a native," Boxer commented.

"Should," Blanchard said. "I've lived here for the past twenty years. My wife is Italian and speaks very little English, though she speaks French and Spanish like a native."

"So you're an American," Boxer said, taking a guess.

Blanchard grinned. "I even did a stint in the Navy. I was a communications officer aboard a supply ship. Not very exciting duty, but duty nonetheless. I have two sons back in the States. One is studying medicine at Johns Hopkins and the other lives in New York. He's trying to make his way as a writer."

The waiter returned with the drinks.

Boxer picked up his glass and said, "I'd like to propose a toast." He waited until the others held up their glasses. Then looking straight at Sanchez, he toasted, "To Mister Morell — may he continue to have a long and happy life."

Sanchez's jaw went slack.

"Drink," Boxer said, touching all of the glasses with his own, before he put it to his lips.

Sanchez took a sip and put his glass down.

Boxer finished his second drink and said, "It's been a pleasure to meet you, Mister Blanchard. I just might take you up on your offer."

"Please do," Blanchard responded.

Boxer reached into his pocket.

"I'll take care of the check," Sanchez said.

"What time is dinner?" Boxer asked.

"We can meet in the hotel lobby about eight-thirty."

"See you then," Boxer said.

"Where are you going now?" Diana asked.

"Back to the hotel," Boxer answered. "I have to make a few phone calls." Then looking at Sanchez, he said, "Stark called me earlier to tell me that Kinkade is back in the hospital. He's not expected to make it out."

"Send him my regards," Sanchez replied.

"Will do," Boxer said and reached across the table to shake Blanchard's hand again. Then he turned and left Sanchez to deal with the bomb he had just dropped.

Boxer used the public phone in the hotel lobby to call Captain Visconti.

"I was just about to leave my office," Visconti said.

"The ball is in your court," Boxer told him.

Visconti lapsed into Italian, caught himself and explained, "All I said was that I am very pleased. You made a good decision."

"The decision was made for me," Boxer said.

"Yes, I suppose so. But that's because you're an honorable man."

"That's because Diana's brother isn't here to protect her," Boxer said.

"I understand," Visconti responded. "I hope you are not angry with me for having made you change your mind."

"No," Boxer said, "I'm not in the least bit angry."

"Good. Maybe we could meet and have a drink before you leave Italy?"

"Good, I'd like that," Boxer said. "But now I have a question I'd like to ask."

"Ask."

"What did you mean when you said I might be set up?"

"Did I say that?"

"Captain, you said it and I'd like to know why you said it," Boxer told him.

For several moments, Visconti was silent; then he said, "To me and my people it just seemed too easy. Morell comes here, takes a small apartment and then you're told he's here in Rome and come after him."

"The information came from Sanchez," Boxer said.

"I guessed that," Visconti answered. "Sanchez has contacts all over the world. I am sure that his people were given the information to draw you here."

"Sanchez —"

"Though he's not loyal to anyone else, I am sure he is completely loyal to you."

"Why should he be?"

"There are probably many reasons," Visconti said, "and we can discuss them when we meet. But probably the main reason is that you're his hero."

"Be serious."

"I am. You're everything he's not and a good deal more than he could ever dream of being. You're really his fantasy of what he secretly would like to be." He found the idea of anyone wanting to be like him very funny. "He's not a boy —"

"Emotionally that's exactly what he is," Visconti said. "He probably has the emotional age of a fourteen year old. In some ways, it's this lack of emotional development that allows him to do the things he does and suffer no regret or remorse."

"Are you telling me he hasn't any feelings?"

"Nothing like that. He has feelings, but when it suits his purpose he can completely ignore them. Case in point, Diana. He probably likes her very much and of course he respects his relationship to the family and his past relationship to her dead brother, but none of these emotions counted when someone offered to buy her. The money he would make was more important than anything he felt for her, the family, or the memory of her dead brother."

"I hear what you're saying," Boxer said, "but I'm not exactly sure I understand it."

This time Visconti laughed. "I promise to give you a better explanation over drinks."

"Tomorrow evening?" Boxer asked.

"Yes... I'll leave word at the hotel where we'll meet."

"Good... Oh by the way, do you know a Mister Blanchard?"

"Another interesting man. He and his wife are well known amateur archeologists."

"I met him. He was with Sanchez."

"Over the years they have had business dealings," Visconti said. "He's well known here."

"Then he's not the buyer?"

"Certainly not," Visconti laughed. "I'm looking forward to seeing you, Admiral. But if I don't leave this office and go home to my daughter's fifth birthday party, neither she, my wife and all the various members of my very large family will speak to me again."

"Go and enjoy!" Boxer said.

"Goodbye," Visconti answered.

Boxer hung the phone back on its bracket and realizing that he liked Captain Visconti, he smiled as he left the telephone booth. He went to the desk and asked if there were any messages for him.

There were none.

Boxer went to the elevator and hoped he'd be able to make it to his floor without suffering too much discomfort.

The elevator doors opened, he stepped into the car, faced front and as the door closed, he took several deep breaths. The elevator moved slowly and he counted the floors as he passed them. Finally the car reached the sixth floor, the doors opened and Boxer stepped out into the hallway. He looked over his shoulder. The elevator doors closed. He took another deep breath, exhaled and went to his room.

In a few moments, he unlocked the door, opened it and stepping inside, he heard the shower going. There was an open suitcase on the bed.

Until he saw his jacket on the back of the chair, Boxer actually thought he was in the wrong room. But if it was his room, then whoever was using the shower was in the wrong room. He went to the bathroom and started to ease the door open.

When suddenly the shower stopped and a woman's leg appeared and then the rest of her came out. Copper colored red hair.

"Francine!" Boxer exclaimed.

She looked at him, reached for a towel and said, "I hope you weren't expecting someone else." And wrapping the towel around her torso, she secured it with a large knot which rested on her breasts. "Aren't you —"

Boxer rushed to her and crushed her against him. "I was afraid I'd lost you," he said.

"I was afraid of the same thing," Francine said. "I couldn't let that happen so I decided to come here."

"How did you find out where I was staying?"

"Stark told me," she answered.

Boxer kissed her passionately on her lips.

"I love you," she said breathlessly.

"Are you sure?"

"Yes … very sure," she answered in a low, urgent voice.

Boxer eased his hold on her.

Hesitantly, she asked, "Do you love me?"

Boxer nodded. "I was coming back to the States after this was over to —"

"Is it over?" she asked, looking up at him.

"It never began," he said, gently caressing her face with his fingers.

"I don't understand."

"I traded Morell's life for Diana's."

"Who's Diana?" she asked with an anxious tone in her voice.

"No competition," Boxer said. "She's Lieutenant De Vargas' sister. It's a very long story. But it's over. I guess in a way I'm glad it's over."

She kissed the palm of his hand. "So am I," she whispered. "I can't begin to tell you how miserable I was. I felt as if my future had been taken away."

Boxer lifted Francine in his arms and carried her to bed. "I love you, Francine," he said.

Kinkade rested against two pillows. Stark was on his right and his successor, Henry Tysin, was on his left. Tysin was the President's choice, not his. The man had made a fortune on the stock market and had become a financial advisor to the President when he took office and now he was a part of the White House staff.

"The admiral has been briefing me on the special nature of Admiral Boxer's assignment," Tysin said, speaking with a pronounced southern accent. "And of course the President has also told me a few things about it."

Kinkade rolled his eyes toward Stark and silently asked, *Why did you bring this man here?*

"I understand that Admiral Boxer is something of a maverick," Tysin said.

Kinkade smiled and said, "Tysin, he'll chew you up and spit you out. He's not a maverick; he's a herd of mavericks."

Tysin flushed. He was a dark-blue-three-piece-suit man, gaunt looking, with pale blue eyes, and very fair skin, with a few freckles on his cheeks and neck, and wispy blond hair that he was continually pushing back.

"What Mister Kinkade means," Stark said, "is that Admiral Boxer has a mind of his own."

"According to the President, such a mind and such a man can be a political embarrassment, as it was just a few months ago when the admiral forced the President to say and do something he had no intentions of saying or doing in the first place."

"Get used to it," Kinkade said.

"I intend to run the Company as a team. If Admiral Boxer can't be a team player, he can't be in the Company. There can be no other way while I'm at the helm."

Kinkade nodded and again looking at Stark, he said, "I can see you're going to be in for some high times."

"Where is Admiral Boxer now?" Tysin asked.

"Last I heard," Kinkade answered, "he went to Rome to kill one of our agents."

Tysin blanched.

"Has he killed him?" Kinkade asked, looking at Stark for an answer.

"I hope you're not serious," Tysin said.

"Deadly," Kinkade responded and again asked Stark if Boxer had killed Morell.

"No," Stark answered. "There were certain conditions, I was given to understand, which changed his mind."

Kinkade made a low humming sound. "He's totally unpredictable. I thought for sure he'd kill Morell."

Stark shrugged. "From my conversation with him, I only know that he didn't and doesn't intend to."

"And you're satisfied with that?" Tysin asked.

"For the present," Stark answered. "Sooner or later, he'll tell me what I want to know."

Tysin took a deep breath and when he finished exhaling, he said, "I'm afraid the situation leaves me no choice but to act. I want him back in Washington within the next twenty-four hours. If he can't get a commercial flight, have him flown here—"

"A real tiger!" Kinkade exclaimed, slapping his thigh. "That's right, Tysin, you win with Boxer and you have it made. The rest of your job will be like playing with Silly Putty. But you won't win. Stark, why don't you set him straight before he presses all the wrong buttons and either makes a fool of himself, or is responsible for the deaths of some of his people or yours and maybe, if he's very unlucky, a combination of his people and yours."

"I want Admiral Boxer in Washington within the next twenty-four hours," Tysin said stubbornly.

"I will not order him back," Stark replied. "He's on a well-earned leave."

"Then I will order him back!"

"I wouldn't do that, if I were you," Kinkade said, adding, "you know, Stark, I'm enjoying this. I shouldn't because I was all too often where Tysin is now. But for some perverted reason I'm having a hell of a time."

"He won't come back," Stark said.

Tysin's face reddened.

"He's on an Italian holiday," Stark said.

"I thought you said he went there to kill one of our people?"

Stark nodded. "That was his original purpose, but now, since he's over there, he intends to spend three weeks to a month there. He has the leave time and even if he didn't, I'd give him the time to rest. The man has had two very difficult assignments, almost back to back. He needs the time."

Tysin pushed back his chair. "Considering his previous assignments and the fact that he didn't kill one of my agents, I imagine I can afford to be generous. He has a month to tour Italy. Then I want him back here in Washington. I want him to know where I'm coming from."

Kinkade smiled. "And he'll certainly tell you where he's coming from."

"I'd rather have it that way," Tysin said.

The conversation between the three of them lapsed. Then Stark said, "Boxer sent you his regards."

Kinkade nodded and looking at Tysin, he said, "I would appreciate having a short time alone with Stark."

"I'll wait outside," Tysin said and shaking hands with Kinkade, he added, "It was a pleasure to meet you."

"I won't keep Stark long," Kinkade said.

"Don't hurry yourself," Tysin answered and left the bedside.

Kinkade waited until the door was closed before he said, "I left everything to Boxer, he's my sole heir."

"Does he know?" Stark asked.

"I told him. But there is one thing I didn't tell him."

"Yes, what is it?"

"When my time comes, I want to be buried next to Trish, not next to my wife." He licked his lips. "I loved Trish —" he stopped.

"You don't have to explain," Stark said, putting his hand on Kinkade's frail shoulder.

"I do," he answered in a low voice and looked up at Stark. "It happened a long time ago. She was maybe fourteen..." He closed his eyes. "You can't imagine how beautiful she was. We were in a row boat on a lake. She was wearing one of those bikini type bathing suits. Nothing more than two swaths of cloth: one to cover her breasts and one to cover her bottom and —"

Suddenly Stark felt chilled. Prickles skidded down his back. He tried not to hear what Kinkade was telling him, but he couldn't shut out the words.

"I made love to her," Kinkade whispered, opening his eyes. "I made love to her and after that —" He shook his head. "I spent the rest of my life trying to forget the pleasure she gave me and at the same time trying to live with myself. I couldn't do either. God, I couldn't do either..."

"I'll see that you're buried next to her," Stark said.

"You understand why I couldn't tell Boxer any of this?"

Stark nodded.

"Thank you," Kinkade said.

Stark shook his hand. "I'll be around in a couple of days to see you."

Kinkade didn't answer. He put his head back on the pillow and with tears streaming out of his eyes, he looked up at the ceiling...

CHAPTER 10

With the explosion of cherry blossoms, spring came to Washington. There was that marvelous feeling of anticipation in the air and out on the river, sailboats leaned away from uncertain wind.

From their table at the Barge restaurant, Boxer and Stark watched the boats. This was their last dinner together before Boxer took the *Barracuda* on her sea trials. The next night at twenty-three hundred, Boxer would give the orders that would take her out to sea. During the last month they had met frequently to deal with the problems that had come up in the final phase of the boat's fitting. But now at dinner, neither one of them mentioned the *Barracuda*, or her sea trials, nor did they speak about Kinkade, who was being kept alive by life support equipment.

Stark had just finished telling Boxer that he had been informed by the State Department that Borodine's visit to the United States had been temporarily postponed, "and no new date has been set."

"What did Tysin say?" Boxer asked. He had met the new Company chief several times since he had returned from Italy and didn't much like him. But then, he never much liked Kinkade either.

"His people are working on it," Stark said. "Translated that means he was caught with his pants down when he was informed about the cancellation, though he did say that it probably has something to do with the power struggle going on inside the Kremlin."

Boxer smiled, but didn't comment. For some time, he had known that Stark shared his feelings about Tysin.

"Did I tell you that DB will be in the Academy's September class," Stark said.

Boxer shook his head. "Mind if I mention it to him unofficially?"

"No … go ahead. The papers will be waiting for him when he returns. That's one young man who'll make a fine officer."

"That's certain," Boxer answered; then he said, "There's something I should have told you a while back, but didn't. It's a condition that I've learned to control. But I want you to know it exists."

Stark raised his eyebrows.

"I've become claustrophobic," Boxer said. He had wanted to tell Stark about it several times in the past. But the situation was never right.

Stark's jaw dropped, but he quickly recovered himself.

"I can control it," Boxer said.

"I believe you," Stark responded.

"While we were in Europe, Francine convinced me to see a Swiss doctor. He's the world's leading authority on claustrophobia. He put me under hypnosis and taught me how to handle it."

Stark took a cigar out of a black leather case and offered one to Boxer.

"Thanks," Boxer said.

"Are you on any sort of medication?" Stark asked, after he lighted up.

"None. I control it."

"Have you tested it?"

Boxer nodded. "Every day. Every opportunity I have."

"I trust you," Stark said.

Boxer blew a cloud of bluish gray smoke toward the ceiling. "If you have any doubts, you could beach me. Cowly and Riggs could put the *Barracuda* through her paces."

"If you haven't any doubts, why should I have them?"

Boxer blew another bluish gray cloud toward the ceiling and said, "When I return, Francine and I will be married. I'd appreciate it if you'd be at the ceremony."

"I'd be honored," Stark replied.

"You and Cowly will be the only ones there," Boxer said. "But the entire crew will be at the reception."

Stark smiled broadly. "I'm glad you're getting married. It's about time."

"I agree," Boxer said with a smile. "It's about time."

"This calls for something special," Stark exclaimed. "How about a bottle of champagne?"

"Another vodka would do fine," Boxer said, raising his empty glass.

Stark nodded and summoned the waiter. "Two more vodkas," he told the man; then to Boxer, he said, "I'm glad you decided not to kill Morell."

"I didn't decide. The decision was made for me."

"I thought Francine —"

"She had nothing to do with it," Boxer said, as the waiter brought their drinks to the table.

"To your marriage!" Stark toasted.

They touched glasses and drank; then Boxer said, "It was either Morell, or Diana, De Vargas' sister."

"How did she become involved in it?"

Without mentioning Francine's past relationship with Sanchez, Boxer explained what the situation had been.

"And you never mentioned it to Sanchez?" Stark asked.

Boxer shook his head. "Eventually, I will. But my guess is that once Diana was taken from him, he was able to put it together. He hasn't contacted me since I came back and I haven't tried to contact him."

"Are you sure he's back?"

"Reasonably," Boxer answered.

Stark shook his head and commented, "A strange man. A very strange man. Combination of hero and villain; good and evil living in the same body."

"More like dueling for the same brain," Boxer responded.

Stark finished his drink and looked at his watch. "Would you believe it's ten hundred?"

"You mean we've been here for three hours!"

"That explains why the maître d' looks so unhappy each time he passes the table," Stark said, reaching inside his jacket for his billfold. "I'll pay the check for this one. You take the next."

"A month from now, same place, same ... only Francine will be with us."

"Fine!" Stark said, motioning to the waiter to come to the table and then asking for the check.

"It has already been paid for," the waiter answered.

Boxer and Stark looked questioningly at him.

"By whom?" Stark asked.

"That man there," the waiter said, pointing to a portly, middle-aged man sitting at a table with a middle aged, dark haired woman.

"The Russian ambassador and his wife," Stark said.

"You're joking!" Boxer exclaimed.

Stark shook his head. "We'd better go over and pay our respects."

The two of them crossed the room.

The ambassador got to his feet.

Stark shook his hand and said, "Comrade Ambassador, permit me to introduce Admiral Jack Boxer."

The ambassador shook Boxer's hand and introduced him to his wife; then he said, "It gives me great pleasure to meet you personally, Admiral, and be able to tell you how much I admire you."

Boxer flushed.

"Perhaps someday you will come to Russia as the guest of the Russian people."

"I'd like that very much," Boxer said. "I was hoping to have Comrade Admiral Borodine here as the guest of the American people."

"Some day soon, he will come," the ambassador answered.

Boxer nodded.

"It was very kind of you to take the check," Stark said.

"It was my pleasure," the ambassador replied.

"Thank you again," Boxer said and he and Stark walked away from the ambassador's table. "What was that all about?" Boxer asked, when they were out of earshot.

Stark shrugged. "It might have even been genuine."

The two of them walked along the river bank. The light coming from the windows of the restaurant was gold on the black water.

"Francine worried about your going back to sea?" Stark asked.

"I suppose she is. But she hasn't spoken about it to me," Boxer said.

"It should be routine," Stark commented.

"Should be," Boxer said.

Stark stopped. "But nothing is ever routine, is it?"

"Let's put it this way," Boxer answered, "damn few things are."

The two of them laughed and continued to walk...

Borodine frowned. "With all due respect Comrade Admiral," he said, "I know nothing about what the *Sea Dragon* can or cannot do. This was to be her sea trials, not a mission."

Admiral Gorshkov nodded. "The matter is out of my hands. The decision to land men and equipment in the democratic republic of Yemen is political and we were charged with carrying it out.

"Comrade Admiral Yuri Polyakov is in overall command. He will issue you your orders when you link up with the invasion fleet. We have eight ships involved in the operation, not counting the *Sea Dragon* and five modified submarines to bring in the initial assault troops. It will be your mission to put your force ashore and seize the radio station and the small airport immediately behind it. Once that's in our hands, the other submarines will come close inshore and the main assault force will come ashore and immediately move inland. They have specific objectives. As soon as those are achieved, the main attack force will land. The operation has been planned to minimize the possibility of intervention by the United States. We do not want a war. We do want to make the United States and her European allies very nervous."

"We may do more than make the United States nervous," Borodine said.

Gorshkov shrugged. "The decision has been made."

Borodine nodded. "That's the problem with decisions, especially when they're political and they require a military action to carry them out."

"I was not in favor of this operation," Gorshkov said. "I made my opinion known, but —" He stopped and smiled. "If it is successful, our position in the Middle East and indeed in the rest of the world will be considerably stronger. Looking at it from that point of view, it is really worth the risk."

"And if it should fail?"

Gorshkov lifted a cigar from a humidor. "It will be a very costly failure," he said.

Breathing deeply, Borodine responded, "Most failures are."

"I have to agree with you on that," Gorshkov said, lighting the cigar and blowing smoke off to one side.

Borodine waited to be dismissed. Up until the admiral had told him about the mission, he had thought he was taking the *Sea Dragon* on her sea trials. But now she would be going into action with him knowing very little about her peculiarities.

"Ah," Gorshkov exclaimed, "with all this official talk, I forgot to congratulate you on your marriage." And he offered his hand across the large desk.

Borodine shook it and thanked him.

"And what does your bride think about Moscow?" Gorshkov asked.

"She's awed."

"Will she remain in Moscow while you're at sea?"

"No," Borodine answered, "she'll return home and resume teaching."

"The three of us must have dinner when you return," Gorshkov said.

"Tanya will like that."

"Then we'll do it," Gorshkov replied. "But now let us drink to the success of the mission and to your marriage."

Borodine entered the apartment where he and Tanya were living during his stay in Moscow. It was a building where many naval officers and their families lived. The apartments usually went to those officers with children, but because of Borodine's rank and his special standing in the Navy and in the country, he was given the apartment.

"I'm in here," Tanya called from the kitchen.

Borodine could see her through the doorway. The kitchen was very small. Just large enough to accommodate a small table and two chairs in addition to the sink, stove and several shelves to hold the dishes, pots and pans. The rest of the apartment was equally small. The bedroom was eight paces in one direction and twelve in the other. And the parlor, or living room, was three meters by four. There were only two things that Borodine liked about it: the bathroom had a stand-up shower and the bedroom had a window that looked out over a small park, whose trees were beginning to turn green.

Borodine put his attaché case down and walked into the kitchen.

"What, no comment?" Tanya asked, looking at him.

"About what?"

"Can't you smell it?" she asked.

Borodine sniffed the air. "A roast?" he questioned.

She smiled broadly. "Yes a roast. But what kind of a roast?"

He sniffed again. "Lamb?"

"Yes. Your mother told me it was one of your favorites."

"But how did you get it?"

"I stood in line," she said. "It cost a small fortune, but I wanted to make something special for you..." She hesitated; then finishing the sentence, she said, "since this is your last night home."

He kissed her gently on the forehead.

"Make yourself comfortable. Dinner will be ready in about an hour," she said.

Borodine retreated into the bedroom. The valise containing the clothes he'd take aboard the *Sea Dragon* was already packed and standing in the corner. Tomorrow morning at zero nine hundred, he and his crew would fly to Kronstadt, where they'd board the *Sea Dragon* and by seventeen hundred, they'd be underway.

He put on an old pair of work pants and shirt, lit a cigarette and went to the window. The grass was darker green than the leaves on the trees. Several of the benches were occupied with old men and women sunning themselves and others were taken up with mothers tending their children. And standing against one tree was a young couple. The man had his back to him, but he could see the woman. She had long black hair and her arms were around the man's neck…

Borodine took a deep drag on the cigarette and let the smoke flow out of his nose. His marriage to Tanya was comfortable. She was a good wife in every way. He was very fond of her and might even fall in love with her, if she'd let him. She never said a word about love. Never asked him if he loved her, or indicated that she loved him. They had come to an arrangement: she wanted to marry and he needed an heir. They were married and she had already missed one period. She said that she wouldn't go for a pregnancy test until she missed a second period.

Borodine sighed. Each of them had kept their part of the bargain, but he certainly wished there was something more. He turned and was surprised to see that Tanya was standing between him and the doorway.

"It was so quiet," she explained, "I thought you had fallen asleep."

There was a momentary expression of ineffable sadness that Borodine caught; but it was so brief and so quickly replaced with a smile that without thinking any more about it, he said, "I was looking at that young couple in the park. They seem to be so much in love."

"They come every afternoon about this time and lean against the oak," she said wistfully.

Borodine glanced out of the window. They were gone.

"I've even given them names. I call the man Vasali and the woman, Ilenia."

Borodine faced her. She looked sad again. "Is anything wrong?" he asked.

She shook her head. "I also managed to get enough soup bones and greens to make soup. It's ready now, if you want to come to the table."

Borodine nodded and followed her back into the kitchen. Before he sat down at the table, he went into the bathroom, flushed his cigarette down the commode and washed his hands.

"I plan to return home by the end of the week," Tanya said.

"You could stay to the end of the month if you want to. We have the apartment until then."

She shook her head. "I wouldn't enjoy it without you being here," she said. "Besides, I want to be back a few days before I start to teach again."

Without commenting, Borodine continued to eat his soup.

"Have you any idea when you'll return?" Tanya asked, going to the stove and removing the leg of lamb.

"None," he answered. "But I wouldn't be surprised if I was away for three months."

She turned to him.

"Maybe it will be shorter," Borodine said. He hoped it would be. He hoped that the invasion would succeed. He bit his lower lip.

"Is anything wrong?" she asked.

"Why?"

"You always bite your lower lip when something upsets you," she told him.

"Nothing is wrong," he said, trying to put enthusiasm in the tone of his voice.

Tanya put the roast on the table. It was garnished with small roasted potatoes, sprigs of parsley and a mound of mint jelly.

"It looks too good to eat and smells better," Borodine said, beginning to carve. "There's enough here for several meals."

"What is left, I plan to give our neighbor down the hall."

Borodine served her first; then carved for himself. "Fantastic!" he exclaimed, swallowing the first bite. "Really fantastic."

Tanya beamed. "Your mother gave me the recipe," she said.

"Did she give you the one for roast goose with prune stuffing?" he asked.

"No, but she told me about it."

For a while, Borodine talked about his mother's cooking; then suddenly he realized tears were streaming down Tanya's cheeks. He left his chair and going to her, he put his hand under her chin and tried to turn her face toward him.

She resisted.

"What's wrong?" he asked gently.

Tanya covered her face with her hands and began to sob.

"Tell me what's wrong?" he asked.

She lowered her hands. "Maybe this is wrong," she sobbed. "Maybe we shouldn't have married."

Borodine was taken aback. "Have I done anything to hurt you?" he asked.

"Nothing."

"Then why shouldn't we —"

"Oh Igor," she wept, "you're not happy."

"Are you happy?"

She shook her head.

Borodine took a step back. He hadn't realized that she was unhappy too. Maybe the marriage was a mistake? Maybe she didn't and couldn't love him the way he wanted to be loved?

"You don't love me," she said. "I've fallen in love with you, but I can feel that you —"

"You've fallen in love with me?"

She nodded. "I love you, Igor … but I can understand why you haven't fallen in love with me. I know you've been with many beautiful women and I know that —"

He lifted Tanya to her feet and then into his arms.

"Put me down," she cried.

He ignored her.

"Where are you going?"

"Where does it look like. We're going to the bedroom. We're going to make love, Tanya. We're not just going to have sex. We're going to make crazy, passionate love." He stopped. "Now do you want me to put you down?"

Wide eyed, she shook her head.

"Remember what I said about the roast?" he asked, carrying her into the bedroom.

She nodded.

"Tell me?"

"It looked good enough to eat and smelled better," she whispered.

He smiled, set her down on the bed and said, "You look good enough to eat and smell better."

"You love me?" she asked, when they were both naked together in bed.

"I love you," Borodine answered, kissing her. "I love you…"

Closing her eyes, Tanya said, "I hope we will have a son."

Borodine raised his head.

"I wanted to give you something before you left," she said. "I was at the doctor this morning. The test is positive."

He crushed her to him…

Boxer and Francine drove up to the gate. "We won't be allowed to drive any further," Boxer said, before a Marine came up to the car, saluted Boxer and informed him that civilian vehicles were not permitted on the pier.

"Park it there," Boxer said, pointing to a graveled area alongside the gate.

Francine shifted into drive and eased the car into a tight turn. A few moments later they were parked next to a blue Chevy.

"Looks like one of my crew got here first," Boxer commented. "But I don't recognize the car."

"Let's hope you recognize the man," Francine said, opening the door and getting out.

Boxer took nylon bags out of the trunk and started to walk.

Francine fell in alongside of him.

Without speaking, they walked out on the arc-lit pier. Earlier they had made love and each of them knew their bodies already had said everything a person could say to one another.

"I never saw a submarine close up," Francine said.

"The *Barracuda* is larger than any other one," Boxer said with obvious pride. "I only hope she does as good as she looks."

"You have doubts?"

"Only the normal anxiousness," Boxer answered. "She's a complex machine with her own personality. By the time we're finished with her sea trials, she and I will be lovers."

"Ah, I always knew there was some kind of a sexual attraction between you and your sub."

"Must be," Boxer answered. "My life and the life of my crew depends on it."

"How long is this pier anyway?" Francine asked.

"A quarter of a mile and the *Barracuda* is tied up at the very end of it."

"Had I known, I would have worn flat heels," Francine said.

"No comment," Boxer laughed.

"Except for the guards at the gate, it doesn't seem to be guarded at all," Francine said.

"It is," Boxer told her. "There are guards on deck, in the mast, and there are two patrol boats close by at all times. There are even periodic helicopter checks. Right now we're being watched by a battery of TV cameras with zoom lenses."

"Are we now?" she asked.

"We sure as hell are."

"Then let's give them something to watch," she said. "Kiss me."

Boxer stopped.

"Put down your bags and kiss me," she demanded.

Boxer dropped his bags and took Francine into his arms.

"You know," she said, "already I ache inside."

He kissed her passionately; then letting go of her, he picked up his bags and continued to walk.

"I promised myself I wouldn't ask," Francine said, "but I can't help it. How long do you think you'll be gone?"

"Two months if everything goes according to the book, but that seldom happens. I'd say three to four months would be a more accurate guess."

"Guess?"

"That's all it is," Boxer answered. "I can't be any more specific than that."

Francine nodded and whispered, "I didn't think it would be this hard to say goodbye to you."

"And it doesn't get any easier," Boxer said. "Maybe it becomes even harder."

Francine shook her head. "That's hard to believe."

"Most wives say it's true," he said.

They reached the end of the pier. Awash with the white light from the arc lamps, the *Barracuda*'s dark gray sail rose above them.

"There's no easy way to do this," Boxer said. Putting his bags down and taking Francine into his arms, he kissed her. "Now turn around and walk back to the car without looking back."

"I love you, Jack," she said.

He kissed her again. "Turn around and go … that's right … don't look back." He waited until she was almost at the gate before he picked up his bags and started across the narrow gangplank leading from the pier to the open bulkhead door in the sail…

CHAPTER 11

The *Barracuda* was running on the surface. Just ahead were the lights of the Chesapeake Bay Bridge. Boxer had the CONN. Cowly was close by and Mahony was at the helm.

"All systems green, Skipper," Cowly reported, looking at the red illuminated SYSTEM CHECK DISPLAY

"Roger that," Boxer answered, pipe in mouth. During the next few weeks he wouldn't have too many opportunities to enjoy a smoke topside. The *Barracuda* would spend practically all its time submerged and on those rare occasions when it would surfacc, it would be for test purposes only. "I don't think we ever left on such a clear night," Boxer commented.

"I was just thinking the same thing," Cowly said. "If there was any kind of a moon, it would be almost like daylight."

The RO keyed Boxer. "Target bearing four-eight degrees... Range ten thousand yards... Speed one-one knots... ID tanker *Henry Mark*."

"Roger that," Boxer answered and keyed the COMMO. "Raise the *Henry Mark*. Make sure he has us on his radar and tell him to keep two thousand yards between us."

"Ten-four, Skipper," the COMMO answered.

Boxer turned to Mahony. "How do you like your new toy?" he asked, referring to the ELECTRONIC HELM CONTROL.

"Well, Skipper," Mahony said, "we're just getting acquainted. You know how it is when you're out with a new woman for the first time?"

Boxer laughed. "I know," he said.

"Well this EHC gadget is like that. She'll give me everything I had before and some things I'm glad I didn't have, like a 3-D display of where we are with relation to all targets within five thousand yards of us."

"I'm sure you'll get to know one another," Boxer said.

"Skipper, if we don't, it's not goin' to be my fault," Mahony said with a straight face.

Everyone on the bridge laughed.

"Do you think you might convince it to keep two thousand yards between us and the *Henry Mark* when it comes up on the screen?"

"Might, Skipper," Mahony answered. "Might."

Boxer looked out over the bow, where the water was parted into two long white ribbons that seemed to be part of the boat. He and the rest of the crew had spent five days a week, sometimes fifteen hours a day, of the last two months going over the *Barracuda* and getting to know her. She was larger than the *Shark* by thirty feet in length and four in width. Equipped with conventional rapid firing, radar directed anti-aircraft guns and twin eight-inch fore and aft retractable gun turrets, she could also launch SAMs, SS, or nuclear ICBMs. She was equipped with an improved UNDER WATER IMAGING SYSTEM, electronic spoofing gear that could project five different targets simultaneously to enemy sonar systems and a BLUE LASER GUN with a five-thousand yard range. With a diving capability of six thousand feet and an underwater speed of fifty knots, the *Barracuda* was an awesome weapons system.

She also had on board two high-speed mini-subs, each of which was armed with the American version of the Russian Killer Darts. And she carried two helicopters, each of which carried a battery of four air-to-surface missiles and an array of other weaponry.

Because of her size and the new electronic gear on board, her crew numbered fifty, against the *Shark*'s forty. And the assault force she carried was larger than the *Shark*'s or the *Turtle*'s. It numbered a hundred and fifty officers and men, none of whom were aboard yet because of a last-minute change in plans by Tysin, who without explanation to Stark, or to him, had sent the assault force for last-minute training to Puerto Rico and ordered that they be picked up at the naval base there three days after leaving Norfolk.

Boxer didn't appreciate the last-minute change and didn't particularly like the idea of surfacing where the *Barracuda* could be easily photographed by Cuban agents. Not that a Russian spy satellite hadn't already photographed her. But why give them the opportunity to get more detailed pictures than they already have. He had sent his objection to Tysin and to Stark.

Tysin had answered with a simple reply. "Follow original directive, number 92A-1003B, dated Aug. 1, 1995."

Stark had said in a phone conversation, "Allow him his way on this one. It's not worth going into the ring with him."

Though he hadn't wanted to, Boxer had agreed.

"Coffee, Skipper?" Cowly asked.

"Not a bad idea," Boxer answered. "Notify all section chiefs to give their men time for coffee and whatever munchies are available. It's going to be a long night. I want every man at his duty station when we dive."

"Aye, aye, Skipper," Cowly answered, and immediately began to contact the section chiefs.

The *Barracuda* passed under the Chesapeake Bay Bridge.

"Skipper, target bearing three-eight degrees... Range five thousand yards," Mahony reported.

Boxer checked the scope. The 3-D display was photographically clear. "If it comes in as good as this in bad weather we'll have an extra measure of safety," he said. "Cowly take a look."

"Damn good," Cowly commented.

Boxer faced the bow again and turning on the infrared glasses, he made a hundred-and-eighty-degree sweep with them. The *Henry Mark* was clearly visible and he picked up two fishing boats off the star'b'd bow.

One of the crewmen came up through the hatchway. "Coffee and Danish for everyone," he announced.

"Give him a hand," Boxer told two of the enlisted men.

Boxer waited until every man on the bridge had a cup of coffee and a Danish before he took his.

"Cynthia says she'll call Francine," Cowly said, moving close to Boxer.

"Good. They might keep each other from getting too lonely," Boxer said, sipping at the coffee. He wondered how the two women would get on with each other. He and Cynthia had been lovers long before he had met Francine; and though he had told Francine about Cynthia and she had said it didn't matter, he wasn't completely convinced.

"Skipper, two thousand yards," Mahony reported.

"Roger that," Boxer answered.

"I might get to like this gadget," Mahony commented.

Boxer smiled, took another sip of coffee and asked Cowly, "How are things between you and Cynthia?"

Without hesitation Cowly answered, "I never believed I could love someone as much as I love her."

Boxer nodded. He felt the same way about Francine. There was something in his relationship with her that he never had experienced with other women ... something almost palpable...

"I actually feel incomplete," Cowly said, "when I'm not with her."

This time Boxer did answer and said, "I know the feeling."

"To Francine," Cowly toasted, raising his cup.

"To Cynthia," Boxer echoed, touching his cup to Cowly's...

The *Barracuda* continued to run on the surface. Boxer alternately called for Engineering to increase its speed to flank and decrease it until the boat was almost dead in the water. He ordered several tight turns and followed a zigzag course for more than thirty-five minutes.

At 0100 hours Boxer switched on the MC. "All hands... All hands now hear this... This is the captain talking... First I want to welcome all of you, old hands and new, aboard the *Barracuda*... We'll be together for a while and it's very important that we develop in the new men aboard the kind of cooperation and level of performance we had aboard the *Shark* and the *Turtle*. This will be one of the few times that a dive will be announced. We will run half submerged for twenty minutes; then we'll go down to one hundred feet and test some of our equipment. The section chiefs will report any change from normal operating conditions. All hands stand by to run half submerged."

Boxer keyed the DO. "Deck awash," he said.

"Deck awash," the DO repeated.

Within moments the *Barracuda*'s hull slipped beneath the water.

"Skipper," the DO said, keying Boxer, "going to two zero feet."

"Roger that," Boxer answered, checking the master operating instructions manual in the COMCOMP. Twenty feet put the deck just under three feet of water and left eighteen feet of the sail completely exposed. He keyed the EO. "Flank speed," he said.

"Going to flank speed," the EO answered.

Boxer watched the *Barracuda*'s speed increase. "Speed holding at four-zero knots," he reported to the EO.

"Ten-four, Skipper," the EO reported. "I have the same reading on the ES panel."

"Roger that," Boxer said.

"Ballast trimmed," the DO reported, keying Boxer.

Boxer acknowledged the report and switched on the MC. "All section chiefs now hear this… All section chiefs now hear this… Switching all systems from manual control to auto-control… Switching all systems from manual control to auto-control." He bent over the COMCOMP and changed the position of several switches. The operational status lights changed from green to amber.

"Skipper," Cowly said, "the *Henry Mark* is off our port bow."

Boxer looked up. "Mahony, what's her range?"

"Two thousand yards," the helmsman answered.

Boxer keyed the COMMO. "Send my congratulations to the skipper of the *Henry Mark* for keeping the requested distance from us."

"Ten-four," the COMMO answered.

Boxer knocked his pipe bowl free of ash, refilled it and lit up again. "So far a piece of cake," he commented to Cowly.

Cowly grinned. "She runs quieter at flank speed than the *Shark* or the *Turtle* did," he said.

"Special anti-vibration devices around the drive shaft bearings," Boxer explained.

The SO keyed Boxer. "Skipper, I've been getting a shadow just beyond our max range."

"Bearing?"

"Six-zero degrees," the SO answered. "But that's not a hard fix."

"Keep monitoring it," Boxer said. "I don't want anyone shadowing us." Then turning to Cowly, he said, "The SO is getting shadow reading beyond the twenty-five-thousand yard range."

"If we were going to be shadowed," Cowly said, "that would be just about where the Russians would pick us up. After that, there'd be too much ocean for them to find us in; unless they were very lucky."

"My guess is that they don't know we're here," Boxer said. "They're probably waiting out there to monitor traffic going in and out of the bay. But once they spot us, you can bet they'll radio Moscow and either have their orders changed to follow us, or have another boat do it. There's probably a buddy around somewhere."

"What do you want to do?" Cowly asked.

"Get them the hell out of there," Boxer answered and keying the COMMO, he said, "Send the following message to Naval Ops. Send it code four. Russian sub suspected at — Get the coordinates from the SO. Take appropriate measures."

"Skipper code four —"

"The Russians can decode it," Boxer said. "I know that. I want them to. Once they have the message, they won't stick around to see us. They'll head out to sea before the planes come."

"Ten-four," the COMMO answered.

Boxer checked the clock on the COMCOMP. "Five minutes before we dive," he said to Cowly.

"It was a good night to be on the surface," Cowly commented.

"No argument there," Boxer said, knocking his pipe against the bridge's out surface. He took several deep breaths to steady himself. He was beginning to sweat. He stood up and looked around him. Everyone was busy doing his assigned task. The time had come to prove to himself that he could control his problem. If he couldn't do it now, he never would.

Boxer switched on the MC. "All hands, now hear this... All hands, now hear this... Prepare to dive... Prepare to dive." he pushed the klaxon button twice. The bridge detail dropped though the open hatchway, while Boxer quickly adjusted the controls for a slow descent to one hundred feet. He lingered a moment to fill his lungs with fresh air; then he dropped into the sail and pulling the hatch cover down, he dogged it shut.

Moments later he was at the COMCOMP. The entire control panel was bathed in red light. He watched the DIGITAL DEPTH INDICATOR. He checked the depth gauge above the COMCOMP. The two readings matched. The *Barracuda* was passing through twenty-five feet.

"Air system on," Cowly reported.

Boxer nodded. A moment before he had seen the system's green light come on.

The red light bathing the interior of the *Barracuda* began to shift to white. The control of the lighting system from night to daylight was operated automatically with a ten minute gradual switch-over, except under emergency conditions, when the delay could be reduced to zero by an override switch at the COMCOMP.

The SO reported the position of the two fishing boats that Boxer had seen through the infra-red glasses. The boats were well astern of the *Barracuda.*

"Going through five zero feet," Boxer announced over the MC.

"All systems green," Riggs reported.

"Roger that," Boxer answered, glancing over his shoulder at him. On his own, he had taken up his position in front of the secondary SYSTEM CHECK DISPLAY unit. Boxer nodded approvingly but said nothing.

The DO officer keyed Boxer. "Skipper, I've got green all the way."

"Roger that," Boxer said, checking the depth gauge and reported to the crew they were passing through seventy-five feet.

"Skipper," the SO reported, "the bottom is two-five-five feet."

Boxer turned on the fathometer and looked at the three-dimensioned profile of the sea floor. It was flat with rills running northwest to southeast. He switched on the UNDER WATER IMAGING SYSTEM and brought the bottom into sharp focus. It was strewn with boulders and here and there were broken hulls of wrecks.

Suddenly a bell sounded and a small green light began to flash indicating that the *Barracuda* had reached one hundred feet.

Boxer picked up the MC. "Dive completed," he told the crew. "Dive completed. Boat trimmed."

"All systems green," Riggs said.

"Roger that," Boxer said; then adjusting the AUTO-NAVIGATIONAL SYSTEM, he placed the *Barracuda* on a new course that would in a matter of thirteen hours bring them to an area off Bermuda, where he could test dive at a depth of two thousand feet.

"Looking good," Cowly commented.

Boxer agreed and said to Riggs and Cowly, "Except for emergencies, there is no need for the three of us to be on duty at the same time. The two of you work out a schedule that will allow each of you to have the CONN and the other to be the EXO on duty. I will take the CONN for all test dives and during any emergency situation. All other times the two of you will command the boat."

Cowly looked questioningly at Riggs.

"Is that all right with you?" Boxer asked, realizing that Riggs was the new man and still had to prove himself to Cowly and the other officers who had served aboard the *Shark* and the *Turtle*.

"I'd rather familiarize myself a bit more with the boat before I take the CONN for any length of time," Riggs answered. "She's not like any boat I previously commanded or served on."

Boxer rubbed his beard. From his experience with Riggs aboard the *Neptune*, he realized the man was cautious. But he didn't expect him to be so cautious. "Then you're EXO to Cowly," Boxer said, "until you feel ready to take the CONN in an operational situation."

Riggs nodded.

Boxer turned his attention to the instruments on the COMCOMP. Every system was green...

The SO keyed Borodine. "Comrade Admiral, target bearing eight-four degrees... Range twenty thousand yards... Speed one-eight knots... Course six-four degrees."

"Roger that," Borodine answered; then turning to Viktor, he said, "That must be the *Minsk*." They were at the assigned rendezvous point of 35 north latitude, 140 east longitude. As part of her shakedown cruise, Borodine had sailed the *Sea Dragon* under the Arctic Ocean and she had performed magnificently, she was much larger than the *Sea Savage*, better armed and equipped with surface to air, surface to surface and nuclear-armed intercontinental missiles. She also was able to launch one mini-sub equipped with Killer Darts and acoustical torpedoes and could put one fully equipped ASW helicopter in the air from a depth of thirty feet.

The SO keyed Borodine again and reported four more targets, each smaller than the primary target.

Borodine acknowledged the report and switched on his sonar display unit. The *Minsk* was two thousand yards ahead of her escorts. He ID'd the vessel he thought was the *Minsk*. It was and the four escorts were the destroyers, *Neulovimy*, *Bedovyy*, *Prozorlivy* and the *Neuderzhbimyy*.

He keyed the COMMO. "Signal the *Minsk*… Use code N… Message to Comrade Admiral Yuri Polyakov… Have you on sonar… Slow to eight knots… Keep present heading… Will surface one thousand meters to your starboard… Advise weather and condition of sea… Signed Admiral Igor Borodine."

The COMMO repeated the message.

"Send it," Borodine said.

"Aye, aye, Comrade Admiral," the COMMO answered.

Borodine knew very little about Polyakov. He had started out as a fighter pilot, but had never been in combat. He had won his rank from a desk and this was his first combat command. He was a member of the Party and, according to what some of the other officers at Kronstadt said, he was very close to the Premier, almost his son-in-law.

The SO keyed Borodine. "Four secondary targets closing on the primary target."

"Roger that," Borodine said. He had been watching it happen on the scope. He turned to Viktor. "Either they picked us up, or Polyakov ordered them into position."

The COMMO keyed Borodine. "Message from Comrade Admiral Polyakov."

"Read it."

"Reducing speed as requested... Weather clear... Sea running three to five feet... All guns will be trained on you... If you surface anywhere other than the place you designated you will be fired on... Signed Comrade Admiral Yuri Polyakov."

"Roger that," Borodine growled and related the contents of the message to Viktor.

"He's probably pissed that we picked him up before he located us," Viktor commented.

Borodine shook his head. "I sure as hell wish I felt better about this meeting than I do," he commented.

"It might go better than you expect," Viktor said. "He might even turn out to be better than you expect."

"I sure as hell hope so," Borodine answered. "I sure as hell hope so." And keying the EO, he said, "Slow to zero-eight knots."

"Slowing to zero-eight knots," the EO responded.

Borodine keyed the DO. "Stand by to surface."

"Standing by to surface," the DO said.

"Helmsman, come to course four-two degrees," Borodine said.

The helmsman repeated the command.

Borodine hit the klaxon once.

"Blowing all tanks," the DO reported.

The sharp whistle of escaping air filled the boat.

"Tanks blown," the DO said. "Diving planes zero-five degrees."

Borodine acknowledged the report and watched the instruments on the COMCOMP. The *Sea Dragon* was down eight hundred feet.

His eyes shifted to the sonar display. Polyakov's ships were holding course. He didn't want to give that idiot anything to shoot at.

"Passing through six hundred feet," the DO reported.

"Roger that," Borodine answered, checking the DDRO.

"All systems green," Viktor reported.

Borodine nodded.

Suddenly a sharp pinging sounded through the *Sea Dragon*.

"Son of a bitch," Borodine exclaimed, "they're using us for practice!"

"Passing through four hundred feet," the DO reported.

"Roger that," Borodine answered; then to Viktor he said, "Should we give them something to worry about?"

"Only if we wanted to be childish too," Viktor answered.

Borodine looked at him, made a face and nodded. He was lucky to have an EXO as steady as Viktor. He switched on the MC and said, "Now hear this... All hands now hear this, the surface craft are using us for practice... The surface craft are using us for practice."

"That should put the men at ease," Viktor commented.

The DO keyed Borodine. "Passing through two hundred feet," he said.

"Roger that," Borodine responded, looking at the section of the COMCOMP where the auto-dive / surface controls and indicators were located. Given the weight of the *Sea Dragon* and its speed of ascent, the computer automatically computes and displays the time left until the boat breaks water.

"All systems green," Viktor said.

"Passing through one hundred feet," the DO reported.

"Roger that," Borodine answered.

Suddenly a red light began to flash.

"Depth to Surface Timer on," Borodine said. "Zero-two minutes and three-zero seconds to surface." He switched on the MC. "Topside bridge detail stand by… Topside bridge detail stand by!"

"Sail up," Viktor said, activating the controls that elevated the sail from its well.

The red flashing light turned to green… A bell rang.

"Bridge detail topside," Borodine said over the MC.

"Diving planes at null," the DO reported.

"Roger that," Borodine answered, as a blast of cold, damp Pacific air rushed into the *Sea Dragon*. He grabbed his foul weather gear and clambered up through the open hatchway to the bridge… The *Minsk* was directly off the *Sea Dragon*'s starboard beam.

The COMMO keyed Borodine. "Comrade Admiral, Comrade Admiral Polyakov requests permission to speak to you."

"Patch him through," Borodine said.

"Aye, aye, Comrade Admiral," The COMMO answered.

"How soon can you come aboard the *Minsk*?" Polyakov asked.

Borodine looked at the sea. The waves were at least five feet. There wasn't much point in risking being swamped.

"The sooner we meet, the sooner we can coordinate our plans," Polyakov said.

"Come to dead in the water and have your men stand by to receive lines," Borodine said. "I'll come aboard by breeches buoy."

"My men will be standing by," Polyakov answered.

"Roger that," Borodine said, ending the conversation; then turning to one of the junior officers of the bridge detail he told him to make the necessary preparations to rig a breeches buoy.

"Aye, aye, Comrade Admiral," the man answered.

Borodine turned to Viktor, "Keep us ten yards away from the *Minsk*."

Viktor nodded.

Borodine keyed the EO. "Stop all engines," he said.

"Stopping all engines," the EO responded.

The *Minsk* continued to move forward for several minutes before she began to lose headway.

"She's slowing," Viktor said.

"So are we," Borodine replied and keying the EO, he said, "Give me six hundred rpms."

"Six hundred rpms," the EO answered.

Then to the helmsman, he said, "Bring us close, about ten yards from the *Minsk* and hold it there."

"Aye, aye, Comrade Admiral," the helmsman responded.

"You take the CONN," Borodine told Viktor. "I'm going below to get my attaché case and then I'll be on deck."

"Good luck," Viktor said.

"I might need more than good luck," Borodine said, as he dropped through the hatchway. A few minutes later he was on deck. His men had already thrown the first two lines to the detail on the *Minsk* and a short while later, Borodine was swinging between the *Sea Dragon* and the *Minsk*. Below him was the lead gray water of the Pacific and as he was slowly moved toward the *Minsk*, it began to rain.

Polyakov was on deck to greet Borodine. He was a big, blond man, with a clean shaven chin, blue eyes and a sensuous mouth. He saluted Borodine. "Safe and sound," he said with a grin. "Come to my cabin and we'll talk privately before we meet with my staff."

Borodine returned the salute and glanced back at the *Sea Dragon*. A wind had come up and she was rolling badly. "It would be a pleasure, but first I will signal my EXO to disconnect the breeches buoy and dive until the sea becomes calmer."

"Not necessary," Polyakov said, with a smile. "Your boat as of now is under my command."

Borodine raised his eyebrows.

"Do not worry," Polyakov told him, "your crew must have the experience."

Borodine remained silent.

"This way to my quarters," Polyakov said.

Borodine nodded and followed him into the cavernous interior of the *Minsk*, up several flights of steps into the island and finally through a door into a room furnished with a real bed, chairs, and a desk. On the desk was a color photograph of a young woman in a bikini.

"Please sit down," Polyakov said. "I thought it better that we have a few minutes to ourselves." He crossed the room to a small cabinet. "Would you care for a drink?" he asked.

Remaining standing Borodine responded, "Yes, thank you."

"I've wanted to meet you for a while now," Polyakov said, as he poured vodka into two small glasses. He recrossed the room and handing Borodine a glass, he said, "Please sit." He sat down at the desk and swiveled around to face Borodine. "To the success of our mission," he toasted.

"To the success of our mission," Borodine repeated, touching Polyakov's glass.

"If we pull this off," Polyakov said, "we will have caught the West with their pants down. There's really nothing they can do. Even your friend Boxer will not be able to help. He and his boat are on a shakedown cruise."

"That's what the *Sea Dragon* should be on," Borodine told him. "The boat is new. We still don't know her."

"Have you had any trouble thus far?"

Borodine shook his head.

"And you came here by way of the Arctic?"

"Under the Arctic."

"And you made the necessary tests while you were underway?"

"Of course."

"Then, Comrade Admiral," Polyakov said, "to paraphrase a famous saying, you have nothing to worry about but worry itself." He laughed and finished his vodka. "To keep a tighter hold on security, we've altered our plans somewhat."

Borodine understood the alterations were probably his ideas.

"Once your assault force takes its objectives, you will be reinforced by paratroops flown in from Afghanistan. They will be sent there in a few days and be in the air by the time my squadron is off the coast."

"And what role will your ships and men play in this operation?" Borodine asked. He liked what he had just heard even less than the original plan.

"We will prevent any interference," Polyakov said. "We will be joined by three other ships, the sister ship to the *Minsk*, the *Kiev*, the *Moskva* and the *Leningrad*, In addition we'll have the *Ivan Rogov* with an additional thousand marines to land, should they be needed. And we have your boat and two more attack submarines."

"Formidable," Borodine had to admit.

Polyakov nodded. "Success must be ours."

Borodine finished his vodka and said, "How do you expect to hide all of your ships from spy satellites?"

Polyakov smiled and said, "We are going to put them in a typhoon. We'll let Mother Nature hide them for us."

"I don't understand," Borodine said.

"We're going to have a typhoon at the right place and the right time. A typhoon made just for us. In fact the operation's code name from this moment on will be Typhoon."

"I still don't understand," Borodine said.

Polyakov grinned. "About a month before this operation was presented to the Premier, I happened to overhear a conversation between two of our senior meteorologists. They were talking about long range weather forecasting and how the state of the art made it possible for them to forecast the long range weather with ninety-seven percent certainty. To make the long story short, I became interested and it turned out that they were able to do this for only two or three areas of the world. One of them happens to be where we will soon be. We will pick up our typhoon in approximately forty-four hours. The storm will track on a path that will enable us to be invisible to American spy satellites until we're two hundred miles from our destination. At that point the storm will turn on to a new track."

The moment Borodine had seen Polyakov, he had guessed the operation had been his idea and now that there was no doubt in his mind, he was less comfortable with it than before.

"Another glass?" Polyakov asked.

"Yes, I think another would be just what, as the saying goes, the doctor ordered."

"What shall we drink to?" Polyakov asked, refilling the glasses.

"You make the toast," Borodine answered.

Polyakov's eyes went to the photograph of the young woman on his desk. "To love," he said.

Borodine nodded. "To love," he echoed and added, "to luck."

Polyakov raised his eyebrows.

"We're going to need it," Borodine answered. "Believe me, Comrade Admiral, we're going to need a great deal of luck before this operation is done and even more if it turns out successfully."

Boxer was seated at the desk in his cabin. With him was Colonel Lyle Dawson, a lean, muscular man in his early fifties, with graying hair, black eyes and a clean shaven chin. He was not the man Boxer had interviewed and had chosen to lead the *Barracuda*'s assault force. "You understand," Boxer said, "I have nothing against you, but you are not the man I expected to see."

"You have my orders," Dawson said.

Boxer looked at the papers on his desk. "According to what is on them, you assumed command three days ago."

"That's right."

"Up until that time Major Williams was in command?"

"Yes."

Boxer keyed the COMMO. "Have you raised Langley yet?" he asked impatiently.

"Coming in now, Skipper," the COMMO said.

"Tysin, this is Boxer," Boxer announced. "What the fuck is going on?"

"What did you say?"

"Listen to me," Boxer said, "if you have half a brain you'll understand that Colonel Dawson doesn't know the men and he's too fucking old to do what must be done."

"What?"

"Are you fucking deaf?"

"The assignment will not be changed," Tysin said, shouting.

Boxer looked at Dawson; then said to Tysin, "We'll fight this one out when I return. I'm cutting the shakedown cruise short.

I'll be back in Washington in three days. I want a meeting with you, Stark and the President, if that's the way you want to go. And I'm telling you now, if I don't get my man back, I will resign."

"Are you finished, Admiral?" Tysin asked coldly.

"Finished."

"Then listen to me," Tysin said. "Within minutes you will receive a code ten red message."

"You're joking," Boxer responded. "That's only used —"

"I know when it's used," Tysin said.

"Out," Boxer responded and switched off the mike. "Did you know about the message?"

"Not the details," Dawson answered.

Boxer leaned back in his swivel chair. "How well do you know Tysin?" he asked.

"We've known one another for fifteen years. We belong to the same club."

"Same club," Boxer repeated. "I don't understand?"

"The same country club," Dawson said. "Lots of attorneys belong to —"

"You mean you're not regular Army?"

Dawson shook his head. "Called back in for this mission. I'm in the Reserve."

Boxer rubbed his beard.

"Skipper," the COMMO said, keying Boxer, "I have code ten red coming in."

"Roger that," Boxer answered. "I'll be there in a few minutes to decode it."

"Aye, aye, Skipper," the COMMO answered.

Boxer focused his attention on Dawson. "Why in hell would you want to be here?"

"I was recalled."

"Cut the bullshit, Dawson. You weren't just recalled and given command of the assault force. That kind of thing just doesn't happen. Even with the screw-ups that Washington makes, that kind of screw-up is —"

The COMMO keyed Boxer again. "Skipper, incoming radio from Langley."

"Roger that… Patch it through."

"Boxer, Tysin here."

"Go ahead."

"Stark has been rushed to the hospital," Tysin said.

"What?"

"He had a stroke and is in a coma."

Boxer gripped the edge of the desk.

"Did you hear what I said?" Tysin asked.

Boxer cleared his throat. "I heard."

"Prognosis doesn't look good."

Boxer took a deep breath. He didn't know what to say. Somehow he never considered Stark an old man.

"If he should die —"

"Contact Francine Wheeler," Boxer said. "You have her address on file. She'll know what to do. And thanks for letting me know. Out." Boxer put down the mike and looked up at Dawson. For better or for worse, as the expression goes, Dawson commanded the assault team. Stark was his last hope of getting the man he had chosen back and now that hope was gone. "You're dismissed, Colonel. We'll continue this conversation another time."

Dawson started to salute.

"We don't salute aboard the *Barracuda*," Boxer said. He stood up. "Now if you'll excuse me, I have some important matters to attend to."

Dawson nodded, turned around, opened the door and left the office.

Boxer sat down again. And pursed his lips. He knew an attack was coming on. He could feel the tightening in his chest and the overwhelming feeling that the walls were coming closer and closer. He looked at the MINICOMCOMP… The boat was down five hundred feet. All systems were green.

The COMMO keyed Boxer. "Skipper, decoder is ready."

"Roger that," Boxer said, "I'm on my way." And willing himself to stand, he pushed the walls back and made it to the door.

Boxer read the decode message twice before he left the communications room and went to the bridge. "Riggs, turn the CONN over to another officer and come with me," he said.

"Aye, aye, Skipper," Riggs answered.

On the way to his cabin, Boxer stopped at Cowly's room and rousing him from sleep, he said, "In my quarters now."

Cowly rubbed his eyes. "Do I have time to wash my face?"

"That can wait," Boxer said.

Cowly nodded and left his bunk.

A few minutes later Boxer was at his desk.

Facing him, Cowly and Riggs were seated on chairs.

"Stark had a stroke," Boxer said. "The prognosis isn't good."

"Christ!" Cowly exclaimed.

"I'm sorry," Riggs said.

"Now for the real bombshell," Boxer said, picking up the decoded message. "This is a code ten red message."

"You mean we've been ordered into action?" Riggs asked.

"That's exactly what I mean," Boxer answered and he read them the contents of the message.

"But we don't know what this boat can do," Cowly protested.

"We know it, but Tysin doesn't," Boxer said. "Our mission is to land our assault force before the Russians land theirs; then we're to hunt for and destroy ships from the Russian assault force and the *S-33*, Borodine's new boat. The message says it is being used in combination with several attack submarines to screen the invasion force."

"I don't believe this," Riggs said.

"Believe it," Boxer answered. "And believe this too," and he told them about Dawson.

"But the man doesn't have the experience," Cowly complained.

"He's going to get on-the-job training," Boxer replied.

"When is all of this going to happen?" Riggs asked.

"According to this," Boxer said, waving the printout in the air, "we must have our men in position within fourteen days from today."

"Where the hell is the Russian attack force?"

Boxer shook his head. "We don't know. There's a typhoon building up and our spy satellites have lost track of the Russian fleet."

"I sure as hell don't like any of this," Cowly said.

"There's nothing to like," Boxer answered. "We'll conduct whatever tests we can while we're en route. Maybe we'll be lucky with the results."

"I thought South Yemen was in the Commie camp," Riggs said.

"Obviously being in their camp isn't enough," Cowly responded. "They want it all, or maybe the natives are getting restless and the Russians are afraid they'll switch sides."

"Okay," Boxer said, "we've got some tough going ahead. As soon as we reach the Indian Ocean we go on combat status. Cowly, I want models made of the coast and our targets. I want the officers and men to know what they're going to face before they face it."

"Aye, aye, Skipper," Cowly answered.

"Riggs, I want you to spend more time at the CONN," Boxer said. "Use one of the junior officers as your EXO."

"Aye, aye, Skipper."

"You men know what the drill is," Boxer told them. "We've got fourteen days to bring everything together. That's it for now." Alone, Boxer stared at the message and shook his head. He knew that the *Barracuda* and its crew weren't ready for a mission and he wasn't either…

CHAPTER 12

Boxer, Riggs, Cowly and Dawson were in the mess area. On one of the walls was a detailed map of the coastal area where the landing would take place. On a nearby table was a model of the area, complete with roads and telephone poles. "There are three places where the Russians can come ashore," Boxer said, touching the map of Yemen. "Here at the radio station. Here at the airport and here on the beach." He was giving Dawson his final briefing.

"Why those three and no other?" Dawson asked.

"That's what the computer says," Riggs answered. "We asked for a landing simulation and that's the readout we got."

"And you figure the Russians got the same thing?"

Riggs nodded.

"All right," Boxer said, "we're here. Exactly thirty miles from the coast at this point. The beach — that's your first objective. You and your men will be put ashore at oh-three-hundred tomorrow morning. You will secure the beach and then divide your team into the two units that will take and hold the landing strip and the radio station."

"How much resistance do you think we'll encounter?" Dawson asked.

Boxer turned to Cowly. "What's the best estimate?"

"Light. The real show will come when the Russians land."

"How long am I expected to hold?"

"The moment you secure your objectives, you will radio me and I in turn will radio the information to our AWACS and they will dispatch the necessary fighter bombers to deal with the Russians. I'd say five to six hours would be reasonable."

"What's the best estimate on the size of the Russian force?" Dawson asked.

"None … but your men will have the element of surprise on your side. Make sure you mine that beach."

Dawson didn't answer.

"Are you sure your men know what they're to do?" Cowly asked.

"We've gone over it as many times as you have gone over this with me," Dawson said. "If they don't know it by now, they never will."

Not caring for his sarcasm, Boxer told him, "If you or they don't know it by now, you and they will be dead."

"I assure you, Admiral, I am well aware of that," Dawson said. He was the only man aboard the *Barracuda* who did not call Boxer, Skipper.

"We'll get as close to the shore as we can," Boxer said, "but we'll be limited by the surf line. Our charts show that two hundred yards will be safest for us."

"I understand," Dawson answered.

"Hopefully there won't be much of a surf up," Boxer said. "If there is, you're going to have a rough ride in."

"We'll manage," Dawson said.

Boxer nodded and asked for questions.

"I have one," Riggs said.

"Okay, let's have it."

"What if the Russians are there before we are?"

Boxer looked at Dawson. "We'll do what we can to rescue as many men as possible," he answered.

"There won't be any to rescue," Dawson said.

"Probably not," Boxer agreed; then looking at his watch, he said, "It's now twenty-one-thirty. We'll surface at zero-two-thirty and launch the assault force at zero-three-hundred."

The three officers checked their watches.

Boxer went straight to his cabin to rest. He was tired and worried about the landing. There would be a fight and he didn't feel that Dawson would be able to take it, let alone make command decisions that would determine whether his men lived or died.

The *Sea Dragon* cruised comfortably at a depth of five hundred feet. But on the surface Admiral Polyakov's battle group was plowing through a raging sea. Two of the destroyers were so badly damaged that they were forced to turn out of the typhoon and head for calmer seas, while the remaining ships stayed close together for fear that the other two destroyers might require assistance.

Borodine sat at the COMCOMP. All systems were green. Viktor was close by and several of the other officers on duty were speaking in low tones. The assault force would leave the *Sea Dragon* in approximately seventy-two hours. Major Georgi Khmyz was briefed and confident that his men would be able to hold until the paratroopers arrived. But what was never made clear by Polyakov was why there was a need for a military operation against a friendly country.

Borodine pushed the question out of his mind and thought instead about Tanya and how happy he was to know that she loved him. Happy was the wrong word. It would never begin to describe the way he felt about her and —

The SO keyed Borodine. "Target bearing four-four degrees... Range, twenty-two thousand yards... Depth, six-hundred feet... Speed, forty knots... ID, American attack submarine."

"Roger that," Borodine answered, touching the battle stations alarm.

The pinging of the attack submarine's sonar echoed through the *Sea Dragon*.

"All sections report," Borodine said over the MC.

One by one all of the section chiefs answered.

Borodine keyed the EO. "Flank speed."

"Flank speed," the EO reported.

The SO keyed Borodine. "Target bearing four-four degrees… Range twenty-thousand yards… Speed five-five knots… Depth six-hundred feet… Closing fast."

"Roger that," Borodine answered and keyed the Fire Control Officer. "Prepare to fire Killer Darts —"

The SO keyed Borodine. "Multiple targets bearing four-four degrees… Range ten-thousand yards and closing fast… Depth six hundred… Six-five-zero and five-five-zero feet… Speed nine-zero knots."

Borodine hit the klaxon three times. "Crash dive," he shouted over the MC. "Crash dive!"

The *Sea Dragon* dropped off at the bow and began to drop through the water.

The SO called off another set of target readings.

"Those fucking Darts are following us," Borodine growled.

Suddenly the *Sea Dragon* was caught between two explosions.

Borodine keyed all section chiefs. "Report damage," he ordered. And immediately rekeyed the DO. "Take us up to four hundred."

"Aye, aye, Comrade Admiral," the DO answered.

Borodine keyed the FCO. "Fire when ready."

"Killer Darts fired," the FCO reported.

Borodine watched the deadly underwater missiles streak toward their target…

Boxer was almost asleep when the COMMO keyed him. "Skipper, code red message from S-two-four," the COMMO said.

"Read it," Boxer said, rubbing his eyes.

"Spotted Russian battle group one-five degrees north lat., fifty-seven degrees east long... Group consists of two Kiev class carriers, two Moskova class cruisers and two Mod Kildin class destroyers and the submarine S-three-three... Engaging the S-three-three."

"Contact the S-two-three and patch me through to the skipper," Boxer said, already out of his bunk and sitting in front of the MINICOMCOMP.

"Aye, aye, Skipper," the COMMO answered.

Boxer keyed the bridge.

Riggs answered.

Boxer repeated the message from the *S-24*. Then he said, "I want a fix on that battle group and an ETA to landing beach."

"Aye, aye, Skipper," Riggs answered.

The COMMO keyed Boxer. "No luck, Skipper," he said. "I tried on all set and special frequencies."

"Roger that," Boxer answered.

"Skipper," the COMMO said, "a code ten red radio signal coming in from headquarters."

"Put it through," Boxer said. He knew it would be Tysin.

"Boxer, you know what the situation is," Tysin said without any preliminary conversation. "Our best estimate is that you go in as soon as possible."

"Negative," Boxer answered.

"That Russian battle group —"

"Is still three days away from here," Boxer said.

"But they must know that we know where they are."

"Probably," Boxer answered.

"Then why wait?"

"I'd even wait longer than we planned," Boxer said. "They have three days before they get here. We can land four to five hours before they arrive. We want to stop them. We don't want a full-scale war to begin over a strip of beach."

"Let me talk it over with some of my people and get back to you."

"Don't take too long," Boxer answered.

Tysin didn't answer.

Boxer switched off the radio and put the mike down. He leaned back and rubbed his beard. Though he guessed he'd be facing Borodine again, he wasn't looking forward to it. Too much had passed between them to make it any easier to hunt and if need be destroy him...

Two soft raps on the door brought Boxer's thoughts back to the immediate situation. "Come," he called out.

Cowly entered. "Riggs gave me the word," he said.

Boxer nodded and gestured toward an empty chair. "We can presume the S-twenty-three is down."

"I know her skipper," Cowly said. "He was a very humorous man."

"Family?"

"Divorced. Three kids," Cowly answered.

Boxer shook his head. "Sometimes I think that to be a submariner you have to be one of the world's misfits."

"That thought has crossed my mind too," Cowly said.

Riggs keyed Boxer. "Skipper, the best we can do on the ETA is between six-five and eight-zero hours."

"Roger that," Boxer answered; then he said, "Have Dawson report to my cabin."

"Aye, aye, Skipper," Riggs said.

"Good man," Cowly commented.

Boxer nodded.

"The men respect and like him," Cowly said.

"I've noticed that."

"That's a substantial battle group the Russians have put together," Cowly said.

Boxer agreed.

The COMMO keyed Boxer. "Headquarters is on the radio with another red code ten priority."

"Patch him through," Boxer answered.

"You have the ball," Tysin said.

"According to our best estimate we have a one-five hour leeway. But my guess is that as soon as they break out of that covering typhoon we'll be able to get a more accurate number. We'll land zero-five hours before they do."

"Your force has to hold until we can get our fighter bombers there," Tysin said.

"Your man has to hold," Boxer answered.

"There's one change I want to make," Tysin told him.

"What is it?"

"I want Captain Riggs to accompany the landing party," Tysin said.

"That's a hell of an insurance policy for your boy," Boxer responded.

"I'll forget you said that."

"I want you to remember," Boxer growled. "I sure as hell want you to remember it... Out!"

"And you thought Kinkade was difficult!" Cowly said.

"That just shows how fucking wrong I can be," Boxer answered; then shaking his head, he asked, "Why is it that nine times out of ten a shithead manages to get into a position of authority?"

Cowly shrugged. "Maybe it's because the rest of us let it happen."

"I can't argue with that," Boxer said.

"You want to tell Riggs now?" Cowly asked.

Boxer nodded.

"I'll take the CONN," Cowly said.

There was a single rap on the door.

"Come," Boxer said.

Dawson entered the room.

"I'll be going," Cowly said.

Boxer nodded and told Dawson to sit. "Riggs will be here in a few minutes and since what I have to say concerns the two of you, I might as well tell you at the same time. You may smoke if you wish."

Dawson lit up.

A few minutes later Riggs entered the cabin and at Boxer's invitation, he sat down on the other empty chair. He waited until Riggs had lit up before he explained the change of plan. When he finished neither man had anything to say. "Then that's it," Boxer said. "We'll land approximately zero-five hours before the Russians arrive." He stood up to signal the end of the meeting and as Riggs started out of the cabin, he said, "Please wait a moment."

Riggs nodded.

"The order to send you with Dawson came from headquarters," Boxer said.

"That doesn't make it any easier to take," Riggs said.

Boxer nodded. "You understand that I can't do anything about it. Maybe if Stark —"

"It's okay, Skipper," Riggs said. "Dawson needs a nursemaid and I was chosen for the job. But you know and so does everyone else on this boat know that he's not the man for the job."

Boxer agreed. "And if it gets real rough and you see him coming apart," Boxer said, "I want you to take command. You know what the drill is."

"I'm not a soldier —"

"You have a good junior officer and good non-coms," Boxer said. "Listen to them. They'll get you out of it."

Riggs nodded.

"You've got to hold those positions," Boxer said. "There are one hundred and fifty in the assault force and we haven't got the slightest idea of how large the Russian force will be."

Riggs nodded.

"It's up to you to hold it together," Boxer said.

"I'll try," Riggs said. "I sure as hell will try."

Boxer slapped him on the back and together they went to the bridge. "I have the CONN," Boxer told Cowly.

"All systems are green," Cowly reported.

Boxer checked the DDRO. The *Barracuda* was down three hundred feet. He checked its speed. It was going twenty knots. Satisfied that everything was functioning properly, Boxer allowed himself a few moments to think about Francine.

"We've been discovered," Borodine said, speaking into the mike.

"What the hell are you talking about?" Polyakov asked.

"We have to assume that the American sub radioed our position and our course. That would be the first thing he would do."

"Did you destroy him?"

"Yes," Borodine answered. "But —"

"I am not interested in your 'buts,' Admiral. Was your Communications Officer monitoring the submarine's transmissions?"

"No."

"Then it's just possible he sent nothing?"

Borodine rubbed his beard. "Possible but not probable."

"We'll continue on our present course," Polyakov said. "I see no reason to alter any of our plans."

"Comrade Admiral," Borodine said, "with all due respect to you, if you do not alter your plans, you have lost the element of surprise and if you have lost that, you —"

"Not me, Comrade Admiral. Not me … you … you did not kill that submarine fast enough. If anything goes wrong, it is because you failed to respond quickly."

Borodine's face turned beet red. He turned to Viktor. "That bastard wants to blame me if the operation should fail."

"Comrade Admiral," Polyakov said, "we will hopefully have no reason to continue this conversation. But I warn you that I am fully prepared to press formal charges against you."

"Go to hell!" Borodine roared and ended the transmission.

"Now you know how he got to where he is," Viktor commented.

Borodine shook his head. "I'm angry, but he's frightened; of the two, I'd rather be angry than frightened."

Boxer had the CONN topside. "Ease her as close as you can," he said to Mahony, who was at the helm.

"My little toy says I got forty feet of water under me."

"Trust it," Boxer answered.

Mahony laughed. "More than I trust the girl I left behind."

Boxer smiled and scanned the hills with the infra-red glasses. "Nothing moving."

"Skipper, heavy surf," one of the lookouts reported. "Waves zero-eight-one-zero feet breaking."

Boxer keyed Riggs and reported the condition of the surf.

"Ten-four, Skipper," Riggs answered.

"Three-zero yards, Skipper," Mahony reported.

Boxer keyed the EO. "Stop all engines."

"Stopping all engines," the EO answered.

"Hold her steady," Boxer said, looking at Mahony.

"Steady as she goes," Mahony responded.

The *Barracuda* continued to slide through the water and gradually lose speed.

Boxer keyed Dawson. "Have your men stand by to move out."

"Standing by," Dawson repeated.

Boxer checked the hills again. Nothing human was out there. He glanced up at the sky. A ribbon of dim light showed in the east.

"Dead in the water," Mahony reported. "Three-one yards from the shore." Then he added, "I can hear that surf."

Boxer keyed Dawson. "Bring your men topside."

"Ten-four," Dawson answered.

Minutes later, fifteen inflatables carrying the one-hundred-and-fifty-man assault force headed for the beach.

Boxer keyed the EO. "Give me two-zero knots."

"Going to two-zero knots," the EO answered.

"Come to course eight-seven degrees," Boxer said.

"Coming to course eight-seven degrees," Mahony responded.

The *Barracuda* gathered speed and turned onto her new heading.

Boxer keyed Riggs. "What's the situation?"

"Approaching the line of surf," Riggs said.

"How bad?"

"I'll let you know when we're on the beach," Riggs answered.

"Ten-four."

Boxer looked back. The assault boats were nothing more than dark specks and the very next moment they vanished from sight.

"Make it," Boxer whispered under his breath. "Make the fucking beach!"

"Did you say something, Skipper?" Mahony asked.

"Negative," Boxer answered; then switching on the MC, he said, "All hands, now hear this... All hands, now hear this... Prepare to dive... Prepare to dive." He checked the fathometer. There was two hundred and fifty feet of water under the *Barracuda* and the bottom was dropping off quickly. He blew the klaxon twice.

"I have the CONN," Cowly reported from the bridge.

"Go to AUTO-CONTROL."

"Going to AUTO-CONTROL."

"Lower sail."

"Lowering sail," Cowly responded.

"Make one-hundred," Boxer said.

"Making one-hundred," Cowly answered.

Boxer was the last man to clear the bridge and dogged shut the hatch. As soon as he reached the bridge, he keyed the COMMO. "Open all channels to assault force."

"All channels opened, Skipper," the COMMO answered.

Boxer stood behind Cowly and waited to hear from Riggs. He looked at the clock. "Maybe twenty minutes to make the beach?" he questioned.

"Thirty at the very most," Cowly said.

Boxer looked at the other men on the bridge. They too were tense and anxious. Suddenly the sides of the hull began to press in on him. Sweat popped out on his forehead.

"Skipper, are you all right?" Cowly asked.

Boxer nodded and took several deep breaths.

Riggs's voice came over the PA. "Sea base, this is force one… Sea base this is force one."

"Read you loud and clear," Boxer forced himself to answer.

"On beach… All craft made beach… Advancing toward objectives."

"Roger that," Boxer said, regaining his composure.

The men on the bridge began to cheer.

Boxer switched on the MC. "Now hear this… All hands now hear this… The assault force is safely ashore."

Every man on the boat shouted their approval and several let loose with wild rebel yells.

The COMMO keyed Boxer. "Another code red ten radio request from Headquarters, Skipper."

"Patch it through," Boxer said; then to Cowly, he commented, "Tysin must be sitting on his balls."

"Ouch! Just the thought of that hurts"

"Better believe it!"

"Admiral Boxer," an unfamiliar voice said, "this is Admiral Chester Mason, I'm the new CNO."

Boxer put his hand over the mike. "Is that who I think it is?"

"Must be," Cowly said.

"Chi-Chi Mason CNO?" Boxer questioned.

"Admiral Boxer?"

Boxer removed his hand from the mike. "Here, Admiral."

"Has the assault force landed?" Mason asked.

Boxer suddenly started to laugh. The idea that Chi-Chi Mason, the last man in his graduating class, the biggest fuck-off who ever had become the CNO was too absurd not to laugh.

Cowly took the mike from Boxer. "Admiral, the skipper is having an attack of — the sneezes."

"What?"

"The sneezes ... very common aboard submarines, Admiral. Has something to do with the refiltered air."

"Is that a fact?"

"Absolutely," Cowly answered. "Here's the skipper again." And he handed the mike back to Boxer.

"The assault force is safely ashore," Boxer said in a formal manner.

"Good," Mason commented; then he said, "I want reports every four hours. I want to be kept apprised of the situation and if any problems should develop, I want to be notified. I do not want you to make any unilateral decisions. Is that clear?"

"Say again?" Boxer responded.

Mason repeated himself.

Boxer broke the connection and keying the COMMO, he said, "Erase everything that Admiral Mason said after I told him that the assault force was safely ashore."

"Aye, aye, Skipper," the COMMO answered.

Boxer looked at Cowly. "Tysin and Chi-Chi — that's some pair of jamokes, wouldn't you say?"

"I'd say if we didn't have bad luck, we wouldn't have any luck at all," Cowly responded.

"That's for damn sure," Boxer exclaimed. "That's for goddamn sure!"

The SO keyed Boxer. "Multiple targets bearing four-seven degrees… Range twenty-two thousand yards… Speed… one-four knots… ID carriers *Minsk* and *Kiev*… Two cruisers: the *Moskva* and *Leningrad* and the troop carrier, *Ivan Rogov*."

"Roger that," Boxer answered and switched on COMCOMP sonar scope. "That's not the standard Russian squadron for this part of the world," he said to Cowly.

"Not by a long shot," Cowly answered.

The COMMO keyed Boxer. "Radio from Riggs, Skipper."

"Patch it through."

"Russian assault craft approaching beach," Riggs said.

"Roger that," Boxer answered. "Where did they come from?"

"Same place we did."

"A sub?"

"A big one. It's lying off shore now," Riggs said.

"Best estimate on size of the assault force?"

"Equal to or slightly larger than our own," Riggs answered.

"Are you dug in?"

"Yes… We're waiting for them."

"Roger that," Boxer answered. "Out." He looked at the sonar display. "They'll move to support the assault force as soon as it runs into trouble."

Cowly agreed.

"That sub is probably the *Sea Dragon*," Boxer said.

"It's the only one large enough to carry that size force."

Boxer checked the fathometer. There were two thousand feet between the surface and the bottom. "We can't let those carriers launch their planes, or those destroyers get anywhere near that beach."

"That means we have to strike first," Cowly said.

Boxer nodded. "They'll take some sort of action as soon as they find out they've put men on a hot beach." he rubbed his beard. "Our fighter bombers are already in the air. They have three hours' flying time. I'm going to have to go for the carriers." He keyed the COMMO. "Keep a channel open to Riggs."

"Aye, aye, Skipper," the COMMO answered.

Boxer looked at Cowly. "I won't lose that force the way we lost the one off the *Turtle*."

"Battle stations?"

"Battle stations," Boxer answered, touching the button. Instantly the klaxon sounded four times and a red light on the COMCOMP began to flash.

All off duty personnel ran to their stations.

Boxer switched on the MC. "Section chiefs report combat status."

One by one the sections reported they were battle ready.

Boxer keyed the Missile Launch Officer. "Stand by to launch two SS. All firing information on Auto-Control."

"Switching to SO bearing and range," the MLO said.

"Roger that," Boxer answered.

"Skipper," Riggs said, "the Russians are on the beach."

"Where are you?"

"Five hundred yards back."

"Dawson?"

"To my right about one-hundred feet."

"Roger that. Good luck," Boxer said; then turning his attention to the COMCOMP he watched Missile Control Instruments display Bearing, Range, Time to Target and optimum firing depth. The *Barracuda* was running too deep to fire its missiles. Every few moments the values changed.

"Target... Bearing nine-four degrees, range fifteen-thousand yards... Speed three-zero knots... Depth... six-hundred feet... ID the Romeo class attack sub."

"Roger that," Boxer answered and switched on a second sonar display.

"Sub's course steady," the SO said.

Boxer acknowledged the report. He keyed the FCO. "Take that sub out with ASROCS. Fire immediately after SS missiles are gone."

"Aye, aye, Skipper," the FCO said.

Boxer keyed the DO. "Switching to manual control. Make three-hundred."

"ON manual control," the DO answered. "Making three-hundred."

Within moments the deck tilted slightly upward. Boxer watched the DDRO. They were passing through the five-hundred foot level. He keyed the ASWO. "Set up three spoofing configurations. One, ten-thousand yards in front of us. Two, spaced eight-thousand yards behind us. Separate them by five thousand yards."

"Aye, aye, Skipper."

"Three-hundred feet," the DO reported.

Boxer looked at the missile firing control instruments. The missiles were armed and ready to go. Three-hundred feet was the maximum firing depth. Boxer switched on the Time To Launch Clock. "Five-zero seconds to launch," he said, sucking in his breath.

Suddenly the pinging of the Russian sonar invaded the *Barracuda*.

Boxer exhaled. "One-five seconds to launch."

The pinging became louder.

"Launch!" Boxer exclaimed.

The *Barracuda* moved slightly up; then immediately settled down.

"ASROC one and two away," the FCO reported. "Mahony, come to course seven-five degrees," Boxer ordered.

"Coming to course seven-five degrees," Mahony answered.

Boxer's eyes were riveted to the instruments on the COMCOMP. "Two-zero seconds til SS impact."

"ASROCS down," the FCO reported.

"Roger that," Boxer answered and a moment later he exclaimed, "Impact!"

The sound of the two explosions rolled over the *Barracuda.*

"Two hits," Boxer said.

The first shock waved caused the *Barracuda* to heel slightly to the port side.

The ASROCS exploded and the image on the screen disintegrated.

More explosions came from the surface.

Greely's voice came over the radio. "The fight has begun."

"I can hear it," Boxer said.

"Something is burning just over the horizon. Lots of smoke and loud explosions."

"Will you be able to hold?"

"The Russians have stopped on the beach," Riggs said. "But I don't think they'll stay there for long."

"How's Dawson holding up?"

"He wants to pull back."

"Negative. If you can hold them on the beach until our planes come, they'll be finished."

"Aye, aye, Skipper. We'll hold them as long as we can."

The SO keyed Boxer. "The *Minsk* and *Kiev* are dead in the water."

"Roger that," Boxer answered. He looked at his sonar display, the *Ivan Rogov* was no longer on the scope. The *Moskva* was standing by the two carriers, while the *Leningrad* was circling the three other ships.

"Mahony," Boxer said, "come to course four-eight degrees."

"Coming to course four-eight degrees," Mahony responded.

Boxer switched on the MC. "Now hear this… Now hear this… So far we've been lucky… Two Russian carriers are dead in the water and burning and we destroyed one attack sub."

The men began to cheer.

Boxer looked over at Cowly, who was smiling broadly. "All section chiefs allow your men in groups of threes a fifteen-minute break for coffee and… All sections to maintain battle stations." He switched off the MC.

"Don't you think you should report to headquarters?" Cowly asked.

"Chi-Chi wouldn't know what the hell I was saying," Boxer answered.

"Just to cover your ass?"

"I guess you're right," Boxer answered and asked the COMMO to raise Admiral Mason.

"You must abandon the assault force," Polyakov said. "You must find and destroy the *Barracuda*."

Borodine switched on the mike. "Where are the two attack submarines?" he asked.

"We can't contact one and the other is here with us. We have severe damage aboard both carriers. We're unable to launch any aircraft."

"Casualties?"

"Heavy."

"Are you returning to base?" Borodine asked.

"The mission has been cancelled," Polyakov answered.

"Those men on the beach —"

"I don't want to hear about those men on the beach," Polyakov said. "Your sole mission is to find and destroy the *Barracuda.*"

Borodine took a deep breath and after he had exhaled, he answered, "Roger that."

"Premier wants that submarine destroyed," Polyakov said.

Borodine didn't answer.

"Did you hear me?"

"Yes, Comrade Admiral, I heard you," Borodine answered. "It would make it easier if you would assign that attack sub to me."

"That's out of the question," Polyakov answered. "It's needed here."

Borodine was about to answer when the SO keyed him. "Comrade Admiral, target bearing three-six degrees… Range twenty-five thousand yards… Speed four-four knots… Depth one-thousand feet… ID negative."

"Roger that," Borodine said; then to Polyakov he said, "I don't have to go looking for the *Barracuda.* I have her on my sonar."

"Destroy her. Out."

Borodine switched off the mike and to the helmsman, he said, "Come to course three-six degrees."

"Coming to course three-six degrees," the helmsman answered.

Within moments the pinging filled the *Sea Dragon.*

Borodine keyed the Special Weapons Officer. "Arm laser," he ordered.

"Arming laser," the SWO said.

Borodine's eyes went to the COMCOMP. The laser was consuming a huge amount of power. A red light began to flash. The automatic fire alarm sounded.

The DCO keyed Borodine. "I show nothing on my system scope."

The alarm continued to sound.

Borodine ran an SYSCHEK. All systems were green. The laser was still arming.

The SO keyed Borodine. "Secondary targets… Bearing eight-four degrees and one-five-five degrees… Range, twelve and fifteen thousand yards… Speed four-zero knots… Depth five-hundred feet."

Borodine checked the scope. The new targets were there.

Suddenly the blower system cut off.

Borodine keyed the DCO.

"Power malfunction," the DCO said.

"Can you override it?"

"Not while you're arming the laser," the DCO answered.

Borodine keyed the SWO. "Cancel laser arming command," he said.

"Laser arming command canceled," the SWO said.

In a few moments the blowers came back on.

The DCO keyed Borodine. "Fire in duct three-four… Aft section of the boat… Detail dispatched."

"Roger that," Borodine answered. He turned to Viktor. "I keep thinking about the men on the beach."

Viktor nodded. "Me too," he said.

"I'm going to get them off," Borodine said.

"With the *Barracuda* on us?"

"With the *Barracuda* on us," Borodine said and he keyed the COMMO. "Open a channel to the *Barracuda*."

"Aye, aye, Comrade Admiral," the COMMO answered.

Boxer saw a 3-D image of the *Sea Dragon* on the scope. It was slightly larger than the *Barracuda* and though he couldn't tell what her armaments were, he knew they had to be as formidable as the *Barracuda*'s.

The COMMO keyed Boxer. "Skipper, I don't know what is going on but I have a Russian on an international frequency who says his captain wants to speak to you."

"Patch him through," Boxer said.

"Aye, aye, Skipper," the COMMO answered.

"Comrade Admiral Boxer?" the man asked.

"Yes."

"Comrade Admiral Borodine wishes to speak with you."

"Connect him," Boxer said.

A moment later Borodine was on. "Jack," he said. "We have no time to waste. I want to pull my assault force off the beach. We know about your planes coming in. I cannot get my men unless you agree to give me the necessary time."

"Hold," Boxer said.

"Holding," Borodine repeated.

Boxer opened the direct channel to Riggs. "What's the situation?" he asked.

"The Russians are dug in."

"Casualties?"

"Light on both sides. I have five wounded, none seriously."

"Roger that," Boxer answered. "Out." He switched back to Borodine. "How long will you need?"

"An hour at the very most," Borodine answered.

"If you don't do it in that time our planes will catch you on the surface."

"I understand."

"I will attack after the hour is up," Boxer said.

"I would expect you to," Borodine answered.

"You have exactly one hour," Boxer told him. He switched off the mike and turning to Mahony, he said, "Come to course six-eight degrees."

"Coming to course six-eight degrees," Mahony responded.

Boxer opened the channel to Riggs. "Put Dawson on the net."

"Aye, aye, Skipper," Riggs responded.

"Dawson here," Dawson said.

"Listen carefully. In a matter of minutes a Russian sub will surface beyond the line of surf. The assault force on the beach will return to it. You are not to fire on them. Do you understand? You are not to fire on them."

"What?" Dawson shouted.

"You heard me. I do not want you to fire on them," Boxer said.

"But you can't do that," Dawson protested.

"Skipper," Riggs said, "the sub just broke water. She's about three thousand yards off the beach."

"She'll come in a lot closer," Boxer responded.

"What the hell are you trying to do?" Dawson yelled.

"I'm trying to save the lives of our men."

"The Russians want to withdraw —"

The COMMO keyed Boxer. "Skipper a code red radio request."

"Put it through," Boxer said.

"Boxer," Mason shouted. "I've been copying this transmission and then your previous one. You can't make private deals with the enemy. I want that Russian sub sunk. Now that's an order. I want the Russian assault force destroyed. Do you understand that?"

"I understand," Boxer answered.

"Do it!" Mason ordered.

Boxer ended the transmission to Mason and to Riggs. He keyed the COMMO. "Get me Comrade Admiral Borodine."

"Aye, aye, Skipper," the COMMO responded.

A few minutes later he was in radio contact with Borodine. "Put out to sea," he said. "Order your men to surrender to my force. I'll take them aboard my boat."

"What?"

"Igor, do what I ask," Boxer said. "The men will be returned to your government. I promise you they will not be held —"

"Agreed," Borodine told him. "My position will be thirty-five thousand yards to the southeast."

"Roger that," Boxer said and he ended the transmission. He switched on the MC. "All hands, now hear this... All hands, now hear this... Stand by to surface... Stand by to surface."

"Standing by to surface," the DO reported.

Boxer hit the klaxon button once.

"Blowing all tanks," the DO said.

"Roger that," Boxer answered.

Boxer watched the depth gauge over the COMCOMP. They were rising rapidly. "Bridge detail stand by," he said over the MC.

"Bridge detail standing by," the officer in charge said.

Boxer switched on the radio. "Riggs, tell Dawson to stand by to accept the surrender of the Russian assault force. I want our men and theirs aboard the *Barracuda* as quickly as possible."

"Aye, aye, Skipper," Riggs said.

"Passing through one-hundred feet," the DO reported.

"Roger that," Boxer said. He turned to Mahony. "Bring her in close to the beach and hold her steady."

A green light began to flash and the surface signal bell rang.

"Sail going up. Bridge detail topside," Cowly said over the MC.

Boxer raced up the ladder and undogged the hatch. A moment later he was at the topside COMCOMP. He keyed Cowly and said, "I have the CONN."

"Aye, aye, Skipper," Cowly answered.

Boxer contacted Riggs. "What's the situation?"

"Dawson will not accept the Russian's surrender," Riggs said.

"You do it in my name," Boxer said. "Get those men into the boat and out to the sub."

The RO keyed Boxer. "Targets bearing four-nine degrees… Range eighteen-thousand yards… Speed thirty knots… ID the cruisers *Moskova* and *Leningrad*."

Boxer looked at the radar scope. The cruisers were moving toward him at flank speed. "Christ," he swore.

The SO keyed Boxer. "Targets bearing seven-zero degrees… Range twenty-two thousand yards… Speed four-five knots… Depth eight hundred feet… Closing fast."

"Roger that," Boxer answered, wondering if he had been suckered into a trap. He keyed Riggs. "Return to beach… Return to beach… Hold Russians under guard."

"Aye, aye, Skipper," Riggs answered.

Boxer checked the time. The fighter bombers were still forty-five minutes away. He keyed the EO. "Give me all the speed you can," he said.

"Going to flank speed," the EO answered.

Boxer hit the klaxon three times.

The bridge detail disappeared down the hatch. Boxer followed. The *Barracuda* was crash diving. He reached the COMCOMP. "I have the CONN. Lower sail."

Cowly moved to his assigned position. "Lowering sail," he said.

"Come to course nine-zero degrees," Boxer told Mahony.

"Coming to course nine-zero degrees," Mahony answered.

Boxer watched the depth gauge — there were only three hundred feet of water between the surface and the bottom. He keyed the DO. "Level her at two-hundred feet."

"Level at two-hundred feet," the DO said.

"All targets closing fast," the SO reported.

Boxer keyed the FCO. "Program for multiple target discrimination."

"Aye, aye, Skipper," the FCO answered.

The COMMO keyed Boxer. "Admiral Mason is on a code ten red radio transmission."

"Patch him through."

"Aye, aye, Skipper," the COMMO said.

"Boxer what the hell are you doing?" Mason roared. "I gave you an order to destroy that Russian sub, not play fucking games with it."

Boxer paid no attention to the voice coming over the loudspeaker.

"The surface ships are the best set of targets," the FCO reported.

"Roger that," Boxer answered.

"What the hell are you talking about?" Mason shouted.

Boxer switched on the mike. "Listen, Admiral, I've got two subs and two surface ships coming at me. I sure as hell don't need you. You want to stay on an open channel, that's fine with me. But now is not the time for chit-chat."

"Chit-chat!" Mason fumed.

"Either you shut up," Boxer said, "or I'll order the channel closed. What will it be, Admiral?"

"I'll stay on," Mason replied.

Boxer nodded and ran a systems check. All systems were green. He looked at the sonar display. The cruisers were closing fast. He keyed the FTO. "Arm and load torpedoes one, two, three and four."

"Arming and loading torpedoes one, two, three and four," the FTO responded.

"Go to Alpha firing sequence."

"Alpha firing sequence," the FTO answered.

The SO keyed Boxer. "Multiple targets… Bearing seven-six degrees… Range twelve-thousand yards… Speed nine-zero knots."

Boxer keyed the ASWO. "Activate ECM."

"ECM activated," the ASWO answered.

Boxer looked at the sonar display. There were six Killer Darts streaking toward the *Barracuda.* Three disappeared from the screen and three continued to streak toward the *Barracuda.*

"Come to five-five degrees," Boxer said.

"Coming to course five-five degrees," Mahony answered.

Boxer activated the torpedo firing mechanism. "Torpedoes away," he announced.

The *Barracuda*'s bow rose slightly but immediately settled.

Boxer watched the Time To Target Clock. "Three minutes," Boxer said. He glanced down at the sonar display. The two cruisers still hadn't changed course. But the subs had. He keyed the DO. "Make four hundred feet."

"Making four-hundred feet," the DO answered.

Boxer looked at the Time To Target Clock. "Ten seconds and counting," he said.

The SO keyed Boxer. "Skipper, the Killer Darts passed under us," the SO said.

"Roger that," Boxer answered.

The Time To Target Clock stopped and two enormous explosions rolled over the *Barracuda.*

"Skipper," the SO reported, "one target dead in the water. The other slowing."

"Get that other ship!" Mason shouted over the open channel.

Boxer had forgotten about him. He glanced at Cowly and said, "Chi-Chi turned out to be a greedy bastard, didn't he?"

Cowly grinned and nodded.

Riggs came on. "Skipper, Russian transports are circling the beach," he reported.

"Do nothing," Boxer said. "Do absolutely nothing."

"Aye, aye, Skipper," Riggs answered.

The COMMO keyed Boxer. "Heavy radio traffic between Russians," he reported.

Boxer acknowledged the report. He looked at the sonar display. The *Sea Dragon* and her companion attack sub were still on course. He keyed the FCO.

"Stand by to fire Killer Darts."

"Killer Darts armed and ready," replied the FCO.

Boxer hesitated. If he fired the Killer Darts, the *Sea Dragon* had no chance of escaping. It either would be seriously damaged or sunk. Then suddenly he realized the Killer Darts fired at him should have seriously damaged or sunk him. They didn't because they had the wrong information. Borodine had fed the wrong information into them. He was just about to tell Cowly, when Riggs came on the air again, "Skipper, our planes are here. They just streaked in out of nowhere and are circling over the Russian transports."

The SO keyed Boxer. "Skipper, the targets are changing course."

Boxer looked at the sonar display. "They're not just changing course," he said. "They're turning. They've broken off the action."

"Ten-four, Skipper," the SO answered.

Boxer keyed the COMMO. "Raise the squadron leader," Boxer said. "Tell him we're surfacing and are going in close to the beach."

"Aye, aye, Skipper," the COMMO said.

Boxer switched on the MC. "All hands, now hear this… All hands, now hear this… Prepare to surface… Prepare to surface." Then to Cowly he said, "Our luck runneth over…"

"Let it run, Skipper," Cowly answered. "Let it run…"

A NOTE TO THE READER

Dear Reader,

If you have enjoyed the novel enough to leave a review on **Amazon** and **Goodreads**, then we would be truly grateful.

Sapere Books

SAPERE
BOOKS

Printed in Great Britain
by Amazon